3/2014

Spiraling: The Forgotten

Valerie Mannebach

Copyright © 2014 by Valerie Mannebach

Cover Image Copyright © 2010 by Madison Nunes of Madison Nunes Photography

ISBN-10: 1496006984

ISBN-13: 978-1496006981

For my family who loves me.

For my friends who support everything I do.

You have gotten me here.

Thank you.

"Strange is our situation here upon earth. Each of us comes for a short visit, not knowing why, yet sometimes seeming to a divine purpose. From the standpoint of daily life, however, there is one thing we do know: That we are here for the sake of others...for the countless unknown souls with whose fate we are connected by a bond of sympathy." ~Albert Einstein

Prologue

August 8, 1995, 7:40 p.m.

Trey Lorec threw open his eyes and gasped. Nikki Lorec, who was lying on the couch next to him, looked over at Trey, worried at the abrupt wake up.

"What's wrong?" Nikki asked concerned.

Trey's blank look quickly transformed into a giant grin.

"Something big is about to happen." His grin grew wider.

"Trey, the last time you predicted that, all that happened was we won a free mocha Frappuccino at the Barnes and Noble Starbuck's," Nikki stated condescendingly.

"Well, yes. But, this time is different. I'm serious. I can really feel it. Something big is about to happen," Trey said, almost pleading.

"I know," she conceded – for now. "I guess we'll see-"

The clock clicked 7:45 pm. Simultaneously, Nikki cut off, and stared at Trey's chest, right over his heart (or where people think the heart is). Eyes wide, mouth ajar, she was just staring down at Trey's heart, and Trey was a perfect mirror of her.

Both of the identical spiral birthmarks that lay directly over their hearts were bursting with light, shining through their shirts. Trey's grin stretched even wider.

"I told you," he said trying to hold back a chuckle.

"Yeah, I guess you did. But how could this happen? I thought the Railey twins were the last," Nikki thought aloud, confused.

1

"I don't know what's going on, but I do know it means something big, and possibly catastrophic or maybe terrific."

Chapter 1

At what point do strangers become friends? At what point does sympathy take action and become sacrifice? Does fate exist or are some more lucky than others in the way coincidental occurrences of life arrange themselves? Are we bound to meet those that we know or does a series of random, inconsequential decisions lead us to them?

Life can be changed so quickly. In a year, a relationship can grow. In a month, war can break out. In a week, a marriage can fall apart. In a day, life can be brought into this world. In an hour, a job can be lost. In a minute, a moment can be made good. In a second, a life can be lost.

And it all starts where everything begins, when what's taken for granted is taken away.

Nearly seventeen years later, July 12, 2012.

I can't breathe.

I can't breathe. Claustrophobia does not begin to describe the feeling of fright at simultaneously losing all senses in an instant. One minute, colorful, tiny pixels are arranging themselves into pictures and motion on the TV, and in the next moment, the world is going dark and still. I can't see. I can't hear. I can't speak or touch or taste or smell. A moment ago I was a fully-functioning, regular human being, much less like every other sixteen-year-old, lying on the couch watching her favorite show.

3

All senses are void in this nightmare far worse than a dream. A nightmare in which you wait for something good or bad to happen, but are unable to make anything happen.

Slowly, as if jumbled and smothered by a muffler, I hear something – voices. They are fuzzy at first, and muddled, but soon become clearer. I do not recognize the speakers though; no one that was in the house when I was watching TV. The strange voices seem to be a man's and a woman's. They start low and hazy and seem to be on every side of me. I am oblivious to all other senses.

"This is her?" The woman says disgustedly. "She's the one who broke Kasten's prophecy?"

I wonder who Kasten is and what "prophecy" they are talking about. As far as I'm concerned, "prophecies" don't stretch beyond the free fortune cookies in Chinese fast food and the Weather Channel.

"Of course this is her," the man replies, rather annoyed. "Isn't it obvious she hasn't discovered her mark yet? In other words, let's hurry before she does get it, the Spell wears off, and she possibly escapes."

"Shouldn't we at least check, though?" the woman asks, unmoved by the man's frustration, becoming aggravated herself.

"Fine!"

I don't understand what is going on for a while. They aren't speaking. Maybe they left. More importantly, who are they

The man begins to speak again," See? There's the spiral. It's her. Now can we get out of here?"

4

He must mean my spiral birthmark that lies over my heart – well, the area in which people wrongly believe the heart lies. No one I know having anything quite like it, the thin, rickety white line appears more to be a scar than a birthmark as it winds itself in botched circles. Needless to say, I prefer conservative shirts as opposed to revealing ones in order to contest some of the staring. Why would these people need to see the mark though? How do they know it's there?

"Yes. You carry her. I might drop her by accident," the woman huffs (and I can tell the "might" would be a definitely and it wouldn't be an "accident").

"Well, yeah, I'm the one with the physical Gift. But you had better strengthen the Spell," *there is that word again.* "We wouldn't want to give her any sort of advantage."

I don't hear her response so I assume she nods. Unless, she is causing the paralysis and this spell causes my hearing to disappear again. That wouldn't make sense though therefore I must be in some sort of dream…Right?

Once again, I can no longer hear. Or sense anything else for that matter, lost in a dark oblivion.

Left with nothing but the ramblings of my mind, I allow my thoughts to wander, grow and multiply until I have a surplus of raging questions and a brilliant flare of confusion and worry. Most of these contemplations spring from the realization that I am entirely more coherent and logical during this occurrence than I normally am in a dream. Therefore is this somehow all real?

Am I being kidnapped at this very moment?

As troubling as it is, it cannot be possible, can it? Strangers talking of spells and marks, loss of sensory functioning; it's all over-imaginative dreaming. Whenever the time comes to wake up, I think I'll laugh at my stupidity. But this conscious black nothing is getting to be a bit tiresome. Eventually I feel myself falling into the next stage, a deeper phase of the sleep cycle, finally progressing into a state more clearly identified as a dream. I can't think quite as clearly and though this dream has returned to encompass the senses, my vision is blurred or maybe the picture is just dark and hazy.

I am being chased by a man and woman in a black expanse. My subconscious understands them to be the man and woman I heard speaking about spells and marks and gifts. I am imagining them to be rather wild looking or so they appear to be in the indistinct dream. The man looks grotesquely built, reflecting the shape and strength much like the Beast but with no hint of kindness. The woman seems to have hair that is literally on fire and the gleam of her eye leads me to believe she isn't on the same stable mental field as the rest of us. They are laughing menacingly, probably because when running in nothing there is nowhere to hide and I am beginning to move at a frighteningly lethargic pace. The woman's laugh is a high pitched shrill of a screech. The man's is a deep bass that carries and echoes in the open space.

Abruptly and rather illogically, the dream seems to shift and I think they have disappeared and given up. I stop and look around, being met with an eerie silence that reveals nothing of the black depths. Suddenly, the man and woman appear again and I feel like they've come out of nowhere. As if by magic the man is now holding something large and heavy but my muddled, sleep-driven mind can't discern what it is. In the next moment, he is throwing the object at me and I am dodging it, falling down in the process. I race to stand and run again but I feel myself being weighed down, my bones leaded, as if gravity is having a much greater effect here than it would on Earth. This fearfully thrilling dream is beginning to shift into the panicking fright of a nightmare. I am breathing faster, feeling like prey being trapped by the cruel and hungry predator.

The woman takes advantage of my immobility and summons her "spell" over me, taking control. I hyperventilate feeling my senses being drawn away again with a feeling similar to the sensation of falling. The last thing I remember is their sneer, evil faces and their heartless laughs before once again I am locked into my cage of empty oblivion.

Suddenly I am consciously jolted awake, aware that I truly am no longer dreaming but still too within the confines of sleep to open my drowsy eyes. I am lying on something cold and hard (yes I know it's called the floor), but where am I? It is too rough and course to be the finished wood floors of my family's house. I realize my hands are entangled with something that resembles a thick, bristly rope. Not entangled, but tied. The sounds around me are unfamiliar, too real to be from a stereo or TV but too peculiar

7

to be real. I hear gasps – and voices, but I'm not awake enough to understand them. It sounds as if people are hurling objects a far distance, but the sound of a bat-ball contact crack, the dribbling of basketball, or the sound of an onset as the ball is hiked never comes. Whatever they (him, her, whoever) are throwing, I never hear it land or hit something. However, after a gasp, sometimes I can decipher a thud as if a person is falling to the ground.

By this time, I have livened up and am too curious to be cautious. I open my eyes, completing my senses. I kind of wish I hadn't.

Around me is complete and utter chaos, or so it appears as I have no idea what is happening. I am not at home. I do not know anyone around me. I do not know what the hell is going on. But I am here. Truly, consciously here. *It can't be possible. That odd hallucination couldn't have been real!*

I pinpoint the two people who seem to have kidnapped me – as strangely terrifying it is to think that something like "kidnapping" could very possibly be a reality right now. I can tell it's them from the sound of their voices when they shout out orders or give arrogant remarks to the couple they are fighting.

The woman appears shallow. It's obvious by the way she looks, speaks, and fights (if that is what they are doing) that she thinks she is superior to everyone else. She holds her head up arrogantly, with a straight back and good posture, to the point of puffing her chest out with heavy pride. Her appearance is crazier, though. She has to be in her late twenties, maybe early thirties and has wild, curly, red hair and brown eyes that seem like vicious bears turned into spheres, packed into her snobbish eye sockets. Both give her a psycho look that also says, "I'm in charge." Now that I think about it, she'd be a really good Bellatrix Lestrange impersonator (hello, *Harry Potter* fan here).

The man looks to be about six inches taller than her, and she has to be around 5'10 (a few inches taller than me). He must be around the woman's age and has a stalky, muscular build with large, strong arms. His hair is cut to his ears and frames his face. It is the color of a starless, moon-free midnight. His green eyes are fierce and spark electricity as if they are tiny eels. Great! A bear and an eel; just what I want the people who kidnapped me to resemble.

After I watch them, I glance at the people fighting them. There is another girl fighting with the strange couple who are against my captors, and the guy is more or less giving her instructions. The girl has to be around my age if not a year or two older. She is athletic and strong. Her hair is also the color of midnight except it shimmers as if the moon really is shining above her. Her blue eyes are lighter than mine (when mine decide to be blue) and resemble a clear, blue sky. She is just about the same height as me. As I am staring at her, the kidnapper guy hits her. Hard. A giant bruise appears on her face then disappears instantly, as if it has healed already.

The man telling her what to do is about as tall as my kidnapper, but has a skinny frame with scrawny limbs. His short, yet wavy brown hair and big warm eyes radiate a soft, sweet personality, the kind of an open-minded, innocent dork.

Then there is the woman fighting beside the girl and man. Both this woman and the man seem to be around the same age as my kidnappers, maybe a little older. Her hair is a beautiful hazelnut color and glows with the radiance of the sun. The woman's eyes are a hazel of green and brown and have an orange tint that resembles a tame, yet fierce fire.

Once I look away from that group and pay more attention to the surrounding area, I realize two things. One, it looks as if we are all in a large, abandoned warehouse with a high cement ceiling, which explains why the ground was so cold and hard. Two, there are several other groups, spread apart. It is uncanny that in each group I can tell which side is with the kidnappers and which side is what I believe to be my "rescuers".

Only a few of these groups are actually making any physical contact – like the girl and kidnapper guy in the first group, who are fighting with others like them with an incredible speed and strength. The rest seem to be concentrating very hard, and then, to my complete horror, something supernatural attacks their opponent. In other cases, people, like the women in the first group, point to something then fling their hands and the object they are pointing at flies in the direction of their hands. Like a telekinesis.

Either way, I consider it all to be…strange.

The group nearest me – three kidnappers and one rescuer – shifts towards me. It almost seems like the "rescuer" is fighting against them to reach me.

Now that I can see him better, I can see that this "rescuer" happens to be, well, hot. He also seems to somewhat resemble the girl in the first group, despite their completely different hair colors. He has brown hair. His eyes are a much darker and deeper shade of blue and shimmer like stars in the night sky. He looks fit with broad, strong shoulders. I am startled, though, when with one flick of his hand, his three opponents are struck down by lightning. While he bends down to catch his breath (yeah, because flicking your hand is hard work), I stand gaping with shock and fright.

These are my rescuers? These supernatural beings! Where are the police, mom and dad, or Haley, my sister? I know I should be escaping (or trying to), but freak-outs were never my thing. Not to mention, I can't move, although this time it is of my own accord.

By now, the guy has caught his breath and is approaching me. What should I do? Should I run away? Should I grab something in case he is one of the bad guys? He flicks his hand as he is still coming towards me. I close my eyes and tense, preparing for the onslaught of pain. Nothing comes, though, but the rope that I have nearly forgotten is tied to my hands, falls to the ground. Eyes open this time, I brace myself for whatever might happen.

I stumble backwards and with grace, fall smack on my butt. He reaches me, extending his hand. He smiles, and says very smoothly, "Hey, I'm Zac."

Just a little side note: he has a nice smile.

I grab his hand and he pulls me up easily. He doesn't seem to strain himself.

"Stay close and try not to get yourself killed," he says dryly with a smirk. Well he seemed nice...until he opened his mouth.

Putting aside his hotness, I can't help but stare at him in disbelief. I had just watched him possibly kill three people without laying a finger on them. Now I know (at least now I think) that the ones like him are here to help me. But this, all of this, is too much.

The girl that looks like Zac's twin dodges a kick by kidnapper dude so the kidnapper hits the sweet rescuer guy smack in the chest and sends him flying. He doesn't recover like the girl. He remains on the ground, until Zac makes his way through the fighting to the man's side. He motions for me to come, and I slowly move towards them. It is all so over the top. By the time I reach them and see the giant bruise and gash from the kidnapper man's foot, bleeding all over the rescuer's chest, I am ready to burst from an overdose of...what would you call this? Fighting? Dreaming? Delirious, mind-spinning hallucinations.

Zac is looking down at the guy very seriously, trying to find a heartbeat.

"His pulse is faint," Zac says, calm in a crisis.

"What's his name?" I ask, choking.

"Trey. Trey Lorec. He *is* a psychic," he speaks with such emphasis on "is" as if he won't let "is" become a "was".

I just nod, squelching the desire to ask him what exactly he means by "a psychic." I look around wonderingly at what was chaos before, is really the rescuer side losing…significantly. Next I see the rescuer woman who is fighting the woman who kidnapped me thrown by an object that hits her. Even though she slowly stands up, all of it hurts me. Which, if you think about it, is strange in itself since I don't even know any of these people – or if they really are here to save me.

I keep thinking how much these strangers are risking for me. Then again, that's exactly what our men and women of service do every day. But there is no way for them, or me, to be sure I am *the* girl they are looking for, the girl who broke "Kasten's" "prophecy."

I hope I am – for them, I think to myself. If that's even what this is all about.

My thoughts are suddenly interrupted by a bright, ultra-violet, white light directed towards me. Even though it is pointed at me, shouldn't everyone be looking at what is causing it? No, they have all stopped fighting to look at me, or rather my heart. I follow their gaze and look down, almost fainting (which I never do) with astonishment.

Right over my spiral birthmark, directly over my heart, a brilliant light emerges. It's as if my mark is the source of the glowing. But how? I pull down the top left part of my shirt to expose my mark, and the light becomes brighter, unhindered. My birthmark *is* the cause of the glowing.

Seeing its strange beauty, the relieved faces of the "rescuers", and the sneer, arrogant looks of the "kidnappers," fills me with some kind of power. I am also filled with anger towards those who have taken me, and are now challenging the people whom I believe to be good people. With a will to protect, I lash out with that power and that anger towards the evil in the room, having not the slightest clue what I am doing, or what the consequences might be.

It seems as if madness has broken out everywhere: blurred explosions and dancing orange lights, dark shadows gliding about, and red. Lots of red. With each scream I feel weaker and weaker. My eyes flutter and close. I collapse. The last thing I see is Zac (I think) running towards me, catching me in his strong arms. I lose consciousness.

Chapter 2

Why am I so hungry? Is the pounding pain my head? I slowly open my eyes that are as heavy as lead. There is a guy, who looks strangely familiar, sitting next to my bed. I jolt up, preparing to scream, fight, or bite – whatever is necessary.

"It's okay. Don't sit up," Zac reassures me as he gently lays me back down. Oh yeah, it's just Zac. Duh.

"What happened?" I ask dazed and sleepy.

"You don't remember?" he questions surprised.

I am about to say "Well, duh! That's why I asked," but I feel as if something is coming back.

"No, I don't think s-"I cut off as last night's events flash through my head. "Wait, I do. I remember," I am nodding my head for some strange reason.

Zac relaxes in his chair. I think I worried him when I didn't remember.

Before I can say anything, he asks, "What's your name?"

I probably should be more hesitant to answer, but I feel as if I can trust him – strangely, "Kira Taylor."

"You're very special. Did you know that, Kira?" Zac says, very enthralled at how *special* I am.

"Let me guess, you think I'm the girl who broke Kasten's, or who's ever prediction," I say, uncomfortable hearing how *special* I am. I'm okay with being the girl, whoever she is. I just don't want to hear it all the time.

His expression turns from thoughtful to pure shock, "How do you know about Kasten and his prediction?"

"I don't know *who* Kasten is or *what* the prediction is, but I heard the people who kidnapped me talking about him. What *is* the prediction that I supposedly did something to?" I inquire curiously, rolling my eyes – like I don't care. Pfft!

"Bret and Tessa," at my confusion he continues, "that's who kidnapped you. And Kasten's very latest prediction said that Lily and I – Lily's my twin. You probably saw her fighting with Trey and his wife, Nikki-"I acknowledge that I had seen her, well, them, "anyway, me and Lily were supposed to be the last Gifted. But then, a year later, you were born, with the mark," he finishes.

"You just threw about six different names of six different people I have never met before in the same explanation all together. I got Bret and Tessa, and Kasten is a psychic…The rest not so much."

"Alright," he says, and I can almost visibly see his brain doubling backwards," Lily is my twin. Dark brown but sometimes looks like black hair, yay-high. She was fighting against your kidnappers, Bret and Tessa. She was with Trey. Remember him? He was the guy that got kicked in the chest by Bret? And his wife, Nikki, was the other woman fighting with him and my sister."

"So you said Kasten predicted you and your sister would be the last… *'Gifted'*…but along came me and I'm… *'Gifted'* also? That's what's going on?"

"Right."

16

"Ok, so the mark…?"

He pulls down the top left part of his shirt to expose a white, spiral birthmark, the exact mark as mine. Subconsciously, I put a hand over mine as if recognizing they are the same.

"But what is it?"

"It's the Gifted mark. It is how we are identified as Gifted."

I pause for a second. Something keeps nagging at me.

"So I broke his prediction? You can't be right all the time," I say.

Shaking his head, he says, "Kasten has *never* been wrong. Every one of his prophecies has come true. Until you."

"But how do you know it's me?" I ask trying to discover a way out of this, a loop hole.

"Well, I know you're special because you're Gifted with four Gifts."

"Gifted? Gifts?" I am lost…again.

"Your mark – the spiral over your heart – gifts you. Gifts are – I'd guess you'd call them 'powers.' Mine is weather. Trey's is predicting, or prophecy. Lily's is extreme physical strength and healing."

"She has two, so why is four so different?" I ask.

"Try to keep up," Zac huffs – *like it is my fault*. "Some come together like a package; you can't have one without the other. Like Lily's or Nikki's," he says very slowly and teacher-like.

"Nikki could only move things with her mind. At least that's all I saw her do."

"Yes, she's a telekinesis, but more importantly she has a Gifted mind. She can do other things also, like communicate with people through their minds. We call it 'Minding' people."

I nod understandingly.

"So what's so different about mine?"

"You have four *separate* Gifts, four Gifts that haven't ever come all together."

"Which are?" I ask, unable to remember any lightning or objects flying around that I had been controlling.

"Fire, water, earth, and air...You must have been in too much shock to understand what was happening last night. After you received your Gift – that's when your mark glowed and you officially became Gifted – you seemed to look angry, and then it happened. Everywhere the Scorned started screaming." His eyes unfocus, remembering last night. A mild look of horror washes over his face. "But, they were all being attacked in different ways. Some just combusted and burst into flames. Others started choking and spitting out water. Some the earth beneath their feet opened and swallowed them whole or vines grew right through the concrete and strangled them. And the rest, the wind would pick up and slam them so hard against the wall you could hear every bone being broken and the life hurled out of them," he stops, his eyes refocusing and coming back up to meet mine.

18

"I sound like a monster!" I yelp in disbelief and close to tears. "Did I kill all of them?"

Zac shakes his head solemnly, and then adds, "Many survived, including Bret and Tessa. They were injured badly and we let them escape – more like they went running. But we needed to know what you were capable of and if you hadn't…we probably wouldn't have made it out of there." He looks into my eyes and I can almost hear him saying a silent thank you.

I blink back more tears and ask," Why was I so tired and ended up passing out?"

"The more you use your Gifts, the more tired you become. Killing takes an even greater amount of energy. It's extremely difficult to even kill one Gifted person. Whoever put us here, wanted to ensure one group wouldn't abuse their Gifts and massacre the other group. Killing as many as you did…we all thought you'd die."

"That's why you had to stop and catch your breath after you knocked out your opponents."

Zac nods and says, "Yeah, and I'm uh sorry for that. You shouldn't have had to see it – not so soon. *Why are you looking at me like that?*"

"I just expected you to say something more along the lines of 'builds character; get over it.' That's all," I smirk.

He quirks an eyebrow, "I have my moments. But if that's how you want it to be then frankly you should get used to the violence and quit being so awkward and uncomfortable when talking about it."

"Okay, mean much?"

"So does that indicate you like my first reply better? I mean, I thought it was more charming myself," Zac smirks. I roll my eyes.

He pauses and looks down. I think he is confused.

"What's wrong?" I wonder what I've possibly done wrong now.

"You said you *heard* Bret and Tessa talking about Kasten. They didn't have you frozen?" He lifts his confusion towards me.

"They did – at least the rest of me was frozen so to speak, but my hearing wasn't. She must have strengthened it when we left my house because I couldn't hear anymore after that. Why wasn't I frozen when I woke up in the warehouse?" I ask.

"Tessa had to use the strength that was freezing you to fight with. It's interesting, though. You were unthawing her Gift and you hadn't technically been Gifted yet."

"How can she freeze someone like that?"

"One of the perks of having a Gifted mind. She can use hers to get inside of your brain and freeze your senses, to control certain segments of your nerves, even parts of your brain. We call it the Spell. She was only able to completely freeze you – well not even completely since you were able to hear. Anyways, she was only able to freeze you by herself like that because you hadn't been Gifted yet."

"I heard them call it that: the Spell."

He nods and then his head drops down, in his own little world. There is a sort of awkward silence; both of us jotting down on our imaginary mind pad what we have just discussed.

"You still haven't told me how I am beyond reasonable doubt *the* girl."

"Because you're here, and that you have the mark is proof enough. But if you need more...How old are you?" he asks, but it seems as if he already knows.

"Almost seventeen."

"See! Lily and I were supposed to be the last and we just turned eighteen. We were born in 1994. If you're about to turn seventeen then you were born in - ..."

"1995."

"You were born a year later, with the mark, causing Kasten's prophecy to become his first false one. And now, everyone knows you have four Gifts, and we're all wondering how Kasten could *not* have seen you coming," his eyes are filled with a glimmering wonder.

I am silent. I look everywhere but at him. How can I be the girl? What are the odds?

We sit here a while silently. I wouldn't say it is an awkward silence like before. We're just thinking.

"So... you and that girl – Lily, you said – are twins?"

He nods.

"Huh, you look alike but your hair is completely different," I smile.

"Yeah, most people guess we're brother and sister but not actually twins," Zac's lips quirk up in a smile.

Awkward silence yet again. But an interesting topic flirts across my mind.

"So why are we here? Why do we have these 'Gifts'?"

"Why is anyone here? How can anyone know? I guess because God – or whoever you believe is out there – wanted us to be, but why? I don't know," Zac looks up at me with wondering eyes that at the start of his next sentence fill with hate. "Although, others have the opinion that we are here to torture and kill people. That, because of our Gifts, we're superior to all. Obviously those opinions come from the Scorned. You can see why we fight."

I can tell it is a touchy subject.

"Why do you call us the Gifted, and Bret and Tessa the Scorned?"

"Because it's our name and that's theirs. You're defined as Gifted or Scorned by your mark. We both have the spiral. When your mark recognizes itself, it glows white if you're Gifted or red if you're Scorned. It's pretty much your classic good vs. evil," he rolls his eyes. "But something extra happens to the mark; at the point they become Scorned, their spiral forms thorns that jet out and connect the rings."

"Can your color/side change?" I ask.

"Well, you're chosen by the content of your heart," Zac articulates the words as if he is almost disgusted by it and explains,"-*yeah because that's not cheesy at all*. If you're really determined, and truly change, then yes. Either way it's painful. It's easier to go from Gifted to Scorned; whereas it's extremely difficult to transfer from the Scorned to the Gifted. Again, typical good vs. evil."

"Have people ever done it?" I ask curiously.

"Well yeah," he says dramatically, smiling.

Here I am, starring and smiling at a complete stranger like I've known him my whole life. As if finding out that the natural laws of existence that you thought ruled your life are completely untrue is no big deal. Acting as if everything is 'A-O-K'. Then again, I'm not the only one smiling now am I?

Before I can start feeling awkward, someone knocks on the door in the far left corner of the room. Only now do I look around the room and see it is an actual bedroom and not a hospital (or loony bin). Though if I was really in a loony bin, meaning I am mentally insane, I doubt I'd be seeing what is actually here anyways. The walls are the color of blue jays and it matches well with the silver-thread bedspread. There are nature pictures on the wall and funky lamps and chairs decorating the floor. It feels very home-y, like someone's own little corner of the world. I see (shockingly just now) that I'm not attached to any type of "machine." In fact, the only "machines" in the room, are modern technology like a TV and a digital clock.

Nikki Lorec (at least I think it's her) walks into the room. "Hello," she greets me and smiles brightly.

"Hi," I return.

"Kira, this is-" Zac begins to introduce us but I interrupt him, hoping to show him I had been paying attention to his account earlier.

"Nikki Lorec, right?" I ask shyly, in case I am wrong.

"Zac here must actually be doing something productive if you already know my name. Nice job Zac," Nikki Lorec applauds him, with mock amazement.

"It is known to happen you know," Zac grumbles.

Nikki and I laugh.

Wait! Her husband, Trey, seemed as if he was critically injured last night. I want to know if he is okay and recovering well, but I don't want to upset Nikki. I look at her hard. She is smiling brightly at me, her eyes aren't puffy and red. Her face isn't tear-stained. I take a chance.

I say slowly and sincerely, "How's Trey – I mean – Mr. Lorec?"

Nikki smiles brightly and says, "You were right the first time; he prefers Trey – as do most adults here." All of a sudden, she begins staring and smiling at the still open door. She continues, "To answer your question, he's fine; a few bruises but he'll definitely be fine."

"A few bruises?" A man shouts teasingly and waltzes into the room. "You call two broken ribs 'a few bruises'?" Trey (well

24

of course it's him) is smiling the entire time, and when he reaches Nikki, he corners her into his arms and kisses her.

With an even brighter smile, she says, "Yes I do, because only your weak bones and fragile body would break after a kick like that."

Obviously she is teasing him, and he doesn't seem to mind. Actually, he rather seems to enjoy it as now he sweeps her up and kisses her again.

However the funniest thing is Zac clears his throat, as if he feels uncomfortable around it. I pretend to cough to cover my giggle.

"Oh, yes, right," Trey turns to us with a friendly smile. "Zac probably already told you, but I'm Trey Lorec. This is my wife, Nikki Lorec. Of course, you've already met Zac Railey, and you might have seen his twin, Lily, fighting with us last night. The rest of the introductions will have to wait until you actually meet the people," he pauses for a second. "I heard you were worried about me, but really I am fine. Two ribs will only take a day or two to heal when Lily is able to heal it. So Kira, how are you?"

How does he know my name? I'd just met these people, and I've only told Zac my name.

Nikki answers my silent, confounded question," You probably have never seen *us* before, but we've been watching you for almost seventeen years now."

Yeah, 'cause that's not creepy.

25

"Alright, so 'watching' was probably not the best word to use. More of... protecting. Haven't you noticed that while terrible things may happen to everyone else, your family has been untouched? You probably haven't seen us, but I'd bet you've felt us; or your dog, when he seemed to be staring and barking at nothing, it was really us.

"And when you feel like someone's in the shadows somewhere watching you, you hurry up and go inside, but it was just us – which, we really didn't mean to scare you at all, but it was necessary for us to be there."

"Why were you there?" I ask what should be an obvious question.

Nikki looks a little annoyed; not towards me though, more so towards Trey. Huh.

"To prevent last night from happening. We knew eventually the Scorned would come and try to catch you, and even here they might," she adds, "so we'd always watch you to scare them off before anything occurred. However, he-" she points her fierce eyes towards Trey, who slyly smiles, "just *had* to get a coffee while we were following you home from your camp."

Getting over the weird fact that they'd followed me (everywhere, it sounds like), I notice her change in tone from annoyed to serious and slightly sad. "Bret and Tessa obviously saw we weren't there – oh I'm sorry, did Zac tell you about them?"

"You have no faith in me," Zac says seriously.

"Well, did you?"

"Yes," he says, grouchily.

Nikki doesn't reply, but she smiles.

"Anyways, they saw we weren't there and well-" her smile disappears, and she acquires that look of 'I'm sure you can figure it out' in her eyes.

I look down and nod. That reminds me of a scary, but important question that makes my heart sink when I remember. I gasp.

"My parents, my sister, my dog. What happened to them? Are they okay?" Tears well up in my eyes at the possibilities.

Something is wrong. No one will look at me. No one is smiling anymore, and they all appear uncomfortable. Zac is looking at Nikki and Trey helplessly. A silent connection seems to pass between them.

"What? What is it?" Those tears are now spilling over.

They continue to ignore me as Nikki shakes her head at the two of them almost warningly.

"Just tell me!"

Now she turns to me.

"Kira, they're okay; it's okay. You can calm down," she says reassuringly. She doesn't look heartened; she looks like she is hiding something. I gaze at her nervously. She tries to smile at me and seems to force out the words, "Your family's okay."

"When can I go back? When can I see them? Do they know I'm okay? Do they know where I am?"

27

"Kira – calm down; too many questions," Nikki stutters, looking overwhelmed and suddenly exhausted. The other two look nervous and worried and they turn to Nikki for guidance again. She pauses hesitantly, as if she is selecting her next words very delicately, "They're not worried about you and we're…working on getting you-"

"Nikki," Zac interrupts, warningly. He looks grim but shell-shocked.

" – better right now," she finishes, turning to glare at him as if trying to say she isn't an idiot.

They aren't telling me something – something bad. It fashions apprehensions and troubles my already worried mind. Why can't they just tell me? What is this bad? They say my family is alright. If they were kidnapped or dead, Nikki wouldn't say they are fine. Would she? Would she really lie? What is going on?

Nikki turns back to me and sees my look of utter anxiety.

"Kira, breathe. They are okay," she punctuates every word to show there is no double meaning, no trick. "Just let it go for now, okay? They are fine; you are fine. Trust me."

For now, I will.

A shadow appears in the doorway; from my angle I can't see who it might be. Whoever it is knocks on the frame and then walks in. It is a guy who has sandy blonde hair and dark pine green eyes with a few pale freckles. He is holding a tray carrying what looks to be someone's breakfast.

Teasingly, he asks, "Someone order room service?"

Nikki smiles and explains, "Kira, this is Sterling. He has an earth Gift – oh wait, did Zac-" She breaks off when she sees Zac's expression as if he is disappointed in her doubt for the second time. She continues, "Well alright, never mind then. Sterling, perfect timing."

"I try my best," he says boastfully, faking a humble tone as he pulls out the legs of the tray and sets it on my lap. "Oh, and Kayla told me to tell you that we're out of pain killers because of last night but there are still people that need them."

Nikki looks solemn, "Alright thanks. If you get a chance, tell her I'll send someone to get some more soon."

He nods and begins to leave after turning back to say, "Nice to meet you Kira."

"You too," I smile cordially. I look down at the food on the tray and see scrambled eggs and a slice of bacon – more like smell it. Suddenly a wave of hunger hits me like a tidal wave and it is as if I haven't seen food in days. Trying to hold some dignity, I fly straight into the food, mindful of the three people still in the room.

I hear Nikki speak to Zac, "Will you go and get those painkillers? I know you've already done a lot, but I also know you've gotten them before and know the exact ones to get."

"Yeah I don't mind. Someone should maybe stay with Kira though," he suggests casually.

"I'll be ok," I say defensively. I don't want them to feel the need to babysit me.

29

"Well actually, I was going to suggest that if you're feeling up to it you could go with him. A little fresh air would probably help you adjust to all this and then you don't have to lie in a bed all day too. As long as you think you can handle it, I'll leave it up to you."

Now that I think about it that does sound awfully nice. Zac looks as if he wants to object but decides to sulk instead.

"I would actually really like to go," I smile, but then add, "Can I finish my food first?"

Nikki giggles then interrupts Zac, who was getting ready to say something probably sarcastic, "Of course, and if *he-*" she motions over to Zac," gives you any grief or pushes you too far, you just let us know."

She winks at me.

I look sideways at Zac to see him frowning and I smirk," Oh I will."

"Alright, we'll let you eat then," she smiles then leaves the room.

Trey smiles and says goodbye before following his wife out the door.

In between mouthfuls of eggs, I ask Zac, "What's your sudden problem?"

"Didn't realize I was a taxi driver," he mumbles.

Luckily, I happen to not have any food in my mouth as it drops open. I turn to glare incredulously at him.

"I'm sorry, if you didn't want to talk to me you didn't have to stay this long and if you don't want me to go then all you have to do is say something," I say defensively. "After all, Nikki only *suggested* I could come with you; she didn't *tell* me I had to go."

"But you want to."

"Yeah but not if you're going to be a jerk about it. I didn't realize how badly you wanted to go alone."

"It's not because I want to go alone. I don't want something to happen if you leave here and don't have enough people around to protect you."

Okay, well that's actually kind of thoughtful but it doesn't explain his curt comment though.

"So you had to be rude why?"

"Because..." he says uncomfortably, "it's easier than being honest."

"What's so terrible as to say you're worried about my security right after I was just attacked last night? It seems like a reasonable concern," I say truthfully.

He avoids my eyes but then looks straight into them, as if desiring to say something that rests somewhere deep within the folds of his mind. He seems to decide against it in the end.

"Yeah, I just overreacted," he says honestly, but it isn't what he wants to say.

I finish my breakfast and he removes the tray from my lap and sets it on the floor. I realize I'm still wearing a T-shirt and shorts from the volleyball camp the night before – before the world I knew flipped upside down.

"Hey, do you think before we leave I could change into something…Oh, never mind, I don't have anything to change into. I guess I can just go in this," I say dejectedly.

"I'd ask my sister if you could borrow some of her clothes but it might take forever to find her," he shrugs. "Besides, I doubt they smell that bad."

I look at him for a moment, not quite sure how I am supposed to respond to that. I narrow my eyes suspiciously and a smile starts to creep on my face. Bemused, I let it go and begin to get out of bed. He stands from his seat. We move towards the door but I stop.

"Should we get the tray?" I ask curiously.

"Uh, no, I'll get it later. Let's just get out of here," he says casually.

"What's the hurry?"

He hesitates as if he is searching for an answer. *Why is he suddenly acting so weird?*

"Some people might really need those pain relievers."

Good save but that wasn't what was really troubling him. For the second time, I shrug it off, but if he keeps acting so odd I will eventually have to ask him what his deal is.

I walk out of the room and he shuts the door behind us. I take a moment to look around. We are at the end of a hallway with three doors on the left and only one door on the right. The floor is a beautiful white marble with swirls of black in it, almost as if painted. I closely follow Zac as we reach the end of this hallway and turn right. It opens up into two new ones. The one straight in front of us is short and only has a couple of doors and a window, but it seems that at the end it opens up on both sides to a longer hallway. Zac begins walking down the hallway to our left that is longer and lined with many doors. At the very end, natural light streams in from a window. As we come closer, I now can see the window makes up the entire far wall. As we reach the end and turn to our right again, the window stops a few feet ahead, replaced by a deep gold-painted wall, but begins again farther down. This hallway is short like the first one I had seen and at the end I see it transforms into a spiral staircase that weaves its way down to what must be lower levels. On the right, it opens onto *another* hallway, presumably the hallway that the first hallway opened up to.

Keeping an eye on Zac who had drifted in front of me, I gaze out the window. First thought: we are high up. Second thought: wherever we are, it is beautiful though almost familiar. What I assume to be the front yard, as there is a driveway towards the left hand side, is gorgeous. Let's just say it is perfectly beautiful. I know nothing about landscaping, but whoever did this was an artist. Striking, large willow trees (at least three) spot the yard; their boughs and branches and leaves gently swaying in the wind. A little pond is found in the center of the yard. Not only the grass but also the leaves of the trees are a deep, healthy, lush green. Beyond the large, open yard is a heavily wooded area that goes as far as my slightly-high view will allow me to see, as if we're immersed deep in a forest, yet safe and secluded in our own open alcove.

"Kira," Zac says, pulling my attention away from the window to see him a good distance in front of me, waiting on the top step of the staircase.

I catch up to him quickly and we begin to descend the stairs. The steps are the same beautiful marble of the flooring of the hallways, and the rail is a twisted, black iron. We walk down and around, in circles; spiraling circles. It seems to be endless. Every so often we come to a landing, but Zac continues on. Sometimes I see a couple people on the floors, but they seem to be going about their business. By the time we finally reach the bottom I conclude there are four floors in this colossal mansion and also that I am exceedingly dizzy. As we approach the final steps, I see a contemporarily decorated foyer. The room is filled with comfortable looking couches, little side tables, rugs, and a glass coffee table arranged in the middle. A sparkling crystal chandelier hangs from a high ceiling. The far corner, the one next to the front doors, is completely consumed by a large, unblemished window that I would love to stop and look out of. However Zac continues flying towards another beautiful feature of what is turning out to be a stunning house. The front door is a double door, made of beautifully stained and glossed wood, and edged in the center of each door are exquisitely distorted, carved glass windows. The entire room in conjunction with the marble staircase and flooring is an absolutely magnificent scene.

Unfortunately, I don't have long to sight-see as Zac throws open one of the doors and begins to descend the front gray slate steps. *Does that boy have to walk so fast?* I am jogging to keep up. The front yard I have seen four floors up is just as striking up close and personal. I follow Zac on the now visible sidewalk that leads to a large, paved driveway. On the far side is a small tin building with about ten garage doors.

Zac crosses the driveway and walks through the door of the garage. You know what? I think he was purposefully trying to get ahead of me as he calls back to say," Just wait out here."

I huff to a stop and stay where I am. Less than a minute later, the third garage door opens and Zac drives out a silver *PT Cruiser*. I don't know much about cars, but given that I can see other cars in the garage, I just thought Zac would pick something…I don't know…a little *sportier*. I stand, arms crossed, watching him with a look of mockery; sarcasm just waiting on the tip of my tongue.

He pulls to a stop, passenger side door just a few feet away. I walk over and get in, buckling my seat belt as the car begins to move. S*afety first. Second,* I look over at him and raise my eyebrows questioningly.

"What?" he asks gruffly.

"Nothing," I shrug nonchalantly, looking away. "I just didn't pick you as someone who liked this type of car."

"I'm not," he says roughly, grunting but then adds in a more pleasant tone, "but the goal isn't to look flashy; it's to blend in." Well I guess that makes a bit more sense now.

"So where are we going?" I ask into the silence.

"Um, were you not paying attention during the exchange Sterling, Nikki, and I had? Well, now that I think about it, you were absorbing that food like a vacuum, probably not even taking the time to chew."

Glaring at him but deciding not to respond to his rude comment I snapped at him, "I heard about the pain killers. I was just wondering if you were going to a pharmacy to get them or a plain grocery store. I was also wondering where we are," I look at him wonderingly.

"There's a local Wal-Mart we get them from," he says casually enough, but then he seems to have the same uncomfortable look as he had earlier when I had asked about my parents, "and I'm not really supposed to tell you where we are."

"You could anyways though," I say hopefully.

"I also don't really want to tell you." You would think he had said that sarcastically or smirking, but no. It was awkward and uncomfortable.

"Why-"

"Just let it go...please." He has a pained expression on his face and he is staring intently at the road ahead of him. "Someone will tell you eventually – maybe it'll even be me, but not now ok?" He speaks with true sincerity and such politeness for the first time

36

I'd spoken with him – which granted hasn't been a long time so far.

"But what is-"

"Kira," he interrupts, sighing, "just trust me for now."

Rather annoyed and disgruntled, curiosity raging inside of me, I say through my stubborn frown, "Fine."

"Thank you," he breaths, relieved sounding.

"You know what?" he asks suddenly, his face constricting with some "deep thought" and he smiles slyly. "You should probably put a blindfold on – just in case you've been to this area."

I look at him with complete astonishment. *He can't be serious can he?*

"I'm not a hostage," I almost shriek, defensively.

"Yeah," he says – like he really means no, "but like I said, you really shouldn't learn where we are – for your own safety of course," he adds with a look of assurance. I can ascertain it is fake as his eyebrows are raised just a little too high and the look in his eyes is sarcastic; then again, when hasn't it been.

"And what exactly am I going to do if I find out this mysterious location? Huh? It's not like I'm trying to get away from you guys; I'm not trying to run."

"I don't know," he says doubtfully, joking," I don't know if I can trust you yet-"

"You don't know if you can trust me, yet just a few minutes ago you were asking me to trust you?"

"*Don't* change the subject missy," he says pointedly, as if he is an interrogator in one of those old, classic cop shows.

"You can trust me," I say skeptically, interrupting him again – he just makes it so difficult *not* to.

"Yeah…" he says dismally, sighing; his features sagging. Suddenly he perks up again, and he is smirking, "I don't think so."

"Zac!" I say astounded. "What do you plan to do when I say 'no, I won't put it on,' because – FYI – that's *exactly* what I'm about to say. No-"

The car screeches to a halt. Instinctively, I throw my hands out in front of me to stop my rapid approach towards the console in front of me.

"Geez!" I yelp. "What was that Zac?" I squeak.

He has already stepped out of the car and is crossing the front, coming towards my side of the car. Keep in mind: we're still not out of the driveway but fully surrounded by woods.

"Zac? What are you doing?" I ask, confounded as he passes my door and opens the back seat's door.

"Now I think," he is obviously mumbling to himself as I have to strain to hear any of it, "someone said there was – Ah, there it is," he says rather gleefully.

"What are you-?"

Suddenly he is next to my door, swinging it open.

"Be a good girl and put this on, okay?" he commands rather than asks me, holding out what looks like a cloth head band that is actually pretty cute. I just have a problem wearing it…over my eyes!

"You think I'm just going to put it on?" I ask, quirking an eyebrow cynically. "When you won't even *ask me nicely?*"

He rolls his eyes then huffs and continues speaking.

"Fine," he says like a little boy who was told he has to wash the dirt off his face," will you *please* be a good girl and put this on?"

"No," I remark simply.

"What was the point of asking nicely then?" he asks incredulously.

"I just wanted to hear you say it," I say.

He looks stupefied and then narrows his eyes scornfully.

"Well you are going to wear this blindfold whether you put it on or I do," he says stubbornly and starts to reach for my head before I defensively swing out at him.

"Hey!" I yelp, ducking my head farther away from him and swatting out at him with my hands as if he is an annoying fly I am trying to shoo away – which, in my opinion, is an excellent comparison.

"Ow! Watch it!" he screeches.

"Then keep that blindfold away from my head," I snap.

Yet the boy tries again. And again he is shocked that I swing my hand at his face. Unfortunately, he has quick reflexes and catches my hand before it makes contact with his nose.

"Will you quit trying to punch me?"

"Will you quit trying to put that blindfold on me?"

"No," he states rather simply.

"Then no, I won't."

"I'm trying to do this for your own good. Trust me. The fact that it annoys you so much is only a bonus," he says, sounding honest at first but now sounding quite elated.

"Here's the thing, you keep saying trust you and you still haven't shown me why I should. The other thing is, how can I or *why should I* believe you when you say not to ask about my parents or where we are, even though everyone has said they're fine?" When I started this rant I didn't mean for it to end up in the grim state it does.

He pales slightly from his normal arrogance.

"I thought we agreed to drop those subjects?"

"Well, you're trying to convince me to put a blindfold over my eyes – *apparently* – for my own good. I can't know where we are. Otherwise, I'll discover some kind of bad news I'm apparently not prepared to hear. Therefore *you* brought it back up."

"I – The thing is-" For the first time today, Zac seems to have the inability to find the words he is trying to communicate. In other words: he's stumped.

I smirk," Right, so you just expect me not to protest at being blind for a while when I don't know if you're making me do it because you want to laugh at how stupid I look or because *I* would really not want to know whatever it is no one seems to want to tell me."

"Do you even realize how confusing what you just said is?"

"Yes I do, but I'm pretty sure you still understood it."

"I *was* joking around with it more than I should have," he admits honestly. He is still kneeling next to me, the car door still wide open. "I know I keep giving you crossed signals but I promise I won't tease you anymore about the blindfold if you'll just wear it until we get back to the driveway. Please?" he sighs, and the symbolic white flag is being raised.

"Okay," I mumble, frowning and rolling my eyes.

"And I also promise not to bring up either of the conversations again," he says, almost smiling, or maybe it's more so one of those half smiles.

"Good," I say expressly, half smiling myself.

"Here," Zac says, slowly handing me the blindfold. "Do you want help?"

"It would be easier if you tie it," I rationalize aloud.

He nods acquiescently. I turn to face the driver's side and hold up the blindfold against my eyes, extending the ends back towards Zac. He takes them from me and gently ties a knot in it, not even yanking any hair.

"See? That wasn't so bad," he says truthfully, but he doesn't sound as if he is bragging.

"You promised no teasing," I remind him, just in case.

"I wasn't," he says defensively. I can picture him backing away with his hands raised in surrender.

41

I hear my car door close and a different one open and now slam shut. I hear the engine *click-click* for a minute before thrumming to a start. I hear the tires of the car grind on the pavement and I know we are moving again.

Chapter 3

The rest of the car ride is quiet. Awkward quiet. I don't like not being able to pass the time looking out the window. I don't like having a blindfold on either but then again you already knew that. It seems to take forever but it is probably only ten minutes. There are a couple of times Zac stops the car as I am suddenly jerked forward. Every time it happens I think we have arrived but it must always be a stoplight or stop sign. Finally, he parks the car and turns off the engine. I can hear him moving – twisting possibly – in his seat.

"I'll be quick. I know exactly where they are and what to get. Don't leave the car and don't take off the blindfold."

Without so much as a goodbye he slams the door shut.

Now if a boy your age, who was arrogant and cocky, told you to do something for reasons you're not allowed to know, would you listen to him? I didn't think so.

I count to a minute in my head until I decide he has to be far enough away from the car. I reach behind me and undo the knot with difficulty.

What did he do to it? I think, frustrated. I undo it eventually though – with sore finger nails might I add. I look out all the windows to see nothing but a wall of cars.

Suddenly in the corner of my eye, I see a flash of movement and jump, startled. In the next second, Zac is opening the door and reaching across his seat to the cup holder where some money is sitting. He has practically grabbed it and is leaving again, when he notices me.

He stops when he sees me and looks at me a moment like nothing is wrong. Then a wave of irritation hits him.

Through his clenched jaw Zac says, "I thought we agreed you should wear the blindfold. Not to mention, I just told you not to take it off."

"Oh," I say, looking as if I am confused, "I thought you just meant only wearing it for the car ride." That's about when I start to smirk, "Also, you should probably be aware that in most studies done, kids don't like following orders from other *kids* and they tend to disobey their bossy companions."

"Put it back on," he says pointedly.

"Nah," I say casually.

"You already agreed to wear it," he says dubiously.

"Yeah, but I didn't agree to how long or under what terms," I say smartly.

"Kira-"

"Zac. See I know your name too," I smile at him, as if this is a game.

"Just-" He shakes his head as if he doesn't know what to tell me. "Just stay right here for a minute. I promise I won't be gone but two seconds. I'm just going to look to see if the Wal-Mart says what city or state we're in."

I roll my eyes but nod passively. He takes about three seconds to peak his head around the cars and look towards the

Wal-Mart. He leans back into the car, using his hands and extended arms to lean on the seat.

"Alright, you can come with me into the store, but you have to stay with me *and* you only have to keep the blindfold on while we're driving. Does that sound fair?" he asks, begrudgingly.

My frown transforms into a fake, cheery smile, "That's much better."

I hop out of the car brightly, like a five year old who is about to go into the candy shop with a ten dollar bill. Zac looks as if he wants to punch someone and crosses his arms haughtily. He stands there grumpily, like the said five year old's brother who has learned that he not only isn't allowed to buy anything but he has to watch his little sister pick out whatever she wants *and* watch her eat it.

"I didn't realize you were one of the Seven Dwarfs," I purposefully think aloud, smiling undauntedly.

He looks at me, puzzled, "What?"

"Oh come on, you know: *Snow White* always had dwarfs around protecting her. There were seven of them, short, lived all together-"

"Yes I know what you're talking about. What do you mean 'I'm one of them'?"

"Right now, you vividly resemble Grumpy."

And with that I pass by him, basically skipping down the rows of cars, but not before seeing his appalled expression. It makes me smile.

"Come on slow poke," I call back to him.

"Why don't you calm down?" he asks snidely, closer than I had thought. He caught up to me quickly. "I mean what? Did you have a *Monster* sometime between I said you could come and the moment you stepped out of the car? You're like a freaking two year old on a sugar high."

I roll my eyes, "It's called optimism, happiness, joy; any of those would work. You're just cranky because I don't have to wear the blindfold and can come with you."

"I'm cranky because I have to babysit the aforementioned two year old on the sugar high," he grumbles.

"Quit whining," I smirk.

We enter the Wal-Mart, the doors sliding away when its sensor detects us. It is packed – like all Wal-Marts are; one of the inconveniences of low prices. The strange thing is, it resembles the Wal-Mart I have back home in Kenosha. The location of the pharmacy, rotisserie, shelves, vegetables, garden section; it's all alike, a near perfect replica. This can't be the Wal-Mart from home. We can't still be in Wisconsin, let alone where I live in Kenosha. Does wherever we are just happen to have a Wal-Mart similarly built to the one I live by, kind of like how all elementary schools in an area have the same basic design? *Is the world really this small?*

"What are you staring at?" Zac asks, giving me the "have you lost your mind?" look.

"It's nothing. This just looks like the Wal-Mart my family goes to back home," I stop swiveling around and focus back on Zac. He appears to pale, but then masks it well. It's as if he doesn't quite know how to respond.

"Oh, uh, that's kind of interesting," he mutters awkwardly.

"Yeah," I say, returning the "what's your problem?" look.

"Just stay close ok? It's really packed today."

He turns away from me and begins a fast-paced approach towards the pharmacy section. I'm not short. I have moderately long legs, but it's difficult keeping up with him even though he is only a couple inches taller than me. Like earlier, when he left me behind on the driveway, he disappears into an aisle right as I make it to the pharmaceutical section, and he comes right back out of the aisle as I begin to turn into it.

I stop and turn around, huffing.

"Come on slow poke," he says, turning his head back so I can see his smirk.

I roll my eyes and begin walking towards him. He waits for me this time and stays with me as we walk to the register.

We are almost there. I can see the long row of cashiers, when *they* catch my eye. I don't know how it is even possible for me to spot them in this mess but there they are. I freeze, paralyzed. Not with fear, but anxiety. It is one of those moments when it's as if your brain has switched off because you have found yourself caught so far off guard, it doesn't quite know how to respond. So it does a restart – like a computer – that should hopefully unfreeze the software and I am left staring at them.

I have been worried they were harmed, but they clearly weren't. Nikki wasn't lying. The problem is the fact I had expected us to be somewhere far away like California or Florida or maybe even a foreign country. If I am still in the same town – or zip code at least – why haven't they come to the Gifted mansion? Even if they know I am okay, I had been kidnapped right under their noses. Shouldn't some protective parental instinct kick in to urge them to *have* to see me? But here they are, all of them, just carrying on, doing their grocery shopping like it is any other day. *They don't even look troubled.*

"Kira," Zac notices he has drifted in front of me and stops, turning back towards me. "Kira, what's wrong?" He turns his head in the direction I am staring but I don't think he sees them – if he even knows them.

Gadgets and dials in my brain begin to turn in circles, slowly and rigidly and now more animatedly, faster and faster into overdrive. Now there is so much going through my mind I don't know what to do first.

An overwhelming sense of *relief* hits me and I want to run straight at them.

I turn to Zac, smiling faintly – distantly – kind of *psychotically*, "I don't know how healed I am, but I think I'll be okay to go home now."

He pales and continues paling, to the color of a ghost.

"Kira-"

"I mean my parents are here. I can just go with them. I must be pretty far along in my recovery since Nikki let me leave. I'll be okay now. Thank you for everything though."

"Kira-"

Next suspicion comes.

Why wouldn't they just tell me where we are? It's not that big of a deal; I'm not trying to run away. They know this is where I live so they had known there was a risk this would happen if they let me go out, but they didn't care. So why wouldn't they tell me? Zac looks as if he is going to be sick – and I absolutely mean that literally.

"Kira, listen to me. You can't. Not yet, just please. You don't understand-" Zac isn't making sense. He is rambling urgently, trying to say whatever comes to mind to somehow convince me not to leave. Will he get in trouble if I leave? Well, considering they let me go, I don't think so. I don't care. They – the Gifted – saved me; they healed me – like police officers and doctors. Now it is time to be checked out.

"Zac, it's fine," I say patiently." Thank you for everything you guys have done. Thank you for rescuing me, for healing me. I can manage from here though. I just want to see my family please. You have no idea how worried I've been."

He looks shaken, horrified. He just stands there with his mouth hanging slightly ajar, his eyes terrified. He looks frozen.

"Goodbye Zac."

I turn and begin to walk away. Seconds later, I feel a hand on my arm pulling me back.

"Wait!"

Zac spins me around and begins to pull me towards the exit, discarding the meds onto a nearby shelf, completely forgotten.

What does he think he's doing? Is he delirious?

"Zac!" I squeak," You're hurting me. Let go! Ow! What are you doing?'

But he isn't listening. He is focusing intently on the exit, dragging me towards it. He pulls out his phone, dialing a number on his speed dial. Whoever it is picks up quickly.

"Help. Her family is here. I don't know how we forgot, but they are here and she's trying to go to them. *I need help*," he speaks fiercely into the phone, unnerved but trying not to yell. There is a pause then he says, "Just hurry. I don't know how this is going to go."

Now there is alarm, dread, and confusion.

I was wrong. I can't trust him; I can't trust them. They are trying to kidnap me too. Why would they let me leave the mansion then? What is going on? None of this makes sense, and Zac's still pulling me through the store, his fingers leaving prints in my wrist.

I begin to panic. I can't go back with him. I can't let him take me back to them, to some place potentially out in the middle of nowhere, someplace no one could find me (again). I begin to struggle against his pull.

50

"Let me go!" I say firmly, twisting my arm and trying to go in the opposite direction, towards my parents.

"Kira – *please* just *please* come with me. Trust me-"

"*You're trying to kidnap me*," I spit at him, venom dripping in my words.

"No I'm not. Please don't do this. *Please*," he pleads, urgency pulling taught his face, clouding his voice. I continue to resist him.

"You're leaving me no choice," I hear him mumble agitatedly. He wraps his arms around my waist and – literally – lifts me off the ground and starts carrying me towards the exit.

"Zac! Put me down!" I start hitting his arms and kicking my legs around, wiggling around as much as I can.

He is stronger than I am; that is a fact. I won't be able to fight my way free.

"Mom!" I shout. She will recognize my voice won't she? She will at least hear someone yelling and look up, then I will get her attention. "Dad! Haley!"

They all look up. They see me. *They see me.* Yet they go back to what they are doing. Right at that moment, I slip free from Zac's grasp and I take off like a race car that has been revving up and the brake is released, sending me hurtling towards them. *Maybe they just didn't recognize me…*

"Mom! Dad! Haley! You guys, I'm here!" I yell, hurrying towards them, dodging about a million people in the process.

I hear Zac calling my name behind me, shouting at me to wait. *Like hell.* I quickly glance over my shoulder and see he is stuck behind a large group of large people, trying to push his way through. A hole opens in front of me. I surge forward. A smile spreads on my face. I made it. Suddenly and quite abruptly, I stop, frozen in place.

There is a little boy with them. He is really cute too. He looks about three years old. He has beautiful, curly blonde hair and crystal blue eyes – like the color of sapphires. He has rosy, cherry, round cheeks. Such a beautiful little boy. But I have never seen him before in my life. Yet there he is, holding Dad's hand as if it is the most normal thing in the world.

They all look over at me; they're eyes resting on me with interest, but not recognition.

"I'm sorry sweetie. Did you lose your parents?" Mom asks, looking concerned.

I shake my head with a look of disorientation, frowning, "I don't understand. What are you talking about? It's me, Kira."

"You must have us confused with someone else," she says sympathetically.

"No. I'm-" I start in shock, but she interrupts me.

"Kira," she mutters absentmindedly. "That's a very pretty name."

Words won't form. I can't help but just look at her alarmed, my mouth is pulled down in disbelief, my eyebrows are scrunched with confusion, and my eyes are wide with terror.

What's going on? I think exasperated. *I. Don't. Understand!* I want to cry; I want to explode into a shower of tears and *scream.* Why are they being like this – like they have forgotten me? Mom can sometimes joke around pretty well when messing around – but the rest of them can't and she couldn't keep it up this long. Not to mention who would joke around after their daughter mysteriously disappeared? The world around me, the loud hustle and bustle of the store, is drowned out. It is almost as if I am going numb. This has to be a joke but I don't know why it scares me so badly.

Vaguely, I feel a tug on my wrist again, and a whisper, a voice that seems far off. Dots are clouding my vision and there is a loud ringing in my ears. I feel dizzy. Then, as if I am suddenly dropped from ten thousand feet in the air, the world slams back around me like a nuclear explosion, crashing and frightening. With a violent jolt, I become aware of the sounds of the Wal-Mart, of the sight of my family's faces staring at me a moment more than turning back to what they were doing and walking off to another aisle, and of Zac gently towing me away.

A late reply comes for my Mom's comment about my name, I whisper hurt, "You gave it to me."

Anger is the final emotion to roll in. Anger and *impatience.*

"Let go of me!" I shriek, ripping my arm away from him.

This time I notice the people stop around us and stare.

"Kira-" Zac tries to reason with me but I don't want to hear his pathetic pleads. My parents are getting farther and farther

53

away. I need to find them and ask what is going on. I run. I run to where they had been and then around the corner where I had seen them disappear. I hear treading feet behind me, several pairs; it must not just be Zac anymore. I don't have time to look back though. I see Mom, then Dad and the boy, and last Haley disappear behind the final aisle at the far end of the store. I chase after them.

As I turn the far corner, nearly slicing into it, I see them by the milk, opening one of the fridge doors and getting out two gallons of skim. We always get skim.

I start towards them, slower this time. Suddenly I fall to the ground, my knees bending and my legs dropping, as I gradually sink. What is happening now? Black and yellow dots circle the edge of my vision and begin to fill the center. It is difficult to still see at this point, but I can and what I see is my family – the people I love more than anything else on this planet – watch me slip to the ground with a look of concern but not worry as if they are interested by the scene, but I am just a stranger. Now I see them looking behind me.

There they are. Zac, Nikki, Trey, and a girl and boy I've never seen before. The girl and boy look oddly alike; maybe they are twins... This is irrelevant though. They are people I can no longer trust and they are people who aren't "normal." I know they are trying to take me away from here – away from my family (that apparently no longer cares about me). I know if it comes down to a fight between them and the surrounding crowd, they'd kick butt.

Nikki looks exhausted and unbelievably sad, Trey looks as if he is in pain, and Zac, well Zac looks to be a combination of nauseas and bewildered. They don't *look* like your common kidnappers.

Zac has stayed by the others, but now he is coming towards me, taking slow steps but long strides, working up to a hurried walk.

"Kira, don't worry-" he tries to tell me comfortingly, and his mouth keeps moving but I can't hear his voice anymore. My ears are popping and ringing and it feels as if there is a pressure causing a constant explosion inside my head. It is becoming increasingly difficult to see but I can make out Zac reaching me, and holding my head up. I can see Nikki, the boy, and girl clasp hands and seem to concentrate hard. Even with my blurred vision, I can see the brighter glow of their marks as compared to mine, Zac's, and Trey's. Nikki has a Gifted mind like Tessa, and Tessa froze my senses because of her Gifted mind. The three of them have to be trying to freeze me now. They are. I know it is over.

With every inch of will I can muster, I try to find the hidden box of power, the "Gifts" I supposedly have. I have to fight the Spell. I squeeze my eyes tight and push the focus from my brain out, as if I am projecting a barricade out from the power. With a grunt, I can feel one forming and can hear a little better, but the more solid it becomes, the more I can sense sweat forming on my forehead, and the tenser I feel. It is becoming grueling. My eyes begin to drift open and I see the three telekinesis on their knees, panting heavily, sweat and exhaustion painted in sheets over their faces. I can feel them taking over again. I can feel the barricade slipping away from me as if I no longer possess the key to controlling it. It seems as if it is in reaching distance but slips from my grasp when I try to hold it again. How can they do this to me? They told me I could trust them; they had helped me. I don't *understand.*

I see it better than I hear Nikki scream, "Zac now!"

Either my eyes are fluttering or the lighting is flickering. In a shower of sparks and explosions, a pure brilliant, naked streak of lightning charges and strikes the air, burning the ceiling and flooring and anything else it touches. Now three more strike. Screams break out. There seems to be a burst of fiery orange that radiates heat to my face, but its edges are blurred and it is difficult to tell where it is or what is on fire.

My vision blurs, fixing in and out of focus. My hearing begins to waver, picking up sounds and voices and now just ringing. My fingers and toes and limbs begin to tingle but not for long. It takes only seconds until I can't feel them at all.

"No!" I cry before the little Gifted power I had found disappears and silence takes the reins, darkness seizing my vision and I am frozen in an empty, endless world of black oblivion, betrayed.

Chapter 4

It's like I was drugged. Most of the time I am out cold. Every once and a while I drift back hazily to the world. The first time someone is carrying me out in their arms and all I really see before I fade out again is the fabric of their cotton t-shirt and spluttering showers of sparks and flashing lights. I think I feel water beginning to rain on me – but we are inside.

Next time, I am in a car that looks familiar. I see a man in the driver's seat at an angle from me. All I can see in the passenger seat is long wavy brown hair. I am lying on something other than the car seat. I look up with distorted vision. The only thing I can discern is a set of blue eyes, gazing intently at me. I watch them curiously trying to remember when I had seen those beautiful eyes before. I hear a muffled, slurred voice say, "She's breaking through."

Then my eyes start to droop and close and I fall back into a blissful numbness.

The final time I awake and don't fade back into the darkness, I find myself thinking clearly and oddly aware of everything. I am back in the room I had been recovering in after the battle. It is exactly the same room only this time its atmosphere is untrustworthy and menacing behind the pretty bright colors and fancy decorations and electronics. There are people sitting around me. The same three people I talked to after waking up following the fight. Only this time, instead of saving me they had lied to me, betrayed me – used me. None of them can be trusted.

Much to my surprise, Nikki is the first to speak (I had thought it be my loud 'what the hell' speech but that hasn't found the correct words yet).

"Kira-"

I didn't care to listen to her try and reason with me – lie to me.

"Don't," I speak harshly, warningly. A fire burns in my eyes.

"Please just listen to us; we can explain. We really weren't trying to hurt you – or kidnap you as you think-" Nikki's usually fierce eyes turn big, brown, and sad; regretful.

"I don't want to hear what pathetic excuses you've come up with," and I really don't want to hear any more of their reasons. It would all just be lies anyways.

"Kira-" Zac tries this time.

"No! You guys have been lying this entire time. You all told me I could trust you. You told me everything was okay. You rescued me – at least I thought you had. Now you might as well be working with the Scorned – for all I know you are the Scorned," I say coldly.

Zac looks vengeful at being called a Scorned, but Nikki looks hurt.

"We weren't lying to you. We're not the Scorned. You are safe with us – as safe as possible. Kira, you can trust us," Nikki says beseechingly.

"Nikki, just forget it. She's not going to believe us anyways," Zac looks derisive. Then – for the first time – his face softens. "I wouldn't either," he mumbles.

"That's the worst part," I shrug and my voice has softened as if the fight and stubbornness has suddenly rushed out of me and I am just left unsettled. "I don't know what to believe."

Part of me – I almost think the weak side – still wants to believe what they say. It's the same side that would like to believe everyone's honest and good – but that's not how the world works. Which is why I normally listen to the other side, the one that trusts no one.

Nikki sighs, "We tried so hard to avoid this, to make this easier. I can't believe we were so stupid."

"What were the odds they'd be there even if you had thought about it, considering *I* had no idea where she lived?" Zac ponders.

"They're both in the same stinking town, so the odds were good. And maybe the odds weren't that high for her family necessarily, but to see anyone she knows? Those odds are sky high," Trey contemplates logically.

"We should have been more careful," Nikki bristles angrily.

"What does seeing my family have to do with anything?" I asked contemptuously.

Synchronized, Nikki says, "It has to do with everything," as Zac says, "You have no idea."

"It's not like I can ask you to explain because it's not like I'd believe you," I admit sarcastically.

"Alright Kira, look," Zac says growing impatient and aggressive, straight forward. "You might not trust us, but you don't need to trust us to know we're being honest and you know we're telling the truth. Like you knew Bret and Tessa were the evil ones the second you saw them. You know we are here to protect you; you know you are just like us. You know it doesn't feel right to think we kidnapped you. You know all this with or without us having to say it, so know that if you ask us a question we are going to answer it honestly and I think you'll know it's the truth on your own," he finishes his rant as if he has solved and proven a highly difficult equation.

I am silent, staring at him stubbornly and then, with defiance in my voice, I start, "So what does – specifically – seeing my parents or someone I know have to do with you guys holding me here? It's just now occurring to you they might report you and try to arrest you? While you're at it, do any of you know why they were acting like they've never seen me before?"

"You sure you don't want to start with something easier, like why the sky's blue?" Zac asks hopefully albeit a little uneasy.

"No. Tell me about my parents and why after seeing them, everything changed."

Something is wrong – more than usual. No one will look at me; no one is smiling.

"What is it? Tell me! You said you would so tell me what it is. Zac? Trey? Nikki?"

Nikki seems to be attempting not to cry. She speaks hesitantly, "You gotta remember it'll be okay; it was for the better." She stops, sniffling and wiping at her eyes. "All of us had to go through it, and we're all okay now." She pauses, "When you leave your home – because you've discovered your mark and become Gifted or you're taken – something happens in time," Nikki hesitates, causing more strain." We don't know why or how it happens, but when you leave, you're erased from all and any normal human being's memory. If it makes it any better, animals remember, especially dogs. I guess it's the whole loyalty thing." She stops and stares at me, tears running down her eyes.

"This is the reason we can pretty much do whatever we want – like setting Wal-Mart's on fire – without having local or federal authorities on our tails," Zac continues somberly after Nikki. "In fact, the bigger a scene or more chaos we create, the faster the Gifted memory acts. I mean of course we make sure no one will get hurt, though."

I register he's referring to whatever they did in the Wal-Mart but I am still too focused on what Nikki said. Her words – the meaning of her words – hadn't really sunk in yet, or what it truly meant. I start getting glimpses though, little pieces of the solved puzzle, until tears are coming fast. How can she say those things, those awful things?

"No. I don't believe you. No!" I love my family more than anything. I love their warm hugs and their laughs and smiles when we are together. I would never even think about giving it up. Even when I was mad at them, I'd never think about life without them, too afraid that I could really lose them if I did.

"Kira-" Zac tries to help but I won't let him.

"No! You knew all along, and you let me be happy and smile! You knew! You all knew, and you were all pretending everything was fine. It's your fault – all of yours' – that this happened! You have to be lying – it doesn't make sense otherwise." Tears are freefalling down my face. Earlier, I had believed and accepted everything so fast – all the supernatural incidents, everything they had told me. Now, I can't seem to grasp a hold of anything – whether because I don't want to, I can't handle it, or I don't trust them, I have no idea.

"Kira you even said your parents were acting as if they had never seen you before in their life," Trey says with big, wide, glossy eyes. He looks like a sad, lonely puppy.

Is that really what happened? Were they really not playing a joke on me? No. I have to get out of here, away from these people – whoever they are.

I do it quickly and so full of energy that they are still in too much shock to stop me.

I jolt straight up and out of the bed, still wearing my shorts and T-shirt from the night before. I run straight past Trey and Nikki and out the door. I just run. Unfortunately, I have no idea where to go. I have only been through the halls one other time and that was being led by Zac and I was taking in my surroundings more than paying attention navigation-wise. Now the halls seem chaotic to me. The house or mansion or whatever this is, is large and twisty with about a hundred different doors. I want to find the exit, but every door I go through, every stairway I run up or down never leads me to the outside.

Of course there are plenty of windows I can see out of and hint to what floor I may be on. Looking out, I see it has become overcast today and foggy. After I frantically dart around for what has to be at least fifteen minutes, my head is pounding hard in a steady beat, my lungs are on fire, and I am tired. So tired.

I can't do it anymore; I can't run like I have my full strength because I don't. Now that I think about it, I am starving. I collapse right where I am on the floor in the room I have somehow found myself in. Since I'd taken so many turns in this giant place, they probably won't find me for a while. Maybe that is a good thing.

They and my stupid birthmark are the reasons why I lost my family forever (well theoretically, since I still won't believe what they are telling me is the absolute truth). I mean, if it was – if it *could* be true – I'd never see Mom or Dad or Haley or even my dog again. I'd never experience one of their encouraging acts of love. Would you accept that so easily? Would you give up all hope of ever feeling loved by the ones you love again, so quickly? Before I know it, I am crying again, violently.

My eyes quickly become puffy and red and add to my headache and the exhaustion that pulses everywhere. A depressing, numbing lull fills me. Hopefully it is a healing lull that will work as a pain killer and wash away my grief – or at least some of it. I allow the indifference to take control, closing my eyes. I fall asleep with my eyelids throbbing, pulsing back to normal.

Chapter 5

My eyes are closed, but I am aware that I am being lifted. I lean my head against the person's shoulder. Although I know they'll be taking me back to Zac, Nikki, and Trey, I don't care. I need food. I need sleep. Then I'll find a way out. I'll go to my parents. I can't *believe* people who are so close to me could just forget me so easily. When I used to try to think about a life without them, an invisible wall would pop up in my head, stopping me. Now that I have the possibility of losing them, that wall has broken and all of those terrible predictions that were hidden and dim are beginning to pass as a startling reality.

Thinking so much about it again is forcing me to cringe and become less drowsy. So I push it away – all of it. I focus on what Zac had said about my mark and "Gifts". How can all of this be possible? How can people control things like weather and people's minds? I never really gave all that happened last night much thought or consideration. I guess adrenaline forced that. I never questioned any of it though, but now I have to prove to myself – to them – that I'm not one of them, that if I go back to my parents they will remember me. *My parents...* No, I won't think about them. Instead I focus on the proof of my Gifted status which is I had "apparently" attacked all the Scorned last night, except I hadn't seen it and how could they be so sure that I was the one doing it all? Another thing, why should I even trust the facts they gave me?

Still trying to keep my mind from anything too depressing, I realize I am cold. That's it! If I can warm myself up with fire I'll know if I really belong here.

So, um, how do I do that? I mean, do I have to say something or do I just think and feel it? I don't want to alert anyone I am awake yet (and because I don't want to seem like a total weird-o), I try the second, silent option. I think about fire and it warming me, not wholly sure I am doing this right. Suddenly the chills smooth away and I am warm and comfortable, other than my heart dropping down into my stomach. My little experiment convinces me that I am one of them. Not to mention the fact that my family didn't seem to know who I was was already a startling debate to argue against. So it has to be true then. The psychological world in my mind is crashing down, as if a giant wrecking ball has smashed into it. I am one of them, and I don't know if I can trust them. Zac is right though; they wouldn't lie to me. I don't know why I have full confidence in their honesty, and yet every fiber of my gut believes them. Because I have nothing else to believe, I have to believe the heart-wrenching truth they are telling me.

I want to cry again, but I won't. I have to get over it. I need to trust that my family not remembering me is so that they won't worry and that way they would be happier. It would put them out of danger's path. From the time I have spent with them, Zac, Trey, and Nikki seem like they are okay – if not a little strange – but I wonder how long it took for them to get here, to the point when they don't always want to break down. Maybe they hadn't been close to their parents and so it really wasn't difficult for them to move on to begin with.

By now, someone has carried me back to the room and lays me down on the bed again.

"Thanks for helping, Lily. It would have taken the three of us by ourselves forever to find her. She was so upset. I can't believe she made it all the way to the piano room before she finally collapsed," Nikki says. Does she sound sad?

"No problem. It's not like she was heavy – and if she was, it's not like I would be able to tell. Do you want me to stay with her or are one of you going to?" Lily asks (I think that's her voice at least). So she carried me? I guess she would have been most capable with the ability of her "Gift."

"That's okay. I think I'm going to stay, but you should probably come back when she wakes up so she can officially meet you," Nikki says.

"Okay. Trey, why don't we go to the infirmary and I'll heal your ribs?"

"Why thank you Lily! It will be so nice to breathe without pain. Zac? Why don't you come with us and I was thinking, afterwards, the three of us could find a way to introduce Kira to everyone without overwhelming her," Trey suggests.

"Yeah, sure," Zac answers nonchalantly, but it almost sounds as if he is somewhat reluctant to go.

Nikki must have used her Gifted mind because it's as if she is reassuring his unspoken thoughts, "She'll be okay. If we need anything, I'll call you first. I'll let you know when she wakes up if it makes you feel better."

He must have nodded because I don't hear him answer, but the door closes as he leaves. I feel someone's presence in the chair next to the bed. I assume it is Nikki. I wonder if they all are worried about me. Speaking of which, why am I still pretending to be asleep?

I open my eyes and realize that I haven't opened them yet because I haven't actually been fully awake. My eyes feel as if all they want to do is stay glued shut.

"Hi there. How are you?" Nikki asks, sensitively.

"Well…" I begin, trying to wet my parched throat and dry tongue, "my parents don't know I exist, my sister doesn't remember me, and the only one who still loves me is my dog – which really doesn't matter because I'll never see him again anyways," I say sarcastically, the drowsiness starting to wear off. The honest truth of reality is a startling bucket of ice water unfortunately.

"I know. I know it's hard but if it helps, all of us are here and we won't be going anywhere. The kids are all pretty great at welcoming a new lost kid into the family. After a while, you won't think about the anguish you feel as much, and you'll be okay," Nikki says, showing the same care as Mom would.

"I don't want to forget them. I don't want to not have them anymore," I whisper angrily and my voice quivers. A deep restraint is the only force holding back the flood gates.

"You don't have to forget them or stop caring about them. I'm just trying to say that eventually, it will be okay. You can get through it and you will – just like every other loss you have encountered in your life. Yes this one is more difficult and heart-breaking, but all things take a little time."

"How do you know? How do you know life will be okay even though the only people who truly know me and love me for those reasons are gone in an instant? Everyone! How do you let them go? How do you move on from that? How do you cope with losing your entire family so suddenly and instantaneously?" I am hysterical. The dam has broken; tears and questions and the endless hurt rush in like a massive tidal wave and collapse my insides, drowning me.

I sit up, looking at Nikki with wide eyes, scared like a child. So many questions are thrown into my mind and I can't put two verbal words together to voice any of them out. She looks at me despondently, apologetically – as if it's her fault. But she hasn't asked for this anymore than I have. Without a thought, I lean forward into Nikki, throwing my arms around her, hugging her tightly. You might think that it's weird: to find comfort in a complete stranger, but Nikki doesn't really feel like a stranger. She reminds me of Mom, and I could really use my mom right now.

I think she is shocked at first and sits stiffly, but eventually she wraps her arms around me, hugging me tightly and stroking my hair. She somehow finds the words that would help to comfort me in this moment, "I *don't* know for sure; no one can know for sure that life will be okay. No one can know for sure if we'll wake up the next day, or if a miracle might occur the next night, but I do know, it's going to be hard at first. However, I also know it's easier when you have people around you who are ready to take their place. There was someone like Trey and I there when I became Gifted who sort of became my new parent figures. I'm not saying someone could ever replace your parents; I'm not even trying to arrogantly assume the position. I'm only trying to say, you don't have to be alone in this."

I know what she is implying. I guess it makes me feel a little better – but not really.

We are quiet for a while, other than my crying and her occasional sniffles. I am in between cries when I speak calmly, my voice muffled by her shoulder, "This reminds me of my mom. Whenever I was upset, she would always sit with me. It would always feel so comfortable and *safe* in her arms and I never wanted her to let go." I don't say it all at once but more like between sniffles and tears. I almost feel embarrassed; like a little five year old who is crying because her ice cream dropped onto the ground. My mom was never judgmental when I was upset, and the similarities between her and Nikki lead me to believe that Nikki will not judge me either.

Nikki doesn't say anything, but I hear a tiny sigh of relief.

Then I wonder why it feels as if I am lying on a damp towel and I realize my tears have created a nice little lake on her shirt. I sit back out of her hug – even though I don't really want to. I dry my eyes and say, "Sorry I messed up your shirt."

"Don't be silly. I just hope you feel better," Nikki replies, just like a mom-*my Mom*.

"It felt good to cry, but…I don't really feel any better about the whole thing."

"Baby steps; baby steps. And that's how you'll heal: one step at a time."

We sit there for a while just looking at one another. It's sort of nice. Then Nikki closes her eyes, and her lips move as if she's silently speaking. She opens her eyes again. A few minutes later someone knocks on the door.

Lily pops her head through the tiny crack, making sure it is clear then walks in. Zac trails closely but pauses near the door.

"I recall saying 'Lily', Zac?" Nikki comments, only slightly serious.

Zac's face looks bashful and a little embarrassed, "Yeah I know, but I thought, you know, I should come incase Kira needs anything-or something like that." He won't look at Nikki, but he is smiling.

"Uh-huh, so what was Trey about to make you do?" she asks, smirking.

"Find EVERYONE and tell them to meet in the kitchen," he says, with long facial expressions, as if finding "EVERYONE" would take forever. Of course, he has a giant grin on his face and is

71

now confidently striding towards us. He stands on the opposite side of Nikki and Lily.

"Well, you've probably already figured it out by now, but this is Lily, Zac's twin," Nikki says looking up at Lily who is standing over her.

"Yeah but the official introduction is still nice," I smile. "I'm Kira."

"Hi," Lily returns my smile. "Do you like the room?" She asks looking away from me and around the room.

"Yes, it's really nice."

Something pops into my head.

"Is it yours? While I've been in here have you had to go somewhere else – because I don't mind letting you have it back and sleeping on the floor or-"

Did she just giggle? Like actually giggle?

"No, no, this is going to be your room."

My room? My room at home –no, this is my home now – was very, quite simple. Nothing as extravagant as this.

"If you don't like it, we can still change it. We wanted to have it done in some sort of fashion as a sort of welcoming gift. You don't like it." Lily pouts and I want to tell her 'I do' but she continues. "I knew we should have done pink and green; no one else would listen but now we have to do it anyways and it's twice the work."

"Lily!" I exclaim, trying to get her attention, but still smiling. "I love it. Is the TV mine too? I don't mind sharing it or anything."

"Nope, it's all yours," Nikki answers my question instead. "You also have a laptop but it is actually your old one from-..." she looks down as the conversation has suddenly taken a downhill turn.

I attempt to fix the situation.

"So all this means I'll be living here then, right?"

They nod.

"Do all the Gifted live here?"

"Well, all of the children and beginners; others can if they would like. You'll often see some older Gifted here one day and then not again for a month. They tend to stop here while traveling," Nikki explains. "This mansion is divided into four floors or four areas. Bottom floor is outdoors, kitchen, and any type of entertainment you can think of: sports, television, music, you name it. There is also the infirmary – if you need something in case someone's injured. It has come in handy for situations like last night when people have gotten severely injured. Second floor is mainly for the older Gifted such as Trey and I, those who help out around here, and guests who travel around. Third floor is guys' dorm – that way it's easier to hear what they're doing since they're the wildest group," Nikki stares, pointedly (and jokingly) straight at Zac-the symbol in the room of all guy-kind.

"Um, I'm pretty sure the girls are absolutely louder, but you're not under their floor to spy," Zac defends.

"You're such a liar. The girls are quieter than you because we're clever," Lily jumps in.

"Oh really? I find that hard to believe. Please share your wisdom. How do you do it?"

"Ways. We have ways that I shall never reveal, so hah," Lily gloats triumphantly.

"Well that's obviously not fair. Nikki, they really are as loud; they just cheat. They try and hide it instead of owning up to it," Zac throws in, hoping to gain a couple points, but really it is no use.

"Hey don't look at me. All's fair in love and war, and this is war. The rule is silence after curfew, and all I know is that the girls are quiet and the guys, well, they move down from an ear-splitting level of noise to only mild-deafness," Nikki referees.

"Hah," I believe that laugh from Lily qualifies her as having "the last laugh."

"Well, we may be loud, but at least we're not – wait, never mind, we're that too…" Zac began but trailed off, smirking and leaving the statement open as if it were some sort of trap for Lily to fall into.

"What were you going to say? Dumb? Dirty? Because either of those would work."

"No actually. I was going to saw extremely handsome."

"Have you looked in the mirror recently-"

74

"Getting back on topic here," I interrupt the argument seeing as it was going down and could possibly go on infinitely, "this means girls' dorm is fourth floor. We're on the fourth floor right now then, right?" I question.

"Yep. Sure are," Lily answers, elated over her victory.

My stomach grumbles rather embarrassingly, loud enough for everyone in the room to hear.

"Look at us. We're terrible! You haven't eaten since early this morning," Nikki preaches condescendingly as if their manners are just plain awful.

"Except if we took her to the kitchen, she'd be swarmed by pretty much everyone in the entire mansion, remember?" Zac inquires.

"Yeah – speaking of which, I don't know if it's such a good idea to even try to introduce her to everyone. Why don't we just let her meet people as she goes…you know, like a *normal* school would," Lily adds.

"You're probably right," Nikki says, sounding rather put out.

"What if you Mind Trey, tell him to send everyone on their way and we can take Kira to get dinner?" Zac suggests.

"That's actually a good idea. Who knew you were capable of it?" Lily says, teasing her brother.

Nikki is smiling at them, but manages to say, "Well it was bound to happen eventually. Okay, shush, so I can concentrate."

Everyone is silent. Nikki closes her eyes. Her lips move as if she is silently talking – like she did before Lily and Zac came in the room.

"I told him. Trey couldn't believe Zac had thought of it, and he said to give them a few minutes," Nikki says, reopening her eyes.

"Do you think I could change quickly? These clothes probably aren't the sweetest-smelling bunch," I ask trying to smile innocently and not seem too embarrassed.

"Oh yeah. We'll step out and when you're done, we'll all go down to the kitchen," Nikki answers.

"Well I kind of need clothes to change into," I say not too smartly.

"Oh, we must not have told you. The Gift transports all of your stuff to where you'll be staying."

"It actually more like *dumps* it *however it feels like* where you're staying," Lily grumbles.

"What?"

She rolls her eyes, annoyed – not at me I hope.

"The Gift has the power to 'magically' transport things and yet it can't be courteous enough to put them in good order in someone's new room. No. We walk into the lounge and see piles of stuff along with dressers and desks like someone decided to make the lounge their bedroom."

"Well wasn't that a nice thing for it to do," I say indignantly.

76

Zac snorts, "It probably doesn't do it for your or our benefit either; it probably does it to keep the secret. I mean, imagine if someone's parents walked into their former child's room and found all the stuff of the child they 'never had,'" he says cynically. "That wouldn't really go according to the Gift's plan would it?"

Nikki gives him a look that basically says 'calm down and be nice.'

"As I was saying, you'll find all your clothes in the dresser. Zac, where did you put the boxes that have the rest of her stuff?"

"In her closet," Zac says sounding bored.

Nikki glares at him, but I just laugh at them both.

"Well then, you can help her move the boxes out of there," Nikki declares.

"Fine," he says reluctantly.

I giggle again, and then say, "Thank you. I should be okay now."

"Okay, we'll wait outside."

Nikki, Zac, and Lily file out.

I get up, walk over to the dresser, and open the bottom drawer. It looks exactly like how I had left it at ho – the other place. Everything is where I had left it. I pull out my favorite pair of jeans and one of my favorite shirts. After I change, I remember that Zac had said I have a closet. I circle around my room, and there in the wall on the left side of my bed is another door. Inside, there are about a twenty brown, cardboard boxes all stacked up.

I guess I never realized how much stuff I have, I think to myself.

On the far wall of the closet is a mirror. It isn't mine so they must have forgotten it. There is a crack running down the side, separating a piece from the whole. Ugh! I look absolutely terrible. There are giant bags under my eyes. My hair is all puffed up and frizzy like it normally is after I sleep.

I walk out of there quickly before the grotesque mirror can pull me back.

"All better?" Lily asks.

"Slightly. I'll be better after I take a shower. By the way, do you have a hair tie?"

"Oh yeah," she pulls up her arm and there are about five scrunches around her wrist. "Here 'ya go."

She hands me the hair tie, and I am thankfully able to pull back my knotty hair.

"So how many people live here? Ten? Twenty? I mean this is a mansion not a boarding school," I say jokingly.

They all look at me like I'm crazy.

"I mean, it kind of is like a boarding school," Zac considers, intrigued.

Lily ignores Zac and explains, "Well if you're just counting how many girls on Level 4, then yes about twenty people. We're rare, but we're not that rare. This is only the home for the Gifted in the U.S."

"How does everyone get here?"

78

"Well, when a new baby with the mark is born in the region you live, everyone else's marks glow – Scorned and Gifted – since the baby is undecided. Then our psychics are able to locate the baby and we send an experienced Gifted to watch over them until it's time to bring the child here. Normally the Scorned do the same."

"Is the U.S. the only place that has the Gifted and Scorned?"

"No, there are Scorned and Gifted mansions like this everywhere, placed in each country so people are able to help those who are newly Gifted or Scorned everywhere. Some smaller countries have to make the journey to larger ones for safety," Nikki chimes in.

"So Zac wasn't exaggerating when he said 'everyone' like it was a big deal?"

"See, I have my reasons," he teases and flashes that oh-so-perfect grin. "Speaking of which, we should probably get going."

We start walking down the hall. This place is giant. Now I know every door we pass is a bedroom and we seem to pass dozens of doors. The path we are taking feels familiar, and I realize it's most likely the way Zac had taken me earlier.

In the middle of the hallway before the long window, they show me a second staircase. The stairs, like the floor, are white marble with swirls of black and there are twisted, iron bars connecting a glazed and polished, mahogany wood railing to the stairs. It's quite a fairytale-esque image.

On our way to the spiraling staircase, we see a few girls. A couple of their doors are open and I get a quick glance inside. Most have a couple girls in them, visiting each other and probably gossiping. A couple are scattered in the hallways but they are wrapped up in their own conversations and don't seem to notice us. We do run into three girls who must have just reached the floor, as we turn the corner towards the stairs. They are the only ones that see us, but they don't ignore us. They are whispering about something secretively. At first they just glance over at us and smile but then they seem to do a double-take and their whispering stops. It's actually rather uncomfortable. I'll give them credit for trying to look as if they aren't staring, but their chatter picks up until their hushed talking is a whirling wind of gossip and shock. I feel their eyes on me even after we pass them and are putting quite a lot of distance between us. When we reach the other end of the hall where the spiral staircase begins I cast a look over my shoulder to see their fixed stares on my back. My cheeks redden with the feeling that they are talking about me and I quickly turn back around, trying hard to brush off the anxiety.

Zac is the first to move towards the stairs.

"Hey Kira, I was wondering if after you ate I could introduce you to a friend of mine?" Zac questions, tilting his head down almost as if embarrassed, but I can see him looking up at me, his hair falling to shade his eyes.

I almost smile realizing how cute it is. I notice what I am about to do though and stop myself. So he won't think I'm thinking what I was thinking, my natural reaction is to be sarcastic – of course.

"Is your friend hot?" It was really meant to be a joke, but apparently I'm not very funny – or so I've been told. Zac looks put out and irritated by the question, but I hear a chuckle off to the right.

I turn to see Lily smiling," Yes. *Yes he is*."

I smile genuinely at her, "Do you *like* him?" and I wink for good measure, hoping she'd "catch my drift."

She blushes deeply and looks away shyly. Meanwhile Zac has turned the color of a fire truck. Had he been a cartoon, this would be the moment steam would come out of his ears.

"Jamie? You like *Jamie*? Because he is *not* right for you – *at all*."

"I never said I liked him!" Lily says defensively and convincingly enough that Zac will buy it and drop the subject. I'm not wholly convinced however. I do know though that talking about it in front of her obviously protective (aka obnoxious) "big brother" is not a good idea. Since I started the whole thing though I feel like I should at least stand up for her.

"Oh come on Zac, even if she did like him, he's obviously a good friend of yours so he must be a pretty great guy. Don't you want that for your sister?"

Almost immediately, he replies, "No. You're right. He is a really great guy. I don't want my annoying little sister to turn him into some mushy, lovesick puppy." He screws up his face with repulsion.

"What is it with all guys seeming to just hate on adorable little puppies?" I ask baffled, more to myself than any of them. I am so deep in wonder that I don't notice Lily look almost offended by Zac's comment, giving Zac a look that could kill while he is just standing there looking anywhere but at the three of us.

Nikki, who has remained quiet and *observant* this entire time, smirks, "It's a jealousy thing."

Immediately, three heads snap and swivel over to look at her confoundedly.

"Excuse me?" Zac asks, like he *could not believe* she had said that. As if he *must* be hearing things wrong, *obviously*. Well then so are the rest of us.

"Boys are jealous of puppies," Nikki arches her eyebrows humorously and continues to smirk, amused. "Not just of puppies but babies, too. Anything cute and small and adorable, *that takes girls' attention away from boys*. It's simple psychology really."

Lily is smirking now, "Says the psych Gift."

"Wait!" Zac says, with the hand gesture and everything. "You mean to tell me, you think I hate puppies – and babies – because girls like them? No. I don't even hate puppies and babies. Granted they can annoy me sometimes and I would prefer to look at cars or play sports-"

"Oh grow up and gain a little maturity," I smile and roll my eyes. I mean, "cars and sports?" *Really?* Isn't that the stereotypical male?

"Jamie's mature," Lily mumbles smartly, but *very* softly, smirking. I can tell that she is purposefully trying to rile up Zac.

I swear the smile on my face is as large as Zac's disturbed, wide eyes.

"*What did you just say?*" he seethes as if he is no longer her twin brother but her *father*.

"Just that I love you," she smiles sweetly and innocently at him, obviously as a ploy.

"Yeah Sis, I love you too," he says rather begrudgingly, eyeing her with suspicion. Shaking his head – probably wishing he could just forget the past five minutes of the conversation and attempting to, he pauses for a moment to take a deep breath before he moves on. "*Anyways*, I should probably go. I haven't gotten anything done since last night and the guys were going to set up a huge x-box live session."

Lily looks absolutely bored at the idea of sitting for hours playing a video game, while Nikki still looks to be highly entertained by the three of us, and I am just standing here awkwardly, not quite sure what to say. I decide that an "Okay," would do. I add, "Hey Zac, about meeting this Jamie-guy, I can stop by after dinner."

"Actually, I was going to suggest that it may be better if you just rest tonight after dinner," Nikki advocates hesitantly.

"You've had a long day and you wanted that shower. I don't want you to do too much and get run down."

"Nikki that's fine," I smile at her. "I guess I'll come by then sometime tomorrow."

Zac starts to walk backwards down the steps and oddly begins to smirk – what seems to be a habit of his.

"Great. So see you then."

It almost seems as if he is snapping at me, sardonically.

"Ok, *great!*" I remark, taken aback.

"Wonderful!" Lily chimes happily, and her smile falls to an annoyed frown, "So go."

"Uh, what does it look like I'm doing?" he asks sarcastically while he is walking backwards down the stairs as we follow him.

"It looks like you're talking to us – and trying to get yourself killed. When you fall backwards, I'm going to laugh," Lily teases.

"Please, I'm too light on my feet to fall," he is laughing now – and not paying too much attention to the stairs he's walking backwards on.

Sure enough, as he's stepping down the stairs, his foot is a little too far off the edge, slides right off and he falls. Lily, Nikki, and I begin laughing.

"Light on your feet, huh? They seem more like lead to me," Nikki jokes.

"Cut it out. I think I seriously hurt something," Zac is still joking, but his face is a little distorted in pain. His nose starts dripping blood.

"Well that's maybe because you have a broken nose. Come 'ere; let me see it. I've been working on my nurse skills." Nikki starts towards him, but he takes a step back.

"Why doesn't Lily just do her whole healing thing and I can-" Zac tries to struggle against the hands that are reaching towards his nose.

"Don't worry. This will only take a second. You won't feel anything." Nikki is on the step above him, and before he puts up a fight, she pops his nose back in place – wait no, just into an even more peculiar angle.

His nose makes a loud crack and more blood flows out. Zac screams out.

"Oh sorry, that must be for arms and legs only." Nikki looks at him innocently – a little too innocently. Meanwhile, Lily is in tears from laughing so hard.

"Okay, I call you two even, now Zac come here so I can really fix your nose," Lily says, wiping away the tears from her eyes.

Zac walks up the stairs, holding and attempting to contain the bloody nose. Lily puts her hand up to Zac's nose but nothing really happens. All of a sudden, his nose produces another snap-sound, Zac lets out a grunt of pain, a little more blood spills out, and finally he seems okay. Although, his shirt and the stairs are covered in blood.

"I'm, uh, gonna go get changed," his cheeks are slightly flushed and he looks kind of pale.

"And afterwards, come and mop this up," Nikki instructs, looking more like the familiar mom figure. He glares at her then continues down the stairs and disappears onto a landing that I assume is the third floor.

When he's gone, Nikki and Lily burst into laughter. I smile at their joy, but comment, "I don't understand."

"I'm sorry Kira," Nikki gasps between laughs. "Zac and I had a previous event and I finally gained revenge."

Chapter 6

Both of them still hysteric, we start down the stairs. About every twenty steps we come to a landing for each new floor. By the time we arrive at the bottom, Nikki and Lily are winded more so than I am. Once we reach the foyer, we head towards a long hallway to the left of the stairs that leads off to some other part of the house.

"This is what we call the lounge," Nikki informs me about this circular room that I had so greatly admired earlier.

We begin walking down the hallway, away from the beautiful doors that lead to the front yard. We don't go through any of the closed doors we pass, but Nikki and Lily point out what they are. It's as if an entire town was allocated into this one mansion with an infirmary, bowling alley, piano and band rooms, library, movie theater, TV and game room. It's incredible, and so large!

Finally, in the very back right corner of the house, we come to the dining room and kitchen. To get there we swerved around corners and I quite honestly felt as if I was overwhelmingly lost – and I was being led around. The magnitude of the size and beauty of this place is overwhelming.

The kitchen/dining room is neat; it has those old fashioned swinging doors-like the ones in *Ratatouille* that separate the kitchen from the dining area at *Gusto's*. On the other side of the doors is a modern kitchen with numerous stainless steel ovens, stoves, microwaves, and dishwashers, along with a lot of cupboards, pantries, and counter space. But the "cooking area" is

87

only in a rectangular room cut out of the far wall across from us and is small compared to the rest of the room.

The whole room is large – not quite the size of a shopping mall food court but at least a good sized restaurant. There are probably about thirty-five-ish circular table, and around the frame of the room are red leather booths.

I don't have time to look around long as Nikki and Lily continue walking towards the actual kitchen. As we approach, I notice the kitchen actually is large. I also notice that there is a backdoor at the very back of the kitchen area.

Nikki spots what I'm looking at and says, "That's our emergency backdoor. It also opens onto the stone patio, built in pool, and the backyard."

Lily interrupts, "Don't forget the shed of sports equipment and motorized vehicles. As long as you sign the stuff out, there are paths in the woods behind the yard that are fun to go on."

"We'll definitely have to show you sometime, but first," Nikki pauses, "let's eat! Max, what do you have for us today?"

Somehow – and only I, being the blonde that I am, could do this – I'd managed to completely miss a man cooking. When she said his name he turns around to look at us. He is tall, broad, and his hands have tiny burns and cuts on them. He has dark, jet black hair and very olive-toned skin.

"Well," he speaks, "my famous Philly cheese steak sandwiches with an assortment of options such as green peppers, onions, and pickles." He turns to me and smiles, "Thought I'd try and start out with a good first impression with our newest member."

"I'm sorry. My hunger got the best of me when I smelled the wonderful melted cheese. This is Kira. Kira this is Max, our special gourmet but also healthy chef," Nikki introduces us.

He shakes my hand and we both say hi to each other; all that stuff that goes with an introduction, yadda, yadda, yadda.

"So do you like Philly cheese steaks sandwiches?" Max asks.

"Yeah, my mom-" my face darkens at the memory but I slowly continue, "she makes them – she *used* to always make them."

Max says, jokingly, to try and cheer me up, "Well good, it'll make it all the more interesting to see whose is better."

I smile, but the waters that had receded for just a moment are starting to rise again and I can't shake the feeling as easily as I had before.

"Well come here," Max gestures towards the stove. "What do you normally like to have on yours?"

I walk towards the stove and nonchalantly say, "Cheese, steak, and green peppers."

"Truly the best way." He leans in towards me and whispers teasingly, "I only make the other things for everyone else."

That does cheer me up a little more. Max grabs a plate and bun and fixes me a sandwich. Lily moves over to the fridge and retrieves out three Vitamin Waters.

"Oh, I'm sorry, do you like Vitamin Water?" Lily asks me.

Nikki adds, "It's okay if you don't; we have other things. Lily's just our little health freak."

Lily and Zac must share the same glare, because Lily's glare now and Zac's earlier are mirror images of one another.

"I like it – especially strawberry kiwi. You do know they have a ton of sugar in them, right?"

"Thank you! She doesn't seem to believe us – or the bottle," Nikki comments.

"No, I just say the water and vitamin part outweighs the sugar. Not to mention, it's way better then soda," Lily proudly defends.

Nikki rolls her eyes; I laugh. I say, "Nice meeting you," to Max. The three of us sit down at a table.

"Max used to be one of the most famous chefs in the United States, but when his mark discovered its Gift, he started cooking for us," Nikki explains between bites of food. "We were really surprised to find out he was Gifted…and that it took so long for the Gift to recognize itself. Then again, some never do so-"

I take a bite of the sandwich. It is amazing.

"He really is gourmet. It's even better than my-" I don't continue, but they understand. I need to change the subject. "It must have cost a fortune to make these for everyone? Who am I kidding? It must cost a fortune for every meal."

"We get all the money from everyone's no longer existing bank accounts when they become Gifted, so that helps. We don't have to pay any kind of bills because people don't know we exist, and we've created a power source from ourselves for running water and electricity. Not to mention, Max was like a millionaire before he was Gifted-" Nikki explains.

"Don't forget the money tree the earth class is creating," Lily interrupts excitedly.

"You guys have an actual, real money, money tree?" I ask in awe.

"Yep, well, we're working on it. We don't use money a lot. We grow a lot of vegetables and fruits, so we only use the money for meat and things we can't grow."

"Can't people just get jobs – oh wait no, because no one would remember you're working for them or who you are," I say. "You guys mentioned an earth class, so does that mean we still have school?"

"Sort of. You take a two hour class every week day with the instructor who also has your Gift; so yes, you could sort of call it school."

"What will I do then, since I have four Gifts?"

"Trey and I are going to conference with your possible teachers later today. We were thinking we would make your classes an hour and you would have to have private lessons with two teachers, since the two hour class day will be over," Nikki explains.

Great, that means I'll probably always be behind since I'll have to make up an hour for each one. Wonderful! I haven't even started yet and I'm already behind!

"Don't worry, though. We'll figure something out."

I can't tell if she is talking about my schedule or is doing the whole telepathy thing.

We all have finished our food and they show me where to rinse and stack my plate.

"Now ladies, I'm afraid it's about time for the teacher conference I was telling you about, so Lily, do you think you could-"

"Hang out with Kira? Sure, I'll let her take a shower and then I'll take her downstairs and really show her our entertainment rooms," Lily answers and I wonder if she really doesn't mind doing it.

We leave the dining room and head back to the grand staircase. On our way, we pass a few girls heading to dinner.

I can't help but marvel at the beauty of the lounge and front door with the setting sun shining in on them, but I keep walking.

We start to climb the fairy tale staircase, and they tell me about the different teachers and stupid stuff the guys have done. And for all of you who think we're being kind of sexist, have any of you actually talked to and hung out with a guy for more than ten seconds? Especially when they are in a group together? I mean, granted girls can be dumb sometimes too.

Nikki leaves us on the second floor landing but the conversation continues. By the time we reach my bedroom, our faces are red and our eyes are drenched.

We stand at the door, wiping our eyes and gasping for air.

"Alright," Lily splutters, "you're lucky because the bathroom is right next door to you. There's a closet in it where you can find a clean towel. You know where the clothes are in your room, so I guess you can just come knock on my door when you're ready for the second part of your tour."

"Okay," I smile, "oh and Lily do I need to try and find any shampoo and conditioner-"

"No, no, that's all in there," she smiles like a hostess would.

"Thanks. I'll see you in a little."

"Cool." She goes over to the door that is right next to mine and walks in, before rushing back out a few seconds later.

"Kira wait! Oh, you're still here. Good. One more thing, this-" she motions to the doorway she is leaning on, "is my room. Easy enough to find right?" she smiles.

I laugh, "That's really convenient actually."

"Yeah, you're just lucky you don't have a brother here right now. It took me ages to remember how to make it to his room – and then to remember which door was his."

"Yikes. Not to mention it's on a separate floor."

"Yeah I know right? Okay, go off and shower now," she beckons cheerily, not at all like she is trying to dispose of me.

93

I laugh again, "See you in a few."

I walk in my room for a minute to find a set of new clothes to put on and bring them into the bathroom with me. The bathroom is large and nice; several showers, white and pearly tile flooring, and a speckled, tan marble counter with gold trimmings.

I don't realize I was so cold until I step under the steamy water. There's something about showers that gives me the feeling of enough security it's safe to cry without the fear of an unwanted fly on the wall. It always seems as if when the first wave of water hits me, so does a wave of suppressed grief. I'm not ready to let it out yet. This is a public bathroom after all, and I can't take forever in the shower. Lily is waiting after all. Wringing my stomach, I pull the panicking anguish back. I focus on keeping my mind empty, humming to myself to get out of the shower as quickly as possible.

A half an hour later, I am knocking on Lily's door with newly blow dried hair.

"Hi," Lily smiles as she opens the door, "you ready for the second part of your tour?"

"Just try not to lose me."

On the way down, Lily checks the time on her phone; it is almost 8:30 pm.

"Okay, curfew is in two and a half hours so we have plenty of time."

"Cool."

A question pops into my head. I ask, "Nikki said you guys can't pay bills because no one knows you exist, so how can you have a phone that has service?"

"We think – since we don't exist – neither do our phones, so the phone companies don't know to de-activate our phones or send us bills. But like I said, we aren't completely sure; we just figured out one day that they worked."

"So my phone will still work whenever I find it?"

"Yes, and actually I have it right here," Lily pulls my phone out of her jeans' pocket. "I happened to be with Zac when he dropped the box it was in and it fell out. Sorry."

"It's okay. It's not like I haven't done worse," I say smiling. "In fact, the only reason I got this phone is because my dog got my old phone off the table and used it as his new chew toy. It still worked – well, except the front screen, but then he got my mom's phone and completely chewed hers to shreds. She had to get a new one, and so I got a new one too."

We are both cracking up when I realize I'd just been able to talk about my mom and Hammie, my dog, without completely breaking down. Although, I am about to ruin that thought, focusing too intently on them now.

It seems as if Lily can sense I am starting to decline down a slope that could have a significant, depressing effect because she changes the subject.

"We'll probably hear from Nikki soon about your classes."

I nod, trying too hard to quiet the crying.

95

We reach the lounge and head down the hallway of entertainment.

"You like to read, right?" she asks.

"Yeah," I am beginning to regain control, "but a more proper phrase would be *love it with a passion* though."

"The box with your phone was also packed with books, so I was thinking I'd show you the library first."

"You mean Zac dropped my books?" I pretend to be worried and taken aback. "My precious books! Are they okay?"

Playing along, she says reassuringly," Yes, yes, no damage at all. In fact, if anything was damaged it was Zac's foot which he dropped the box on."

We come to what must be the library door. Inside is the example of my dream home-library. The walls are all lined with ceiling-high, furnished wooden shelves, filled with hundreds of books. In the center of the room are comfortable lounging chairs perfect for reading and tables also overflowing with stacked books. Lily and I split up and look around. There is a large range from fiction and fantasy to nonfiction and biographies. I am able to find a few of my all-time favorites like *The Hunger Games, Harry Potter* series, *Impossible, The Perks of Being a Wallflower*, and the *Divergent* trilogy, that I have copies of in the box Lily had mentioned.

If there is anything I appreciate in this world, it is an ideally-filled, large, organized library.

"This place is categorized by author's last name, if you haven't figured it out yet. This list," she points to a sheet of paper that runs from the ceiling to the floor with one hundred lines, some filled in, some still blank, "is a list of books read by people here that are some of the best they've read. If someone ever needs something good to read, they can come over here and look for one they haven't read. If you ever want to add one, you can use the pen right here and write the title and author of the book," Lily explains.

"How did you guys get all these books?" I ask wonderingly.

"The same way we get food and clothes; we buy them," she teases. "Some are donated when people become Gifted. There's a few famous authors that, when they've become Gifted, all of their books are transported to the nearest Gifted mansion *'cause I guess they can't just go poof into thin air*, and then, depending on how many copies there are, that Gifted mansion sends them out to others. Not to mention, the collection has accumulated over time. They started with a few and it's grown to this," Lily motions around the room. "Just make sure if you take one out, you sign the book in and out on this paper." She shows me a paper like the Favorites' List only this one also has a spot for Time Out and In and who has it.

"Okay."

Both of us look around a little longer before Lily says, "We should probably get going, so you have enough time to see most of the rooms."

Next we move across the hall to very briefly check out the bowling alley. Basically we peek our heads in, look around, see no one is here and leave.

We move down the hall, passing a couple of corners, and walk into the Game Room. On the left are a couple of girls playing foosball. Lily quickly introduces us as we don't want to interrupt their game. There is Kyllie and Alex versus Terra and Cammie.

There is one other foosball table, two ping pong tables, two air hockey tables, three of those Sky ball machines, and three Pac-Man arcade games. All in all, a very cool game room.

We exit the room, but before moving anywhere, Lily comes to a stop as I see her texting.

"Hey Kira, how much are you liking this tour?"

"It's pretty good," I say nonchalantly.

"I'm bored. Are you bored?"

"Yeah, just a little. I mean great tour guide, interesting places to see, but-" I shrug.

"Exactly! So I was thinking we could go hang out with my friend Tess in the TV-and-Computer Room."

"Sure. That sounds fun."

There are a few people in the room – Becca, Tess, Lesley, and Sterling. Becca and Tess are sitting at two computers. There are about fifteen. Lesley and Sterling are watching a baseball game on a flat screen TV. There are small rooms connected to this large one, branching off in a star pattern. In the rooms, a TV hangs on the wall in each – probably so people can watch what they want without arguing.

All of a sudden, Lily zones out, and she stares into space.

"Lily?" I ask worried.

Tess and Becca turn around and calmly explain, "It's okay. Someone's just Minding her."

So that's what it's like when you're being "Minded." After just a moment, Lily is back to normal, and she informs me that was Nikki saying I would be having the four, one-hour classes, starting with earth, then air, fire, and last, water.

"Why didn't she just Mind me?" I ask, maybe slightly offended.

"She probably didn't want to scare you or she didn't know if you'd feel invaded."

I feel bad. Nikki was trying to be nice and give me space, even though I wouldn't have been mad if she had Minded me. How would she have known that, though? She hadn't meant to hurt my feelings.

Lily pulls a chair from a nearby computer to sit next to Tess and Becca and starts chatting. She didn't mean to leave me standing by myself. She didn't.

Naturally, because I'm awkward in new situations, I stand here for a few minutes while the three of them talk about whatever. I clumsily go and get a chair, clanking it against the metal bars of the table. After finally flipping it around I see everyone starring; the two guys' heads turned over the back of the couch, the girls glancing at me. I smile to shrug it off. I don't want to smile though. I feel like I shouldn't be sitting with them. They could start talking about something private or worse, me. Then what kind of awkward situation does that leave me in? I don't want to blow them off to go watch baseball; not to mention I don't want to go sit with the guys by myself – that's more awkward than the girls.

It's not like I don't know how to talk to people; I just don't know how to act in a group – especially a group of strangers. I tend to tense up and mumble things, making it awkward. I don't like awkward, which is ironic because I am awkward. I'm rambling. This is what happens.

I'm sitting here, kind of staring at the ground or looking around the room, more consumed in my own thoughts than the girls' conversation. I tune in for a second to listen.

"Oh my god, stop!" Lily says, frowning and blushing.

The girls just smile. One of them, Tess, shakes her head, "Look Lily, your brother is hot-"

Are they talking about Zac?

"-and if he was as concerned about me as he is about this girl – even if he tries to act otherwise – let me tell you, I would definitely not have a problem with it."

"Okay, ew!" Lily shrieks, covering her ears. I smile at her silliness.

I turn back to Tess. She is staring at me intently with her eyebrows furrowed.

"I don't think I've seen you around here before," she looks as if she is trying to remember.

"No, I'm Kira. I just got here last night," I say it so casually but it tastes like something sour. *Ignore the awkwardness you feel.*

She frowns and looks guilty, "Oh that means you're – I'm sorry. I'm really not that interested in Zac. If there's something going on there, I won't be in the way-"

Stupidly, I respond, "What?"

"You *are* the one with four Gifts that broke Kasten's prophecy right?"

"Yes but why would you think there would be something going on with Zac and I?"

"Kira, it's obvious," Lily says exasperatedly.

"What? The fact he's arrogant and sarcastic? Yeah I got that part."

She smirks, "That is true – which is normal for him-"

"Then why would you guys think – what did you say? He's 'concerned' about me?"

"Maybe it's because you don't know him like we do, but honestly that arrogant, bossy, sarcastic, conceited-"

"Lily, we get it. Keep moving," Becca smirks.

"-it's all just an act."

"Okay, but-"

"He was there when I became Gifted and he sure wasn't checking up on me every five minutes," Tess says sounding brusque.

"He's not checking up on me every five minutes either," I say.

"Kira, when you passed out last night and the ordeal at Wal-Mart this morning, he was trailing along everywhere until we finally had to send him away. Granted, he wasn't begging to see you or know if you were okay. He was quietly sneaking behind us or crouched in the background, but that's only because he thinks if he does that, we won't think he cares as much as he does," Lily explains frankly, adamantly.

"Guys, come on. He hasn't even known me a day. Think about it."

"Girl you know your heart fluttered a little when he caught you at the warehouse."

"I was kind of too busy passing out from exhaustion," I shrug sarcastically.

"What about when he was the one sitting next to you when you woke up the first time?

"Again sorry, I was too dazed and confused from passing out and waking up in some unfamiliar place. Besides what does this have to do with how he feels?"

"If you can admit *you* are attracted to *him*, then you can accept that he might like you."

"I don't like him though. I've known him less than twenty four hours and what I do know is he's smug, cynical, and rude-"

Lily snorts, "Ain't that the truth-"

"-That's not all there is. I mean, he has been occasionally nice to me. But let's keep it real here. Would a guy like Zac have a crush on someone after about five minutes with her? Especially when she doesn't just roll over and let him walk all over her?"

"Hey, maybe we're wrong," Tess says, "but I think – eventually – we'll be right. Maybe he doesn't like you now, but he's pulled to you and once he gets to know you, then there's no way to deny he may like you."

I smile. They are so positive. He doesn't like me. He couldn't. He doesn't.

The subject of their conversation changes directions and I am no longer involved. It seems like the farther away their conversation gets the more distant my own mind starts to fade and I realize I am having a difficult time keeping my eyes open.

"Hey Lily?"

"Yes," she asks, mimicking my dreamy, light tone.

"I think I'm going to go now."

"Sorry, we didn't mean to exclude you. We can-"

"No, it's not you guys. I'm just getting tired."

"Alright, well I should probably go to sleep too," she stands up and moves to put back her chair.

"Don't feel like you have to leave because of me. You can stay here and talk. I think I can find my way upstairs; if not, I need to learn anyways."

"I feel bad just…well, basically throwing you to the wolves," Lily frowns, remorsefully.

"Don't," I smile.

She looks conflicted for a minute but then resigns to stay.

"I'll see you guys tomorrow," I say politely, putting back my chair more gracefully than I had taken it out.

"See 'ya."

"Bye."

"Nice meeting you."

The guys either aren't paying the slightest attention to us or don't care to say good bye – possibly both.

I close the door behind me when I step out and lean against it, suddenly needing support. I feel overwhelmingly exhausted like on those Friday nights after a long, stressful week and I'm passed out by ten. I take a deep breath and keep moving, thinking I just need to make it to my room and then I can sleep, as I slump up the stairs. There has never been a day in my life when I have wished harder for something than in this moment for an elevator. I've made it to the second floor okay, but I still have to climb two more flights of stairs.

I make it to the top floor jubilated but fatigued, wanting to fall to the floor and sleep right here – but some people would probably find that weird. Like a lazy bum, I walk on the wrong side of the hall so I can lean on the wall. It is pretty sad when my own knees give in, protesting. It's not a pleasant feeling having your legs give out and suddenly stumbling to the floor, frightened by the imposing impact. Well, it would have hurt had someone not have turned the corner and had stunning reflexes. He almost runs into me but stops himself, instinctively reaching to steady me.

"Woah, are you okay?" he asks.

"Fine," I say with a sigh, dazed and grasping the arms that are currently all that is holding me up. "Just trying to get to my room," I mumble, looking up at the guy.

Do you remember when I said Zac was 'kind of, well, hot?' Well this guy is most definitely dreamy. *Wow…I didn't mean to sound that shallow…* He has beautiful green eyes that remind me of the ocean on a breezy day when the waves are barely rough. He has brown hair that seems to drift in the slightest draft of air. This guy is tall – somewhere around six foot – and has broad shoulders and strong arms. He is in shape, similar to Zac. Sheesh, are there any guys here that aren't in shape?

"A little tired there?" he grins, flashing a knee-weakening smile.

I grunt – not the most attractive thing to do of course. I add sarcastically, "Yeah, a little; I guess you could say I've had a long day."

"Do you think you'll make it to your room or should I carry you?" he smirks.

"Here I thought chivalry was dead," I smile in turn, rolling my eyes.

"Sounds cynical. So you've met Zac Railey then," he says, his smirk growing wider, more amused.

"You know him?"

"Yeah."

"Is he always so…?"

"Yes," he nods his head, pinching his eyes closed for the same reasons someone would sigh.

"You sound like you know him well."

"Pretty well actually. Our rooms are right next to each other."

"Oh, I'm sorry," I shrug.

"Why?" He looks at me genuinely confused.

"You sounded like you were unhappy about it."

"Well Zac's a jerk," he shrugs, "but he's my best friend."

My eyebrows lift half with disbelief, half questioning his sanity.

"Surprised?" He asks trying to hide his entertained smile.

"Um…you two just seem, well different."

"We are – sometimes. Sometimes…" he trails off with a mischievous, wide grin.

I shake my head, smirking. This brief moment of forgetting my exhaustion ends abruptly when my arms develop a tremor.

"Hey are you sure you're okay?" he asks, his face morphing into a front of concern.

"I'm fine. I'm just drained."

"In that case I should definitely escort you to your room. Can't have you passing out in the middle of the hallway now."

"Either you're really into the chivalrous thing or you're just waiting to see me pass out in a couple minutes and have a good laugh," I say sarcastically.

"All innocent intentions – I swear. *Some* of us still carry the practice. Now if you've been around Zac, I would see where you might think that I'd want to take advantage of the situation," He winks. I smile.

We start walking down the hall. He walks near to me without actually touching me, waiting in the wings in case I drop like a fly. It nearly causes me to blush. Thankfully we make it to my room quickly.

"So you *are* the new girl," he states rather than questions, as if confirming his suspicions.

I nod, "What's your name?"

I notice he is staring blankly at me – absentmindedly. The look of being Minded.

"Oh-kay, well then…you can't hear me and here I am babbling," I shake my head, turning away. "Well, I'm going to go now, before I act even more like an idiot. Nice to meet you, whoever you are."

Little did I know he caught on to the end of my rambling and as I open the door I hear him say, quietly, "It was nice meeting you too."

I stop and turn my head back to him to smile politely and see him smiling amusedly.

Great! He probably thinks I'm some kind of idiot and he's just standing there laughing hysterically at me on the inside, I think glumly. *This whole thing was probably such a joke to him.*

"Bye," I mumble sullenly not even waiting for a reply before closing the door as I enter the darkness of my room.

I flip on the light and squint as my eyes adjust to the light. All my old things are here yet this place isn't familiar at all. I open one of my drawers and throw on my pair of pajamas that have the nice, soft, cotton pant. The left over feeling of a recent shower and the pajamas' comfortable feeling bring me back to a lot of nights when I'd be up late, mostly for school purposes back at-.

I turn off the light and crawl into bed, pulling the same-old, homemade covers over me that my mom had made oversized for me when I was only about four so I could still use them now. Although, if I grow any more, they probably won't be big enough. At sixteen though, I highly doubt I will grow anymore. A bittersweet smile creeps onto my face along with a bittersweet sadness.

It is on its way; the overwhelming depression, the controlling fear. *She's gone. They're gone.*

I know it is safe here – to cry – in the dark. Alone. Everywhere quiet, everyone asleep. The tears surge out, streaming in waves. It is like a vast, immense ocean has been building up inside me, overflowing now. The grief is endless.

How is it possible for my heart to physically hurt this much? How is it possible for a heart to hurt at all? Your heart really has no connection to feeling or love, does it? So how can it physically ache this much as if an elephant has sat on it? Still the tears pour out along with all the misery that managed to stay around instead of exiting this morning when I broke down in the piano room and a second time with Nikki. But even though there is so much pain, it feels good to cry, as if a giant weight is being lifted off my shoulders.

So I continue to let it out, my face contorted in anguish and pain, my body curled into a tight ball, my covers and pajamas seemingly soaked. Finally my eyes run out of tears; my mind too numb – too tired to process why I am so sad anymore. I quickly say my prayers – the prayers I have said every night since before I could say them and my mom would instead. Now, even still curled into a tight ball, I close my eyes as my breaths are stuttering to calm down. A numbing pulse runs through every part of me and I fall asleep to its rhythmic, soothing beats.

Chapter 7

Opening my eyes in the morning, I feel disoriented and discombobulated. It feels wrong waking up in this new place, as if the sun shining on me here is different from the sun that used to wake me up, therefore it is wrong. I lay here in bed for a while, staring around at the walls. So many old things from an old place, so many similarities. Because of these old things, this room feels familiar – quaint but it is foreign.

I get out of bed and walk into the closet, trying to rummage through the boxes. The problem is that there are about twenty boxes all piled on top of each other, some of them heavy – and I am not the strongest person in the world you know. I give up on that and dress for the day. Now I'm stuck. Should I just start wondering the halls all by myself? Is that really a good idea? Should I go knock on Lily's door? What if she's still sleeping? I shouldn't wake her up.

I decide to attempt to find my way to the kitchen; I think I can manage. When I walk out the door, it feels as if I am stepping out of my hotel room, going down to the lobby for breakfast; not quite belonging here but having a place nonetheless.

This house – well it doesn't really qualify as a *house* – is remarkable that it still strikes me as spectacular. I still feel blown away by the marble flooring, spiral staircase, and the living room – especially now, with all of it basking in golden morning light. I feel like a little girl again, like a princess in her castle. I find myself faintly running the tips of my fingers against the iron railing, feeling its coolness. I feel the smooth, polished wood of the front doors and once again the cold, brittle texture of stone: the door handle.

"You wouldn't be trying to run away would you?"

I turn around to see Zac standing in the hall entryway, hands in his pockets. He is smirking, but this I can tell is an act. It wavers and quivers until he looks down and hides it completely.

"No," I say, almost smiling. "I was just admiring this place. It's a lot to take in."

"Yeah, and if you try and take in too much, I bet it'd make you want to run away..."

"No," and that's all I say before I start to walk towards the hall.

"I wouldn't blame you," he whispers as I pass him. "I mean that."

"Are you trying to convince me to run away? Do you *want* me to run away?"

"No," he says grimly and then walks up the stairs.

Is it me or does he take more twist and turns than a bendy straw?

I have an easier time than I thought I would finding the kitchen. It isn't too awkward when I walk in. There are a couple of groups already awake and eating breakfast; only a few people look up at me. I stare straight ahead at the kitchen keeping their stares out of my line of sight. Max is in there flipping eggs, frying bacon; breakfast stuff.

"Why hello there Kira," he says happily. "How are you feeling this morning?"

"Hungry for some gourmet breakfast," I smile.

"You're really going to have to wait until I make my French toast then."

I moan, "French toast is my favorite."

He laughs.

"Do you think you'll be okay with eggs today and I'll see if we have enough ingredients to make French toast tomorrow?"

"Eggs sound great!"

They taste great too. Good thing, because as long as I'm eating I won't notice the fact I'm sitting by myself in a room of groups. If there was no one in here, I wouldn't mind sitting by myself. It's that I'm like an outcast now – well, I am an outcast.

If they haven't been paying attention to me yet, they certainly must notice me as Lily comes sprinting into the…is this a dining room or a cafeteria?

Hardly panting, she announces loudly, "Has anyone seen – Oh! Kira, there you are. Whew! Never mind everyone else." She starts walking over to me. "I knocked on your door this morning and you didn't answer. When I peeked my head in and didn't see you I got worried, and then you weren't in the bathroom or even on the fourth floor."

"Yeah, I came down for breakfast. I didn't want to knock on your door in case you were still sleeping. I didn't want to wake you up."

"I was probably awake anyhow. I'm glad you made it down here alright by yourself. That's kind of an impressive thing around here when you're new," she smiles.

"Believe me, I'm just as surprised as you are."

"I'm actually not surprised at all. Oh and I passed like eight people on the way here; none of them had seen you."

"Did you see Zac?"

"Yeah – on my way down the stairs."

"Did you talk to him?"

"He said he hadn't seen you – then something about 'not her babysitter' but I tend to tune out his ramblings so I didn't catch it."

"Hm."

"Why? Did you see him?"

Why did Zac lie?

I decide to ask him about it later and keep this as a little secret between me and him.

"Oh, no. I just thought maybe he would have helped you," I shrug. That's a complete lie. He definitely would not have helped her.

"Okay, well, you need to finish your breakfast and I need to get some breakfast. Then I'm sure Zac's gonna want you to meet Jamie," here she winks at me, "and then we'll have to find something to do until class starts at 2:00."

"Alright. What are you standing there for?" I look at her like a total diva. She gapes back at me with complete disbelief, but soon I continue, "Go get yourself some food girl."

I smile.

She laughs and walks over towards the stoves. I giggle and return to eating my eggs. A few minutes later there is a figure standing in front of me again. Trying to stab a piece of egg that keeps splitting apart I don't look up to see who it is. I just assume it is Lily.

"That was fast."

"How do you figure?"

That – is not Lily's voice but Zac's.

I look up and there he is, leaning forward with his hands placed on the table.

"Sorry, I thought you were your sister."

I don't even give him a second glance; instead, I revisit my more interesting and less offensive eggs.

"She beat me here? Damn, I thought she'd at least go outside first to see if you were trying to escape. Don't look at me like that! She just tends to panic most times and jump to conclusions."

"Must run in the family."

He rolls his eyes.

"Have you talked to her yet?"

"Yes."

"Did she mention me?"

"Are you that conceited that all you can think about is yourself-"

"Just answer the question Blondie."

"She didn't mention you per say…"

"What do you mean?" he peers at me cynically.

"Well…I might have mentioned you," I say hesitantly.

He looks uneasy, "You didn't tell her you saw me did you?"

"No. I didn't it," I say coldly, looking down at my plate. "You want to know why? Because before I could, she said she saw you and *you* said you hadn't seen me. You want to explain that Mr. Sarcastic?"

"First of all, I prefer *Sir* Sarcastic. Secondly, I didn't say anything because I didn't think it would be a good idea to go around telling people it looked like you were trying to leave-"

"-But I wasn't-"

"-and then she would have freaked out and yelled at me because '*I saw you trying to run away and let you out of my sight.*' Then you know she would have come down here and found you and yelled at you for seeming to run away and so I figured you would appreciate it as much as I did not getting yelled at," he finishes smugly.

"Oh how nice of you to think of me. I'm sure that's exactly what you were worried about."

"Fine you don't have to believe me but let me know if you're going to say something to Lily."

115

"I'm not going to say anything to her but I don't like the fact you're treating this like some deep, dark secret. It makes me feel like I'm keeping something bad from her. Maybe you should be a little bit more concerned about *that*," I say defensively.

"We're not lying, especially not about anything important. We're just choosing not to tell her something that's unimportant."

"Whatever dude. Whatever helps you sleep at night," I roll my eyes.

"A peace of mind…and a nice back massage," he wags his eyebrows.

"Aw," I say empathetically, "I bet you like that from your boyfriend."

He just about chokes on *my* drink.

"I'm sorry," he says spluttering, "but did you just call me gay? I'm straight sweetheart," he smirks.

"It's okay," I touch his arm sympathetically, "I understand. You're not ready to come out of the closet yet. I won't tell anyone."

He clenches his jaw and glares at me. He opens his mouth to bite back a remark but is cut off by Lily coming back with her food.

"Hi there Zac," she is looking at him as if he is speaking to her in fluent French. "I thought you already ate?"

Mental note to self: Zac can lie very well and on the drop of a dime.

"Yeah well I thought maybe I would check the kitchen for Kira for you…Found her!"

"You're *so* helpful," she scoffs.

"I try. Anyways, Kira," he pauses and looks me in the eyes, "do you think you'll be up to meeting some of the guys after you and Oinkers here are done eating?"

Lily reaches across the table from her place next to me and smashes Zac's arm with the back of her hand.

"Ow," he articulates.

"Quit being a baby…*Whiners*," she sticks her tongue out at him.

"Real mature Lily."

To avoid another full-out twin feud, I interrupt loudly, "Yeah Zac, we'll see you after breakfast. You can go away now."

He nods at me, glares a second at Lily, and then stands up and leaves.

Lily shrieks next to me.

"I am not a pig! I can't help it; I have a strength Gift."

"Lily, you know you're not fat and that you don't overeat. He's just trying to bother you."

"Yeah, I guess," she says dismally and starts eating.

My eating slows down after our little encounter with Zac, and Lily is a pretty fast eater so we are out of here in no time. We pass Nikki as we head towards the front staircase. She is heading out of a hallway that leads to the infirmary I think.

"Good morning girls," she chimes warmly. "What would you two be up to?"

"I'm going with Kira to meet Jamie and some of the guys on 'Toxic Level Three,'" Lily frowns disgustedly.

I'm not sure if Lily says that because of the friendly rivalry with her brother or if their floor is really dirty.

"I can't believe I'm saying this but could you use some company?" she asks, shaking her head as if she already regrets the offer.

"We'd love to have you, but it's your choice if you want to risk contracting a disease."

"I have to go anyways," she frowns, "I already told Zac to prepare the boys for an cleaning inspection."

Lily turns her head and smiles slyly, "Oh good we get to watch her yell at them."

I giggle.

As we walk up the stairs, Nikki explains that Lily and herself are slightly over-exaggerating. We proceed to share horror stories from the show "*Buried Alive*" about hoarders.

"Can you imagine never being able to throw something away?" I wonder aloud.

"Some things I could understand wanting to keep, but a lifetime's worth of stuff is just so much junk."

We come to the third landing and the conversation halts. Nikki and Lily look around suspiciously. I notice an aroma in the air that is a very strong mixture of something disgusting and a ton of Febreeze, but as soon as I notice it, the bad stench vanishes as if a breeze blew it away.

"At least you can't smell the fungus anymore," Lily comments, but I can't tell if she is kidding or if there really has been fungus growing up here. You wouldn't think so, but it wouldn't surprise me after learning everything else that seemed impossible really is possible.

We start moving down the hallway right to the left of the landing, instead of down the hallway straight ahead that would lead towards my room if we were on the girl's floor. We cautiously approach each of the rooms as if it is a toxic waste zone, but we find all of them to be at the very least sanitary with a little bit of clutter on the floor or on the desk and dressers. Nikki and Lily seem a little surprised to find the guys' rooms so clean.

In the first half of the rooms, they introduce me to whoever is in there distractedly as they glance around the room, searching for a clue as to where the mess could have gone.

We have made it all the way through the first half of rooms and none of us have seen or smelt anything the least bit gross. I am starting to think that Nikki and Lily were hugely over-reacting earlier. Their completely baffled looks, however, are highly hilarious. Along the way, I have met Erik, Kaleb, Lesley, Damen, Gavin, Christian, and Emmitt – and no signs of a foreign species. (Try and ask me who all those people are in five minutes and I won't be able to name half of them.)

119

We still have a few rooms left on this hallway but they are starting to turn down a different hallway to the right, which I think I know where it will lead.

"What about those guys?" I point at the three doors left that we hadn't gotten too yet down the hallway we came from.

"You've already met them in other people's rooms."

On the second half, instead of heading to the section where my room would be on an alternative level, we head up the hallway that will take you to the long window and around to the staircase. No one in the first few rooms answers the door when we knock, either because the room is empty or they decide not to answer.

Well, fine then.

We give up and turn back around to head towards Zac's room. Zac's is the third on the right from the end of the hallway. He is another one who, once again, doesn't answer. Lily is about to open his door and look in, but Nikki stops her, "Lily you know the rules. No going in someone's room unless the door is open or they let you in."

"Oh come on! One peak? I'm his twin for goodness's sake!"

Nikki's serious gaze doesn't falter.

"Fine," with a huff, Lily gives up.

I realize that I didn't know that rule and might have walked in – well I mean, if he wasn't a total stranger – and we were close. Not wanting to anger anyone (like only I could) in the future, I ask,

"Are there any other rules I should know before I do something really embarrassing – or stupid for that matter?"

They both smile. *I didn't realize I was so funny.* Nikki says, "Of course, but you already have enough to remember right now. Everyone will know you're new if you do something wrong and they'd give you a break. I highly doubt you'd manage to do anything too bad anyways. The rules are pretty basic around here, but we'll inform you on them when there's a little less on your plate."

That isn't a lot of help, but I guess she's right. I have so many things to try and comprehend; my brain's going to be fried from overload soon. We move to the door next to Zac's room, which – finally – someone comes to the door.

This guy appears familiar…*He is the guy from last night that walked me to my room.*

"It's about time we found someone. Kira, this is Jamie Brisk. He has the Gift of air," Nikki introduces us.

All of a sudden, a breeze picks up and tousles my hair. It blows down towards my hand and it feels as if there is actual skin touching my hand, shaking it in greeting. Jamie has clearly been controlling it (hello air Gift), and I smile brightly.

"Hi," I say, still smiling like a blundering idiot.

Jamie Brisk gazes at me and says sort of dazed, "Hi, I believe we've already met though."

I try to stifle the chill that is running through me – an affect from his deep, sea green eyes. *Breathe Kira, breathe; it's just you don't meet someone this cute every day.*

"Well you knew who I was, but 'someone' never told me *your* name," I smirk.

I am still smiling (like a dork, probably) and he is actually lopsidedly smiling back.

Zac suddenly pops out of Jamie's room. After he sees we are out here and takes a look at Jamie's and mine smiling/staring game, I swear I see him frown. Just for an instant, but his face returns back to normal in a flash, leaving me wondering if I had imagined it.

"Think it took you long enough to eat?" Zac is definitely back to his usual, sarcastic self.

"Well, we wanted to make sure you had enough time to disinfect the floor level," Lily replies in return.

"As you can see we are well past clean and have just been hanging out for a while now."

Zac leads us into Jamie's room, where we find what is possibly the entire second half of the floor's missing guys. There are four other guys in the room, either on the computer or playing some weird video game. They each stop what they are doing though to introduce themselves.

Matt Fieldson – who's a telekinesis – and Troy Dally – who has a water Gift – are the ones playing the video games. Taylor Lagner – who is a psychic – and Mitchell Hast – who has a fire Gift – are the ones on the computer. Matt has black hair and blue eyes, Troy has blonde hair and green eyes, Taylor also has black hair but with green eyes, and Mitchell has brown hair with brown eyes. A couple of the boys have more of that sweet, smart guy look while the others have that subtle, jock look.

Nikki interrupts my thoughts when she asks Zac and Jamie, "Where are Sterling and Jake?"

"Did you check their rooms?" Zac asks, not the least bit curious or concerned.

"Their doors were closed and they didn't answer when I knocked."

"Maybe they left their rooms and went downstairs, thinking that you had skipped them or they hadn't heard the knock since it took you guys so long," Zac obviously improvised that solution because he/they are clearly hiding something. That was too much of a rambling statement for nothing suspicious to be going on – it was too well thought up.

"Alright, I guess I'll just Mind them."

Jamie quickly whispers, "That's our name for calling someone with your mind; of course only the people who are telepathic can do it though."

"I know," I smile.

Nikki starts to concentrate when Zac quickly turns towards Matt – also a telekinesis in the room – and lifts his eyebrows in a gesture like 'Hello? Are you going to do something?'

"*I don't know* what to do!" Matt whispers, exasperatedly.

"Do *something!* You're the only telekinesis here!" Zac whispers, exasperatedly in return while Lily and I just stare at them.

"Fine," and in a louder tone Matt says, "Wait, Nikki..."

She doesn't open her eyes but she frowns.

"What?" she asks evenly.

"Can I Mind them? You know, for practice."

Now she opens her eyes and glares suspiciously at him. After a moment, she agrees, "Okay, but make sure you tell them to hurry."

Matt nods and begins to concentrate as Nikki always does. Just like Nikki, his lips start to move as if he is attempting to speak but no sound is vocalized.

All of sudden something flies down, past the window. There are many giant crashes and an awful smell similar to dirty laundry wafts everywhere. Matt of course loses his concentration and comes back to us. To complement the weirdness, two guys appear in Jamie's doorway.

All the boys stand in place as if they've been caught red-handed in the act as Nikki, Lily, and I race towards the window. There below us are dirty laundry, old moldy food, and weird, random items. The terrible stench has been coming from the heap and Jamie or another air Gift has been blowing it away from the boys' floor.

The three of us turn to the guys now, understanding why it has been so clean. The guys have used their Gifts to momentarily hide their mess. I'm guessing Sterling and Jake are the two guys that appeared at the door and are probably the ones that were hiding the stuff while everyone else was introduced. My guess is when Matt had to "Mind" them, they must have lost their concentration, dropping the trash. Therefore, Jamie – at least I suspect it was him – lost his very delicate concentration, bringing back the terrible smell I had gotten a tiny whiff of when we first arrived on Floor Three.

"Well, well, well, and whose brilliant idea was this?" Nikki asks sarcastically.

They all turn like a bunch of unloyal foxes, "Zac's and Jamie's."

"Hey!" Zac and Jamie both remark.

"In our defense, we just wanted to show the girls that if they're going to 'hide' their mess with their Gifts that we can too," Zac defends, referring to the Battle of the Twins yesterday.

"We still did it better since we didn't get caught," Lily says, gloatingly.

"Well it would have worked if Lesley and Gavin had come to replace Sterling and Jake like they were supposed to. Instead, Nikki – well Matt – had to Mind them," Jamie says, but it seems more like he is berating himself for not coming to this conclusion beforehand and could have come up with a spontaneous solution.

"It still didn't work, so girls still win," Lily concludes, filled to the brim with triumphant.

The guys are about to say something snappy back, but Nikki interrupts them, "Alright, alright. First of all, Kira, this is Sterling-" she points towards the new blonde hair and pine-green eyed boy with a few pale freckles," and Jake-" here she points to the other guy who also has blonde hair but chocolate colored eyes. "Sterling has the Gift of earth and Jake has the Gift of extreme physical strength."

We say hello to one another – which is probably the hundredth time I've been through an introduction in the past two days.

"Actually," Sterling punctuates, "we've already met," he smiles kindly.

"Right," I return the smile. "You were the kind delivery service who brought me breakfast."

Nikki starts chastising the boys again, "Now, secondly, all of you boys and any other guys whose stuff is down there are going to manually bring the items up yourselves." Nikki glares at Jake as if warning him not to do it for them. "Then all of you will truly clean this whole floor and really clear away that awful smell. And now that that is taken care of – ladies, I'm afraid I have some business to attend to, so Lily, do you think you could-"

"I have no problem at all spending more time with Kira. I'm sure we can find something to do for another two and a half hours," Lily answers cheerfully.

"All righty! Guys I'm serious: all by hand." There's that motherly discipline intervening again before she is gone.

Zac walks over to the wide open door and peeks out after her.

"And...we're clear! Jamie, Sterling, if you would please," Zac motions towards the window. The two boys walk over to the window and start drawing up the disgusting junk.

"You're going to get caught," Lily smiles tauntingly.

"Not unless either of you plan on snitching," Jamie says with just as much provocativeness.

"Are you guys always like this?" I ask jokingly.

"Sometimes...okay, most of the time."

While Lily and I have been talking, the guys have, unfortunately, gotten all of the stuff up and into the room without getting caught. The mess is larger than it looked three floors down; it pretty much covers everything and even spills out into the hallway. Lily and I fly out of the room, completely disgusted. We start toward the hallway stairs, but Zac quickly stops us to ask Lily if they are still planning their weekly movie night tonight.

"I think so. Kira, do you like movies? If you're not a movies kind of person, we can wait to do it until you have other people to keep you busy or you have things to do. Oh, I – other people – I didn't mean-"

I start laughing, and she looks relieved, "I love movies, but I don't want to intrude or anything..." I've already made Lily and Zac spend so much time with me and I have only been here for a day.

"Don't be silly," Lily smiles, "and it's not just the two of us anyways. The movie plan is more like a weekly party that anyone can come to. Zac and I started the event to make sure we'd always see each other, and although not seeing each other for more than a few hours hasn't happened yet, it's something fun we like to do."

"Sure, what time is it at?"

"Eight, but I'll probably find you again at dinner after class and sit with you. If not me then Zac."

I feel a little uncomfortable.

"I still feel like I'm boring you, making you show me around and helping me out all the time and practically baby-sitting me. If you ever want – or need – to go do something-" As you can see, it's possible for me to feel guilty and self-conscience about pretty much anything.

Lily is laughing genuinely at my freak-out, not meanly though. She smiles, "Kira, you're not boring! You're even sometimes a tad bit funny. It's like you see yourself as a bother sometimes, and you really aren't. Honestly."

I smile back at her, breathing normally again. I feel a little better, but how can Lily say she is completely happy walking around the entire mansion, showing me everything and not getting the least bit bored? I'm not saying that I wouldn't want to do that, but I'm me and Lily is Lily – who I'm still getting to know. We had only really met late yesterday and she is treating me as if we've been best friends for years.

"Don't worry will 'ya," she wraps her arm around my shoulders and we head down the hallway.

"That might be a problem since I was genetically programmed to do nothing but worry and stress."

"Really?" she asks, bewildered.

The smile on my face disappears for a second. Does she think I'm actually genetically programmed like that?

"I don't have a disease or anything. I just tend to worry a lot."

I think she is realizing how she reacted and laughs at her mistake.

As Lily and I are about to descend the stairs, we hear a faraway Jamie whistle, and yell, "Guys!" The problem is that since we are on the guys' floor, we're not sure if he means literally "guys" opposite of girls, or "guys" as in "hey you two."

"If we sent something of yours out the window, come and get it in my room, not Zac's!" Jamie announces to all of the boys on the floor.

We start down the stairs as he isn't talking to us after all.

"So what do you want to do?" Lily asks.

"Oh I don't know. If you have some friends hanging out somewhere we can go see them."

"I think most people are just getting up or eating. We could get those boxes out of your closet."

"You sure you want to do that though? I mean, that's really nice of you but wouldn't you rather do something else?" I ask tentatively.

"At this point there's nothing else to do. Besides, I would be way more help than Zac."

I laugh, "That's true."

We stop and turn around, heading up the stairs now. As we pass the third floor's landing, Zac nearly runs into us.

"Um, watch it," he snaps without looking at us.

"You think being his twin, he'd at least apologize for nearly catapulting me down the stairs," Lily says to me hypothetically.

Zac had started walking down the stairs but stops when he hears Lily speak and now turns around.

"Oh, it's you guys. Sorry," he mumbles.

"Wow, that was really sincere," Lily rolls her eyes.

He ignores her and continues talking, "I was actually going to look for you two."

That catches our attention.

"Jamie and I thought you could wait a couple minutes and then we could hang out together, since Kira didn't really get to meet him properly."

"First of all, don't you two need to clean?" Lily quips, quirking an eyebrow. "And secondly, I was about to go help Kira remove the boxes from her closet."

"Eh, my room's decent. And Kira, you don't need any of that stuff yet do you?"

"Well I guess not," I shrug. "But actually Jamie and I met before this morning."

"What?" Zac asks as Lily asks, "When? You never said anything to me."

I look at Lily, "Last night. When I left you in the TV and computer room. I ran into him on the girls' floor. I didn't know who he was at the time, but we stopped and talked for a little."

Zac looks confused and Lily is smiling.

Zac recovers, "Then I'm sure you wouldn't mind talking to him some more-"

"Zac, we already decided to get her boxes out; I'm sure she wants to get her stuff all unpacked."

"Fine," Zac says grudgingly and walks away.

"Is it me or was he marginally crankier than the last time we saw him?" I smirk.

Lily snorts. She laughs, "Come on."

We start racing each other up the stairs, bumping into one another, holding each other back, laughing. It probably isn't very safe, but it is a lot of fun. Lily beats me by far; she does have more of an advantage.

Once we make it to my room, Lily immediately walks over to the closet and starts lifting boxes out and puts them on my bed. I hem and haw, trying to stay out of her way while trying to help move the boxes out of the closet.

"Kira, honestly, you can just let me get the boxes out," she says as she manages to get another two boxes out and she places them on the floor. She doesn't even sound strained as she speaks.

"I'd feel too bad letting you do all the work," I manage to slip into the closet and pick up a box with some difficulty. "Besides, if there are two of us, it'll take less time to get them all out."

"Alright, but I really don't mind."

We are able to remove all of the boxes from my closet but in doing so fill all the empty space in my room. I open one of the boxes on the bed, finding a picture frame inside.

"Would you like me to help you unpack all this stuff now?"

I don't really hear her; I am too busy staring at the picture of my family from a couple of Christmases ago.

"Kira...Kira?"

"Oh, sorry. I think I'll just take care of it, but thank you for all your help."

"No problem. And I get it; lots of memories. When you're done, you can just call or text me. I put my number in your phone if you ever need anything. Zac's number is also in there, but he would probably be less than helpful."

We both laugh.

"Thanks again Lily. I'll see you later," I smile with genuine appreciation.

"See 'ya Kira."

She steps out, closing the door behind her.

"Time to move in," I mutter to myself.

It seems so weird to me. Opening up the boxes, removing the items inside, and putting them in what their regular places would be at home. Then I remember this is home, and yet I keep thinking that at some point I'll have to pack it all up again and return home.

Music. I need something to distract me while I go through this stuff. I look around the room, wondering if my stereo is packed in a box or set up already. Interestingly enough, it is on my nightstand, right in the corner where it's always been. There even is a CD still in it. Not caring what CD it is I push the play button and start to listen, returning to unpacking. I hum along and for a while my thoughts are contained.

Over an hour later, all the boxes are empty and the room is officially moved into. Suddenly this feels permanent, not just a weekend vacation. Here are all my things, almost exactly like how they were at home, but here instead, like there is no other place to go, as if that other place doesn't exist. I sigh, as if suddenly aging a couple years.

I sit down on the bed and pull out my phone. I've had this same phone for a while and it's always looked normal to me, but now in this new place, even my phone feels unfamiliar. I open my contacts. I am disappointed but not surprised to find only two numbers: Lily Cell and Zac Cell. I just wonder whether the Gift erased the other contacts or Lily did.

Lily picks up on the fourth ring.

"Hi Kira. Everything all right?" she asks concerned.

"Yeah, I finished unpacking so I was just giving you a call like you said."

"Oh okay, cool. Well I'm just hanging out with some friends in the room we were in last night. Do you want to come meet me and we'll get some lunch before class starts?"

"Sounds good. See you in a few."

I hang up and pull myself together, leaving my room. Hopefully once I make it down to the main level, the TV room door will look familiar, otherwise I am going to have to wander around, opening random doors until I find it – or I guess I could call Lily again.

Finding my way downstairs is becoming increasingly easier, but finding the right door out of the fifteen different doors is more difficult. Surprisingly I find the TV room in only a few attempts.

I walk in and find it livelier than last night with at least ten people inside. Most stop and look at me before returning to whatever they are talking about. I see Lily in a group of four others and I wave at her. I recognize one of the two guys as Sterling and one of the girls as Tess; the other two in the group are unfamiliar.

"Kira," Lily calls and waves me over.

"Hey," I greet her, coming to stand next to her.

"You ready to get some lunch?"

"Yeah, as soon as you're ready to go," I smile.

"Actually I was hoping you wouldn't mind if they come with us," she looks at me shyly.

"Of course they can come!" I stare at her as if she is crazy for thinking I would say otherwise.

"Let's go get some lunch then."

They laugh at her but start to walk towards the door.

"Oh by the way, everyone, this is Kira Taylor, our newest member if you haven't heard."

The unfamiliar guy asks me what Gift I have. Before I can answer, Sterling asks the guy if he is a) stupid or b) lives under a rock, and then Sterling proceeds to hit the guy in the arm.

"Wow man, take it easy. We're not all in the loop like you are. I think I was actually being very polite to the lady; thought she might like someone actually asking her a normal question."

"More like-"

"Sterling," I interrupt him, "it's fine." I smile reassuringly at him and turn to face the other guy. "I have an earth, water, fire, and air Gift."

His eyes widen for a second and I think he chokes a little on the air he is breathing. He recovers quickly though and reaches out his hand, smiling.

"Nick Peterson at your service."

I shake his hand but stare at him with interest. I keep seeing flashes when I look at him. Explosions and rain, and his face seems to fit in with those scenes of confusion. Why does he seem familiar?

"Have I met you before?" I ask warily.

I notice Lily has stiffened with uneasiness and Nick looks somewhat uncomfortable.

"Well," he starts hesitantly, "I was kind of one of the people who was called to uh…um help out at Wal-Mart yesterday." He is shifting awkwardly and avoiding my eyes.

When he explains, the picture becomes clear and I see him standing next to Nikki and some other girl in the Wal-Mart, eyes closed in deep concentration.

"Oh," is all I say – all I can say. At a certain point yesterday, if I had met him I might have hit him, but now it seems childish and wrong. I'm still not sure how to feel about it though. I guess I should probably let it go, since I seem to have already forgiven Nikki.

"I suppose you don't really want to talk to me now?" he questions, desolately.

"No, it's fine," I force a smile because I'm really trying to not make him feel bad. "So based on yesterday, I'm going to guess you're a telekinesis, right?"

"Both my twin sister and I are, actually. She was the other person with us…" he trails off again, guiltily.

"Twins really do seem to run in the Gifted DNA, I see. Weird," I comment curiously.

"Makes you wonder about things," Nick smiles.

We made it to the kitchen and now form a line to get food.

From behind me, Lily asks, "Hey, are you alright?"

136

I look back at her, "Of course. Why?"

"I just wanted to check – you know, with you talking to Nick and everything. I didn't want it to upset you but I didn't know if it did. I didn't even think about the fact the he was-…"

"I'm okay," I say firmly, smiling at her. "It's okay."

When we make it to the front we find Max has made club sandwiches for lunch. I look around but don't see him anywhere. This is the first time I don't see him in the kitchen.

"Is Max not here?"

"Well it's not like he lives in the kitchen Kira," Lily teases. "He does occasionally leave."

"I was just wondering," I say defensively, throwing my hands up in surrender.

As we sit down to eat, I pay attention to the conversation the five of them are having but don't really participate in it much. The sandwiches are delicious as all the food here is and I find that the time passes rather quickly. We all finish lunch but remain at the table laughing and talking.

Nick turns to me and asks, "So what's your schedule like since you have four Gifts?"

The other four stop talking and suddenly start to pay attention to what I am going to say.

"I have to take four one-hour classes unlike you guys who take one two-hour class."

"You'll have class until six that means?" Sterling asks, looking disgusted.

I stare at him curiously. Lily sees his expression and hits him on the arm.

"Quit it before you get her thinking that she's going to hate it before she even gets to her first class."

"Oh no, that's not it at all. All of her teachers will be great and she'll have a lot of fun in each class. I was just thinking how draining that's going to be on her energy supply though."

"She can manage; that and her teachers will know if she's being over-exerted and they'll take it easier. She'll be fine," Lily says confidently and almost pointedly to Nick. "Speaking of which," Lily says, pulling out her phone, "it's 1:55 now, so we should get ready to go."

Everyone starts to stand and move back to the kitchen to take care of their dishes.

When we all convene again, Lily stops and talks to Sterling, "Would you mind taking Kira to the earth class?"

He nods with a smile, "Sure thing."

Lily turns back to me, "Okay. One more thing to tell you that's important. Nikki and the telekinesis class programmed all the electronics – phones, watches, TVs – to go off at 2:00 and 4:00. Yours – meaning whatever electronic you have on you, so your phone – will probably also go off at 3:00, 5:00, and 6:00 to let you know your classes are over. Oh, and from your fire class, you'll have to go straight to the kitchen for dinner at 6:00. You may have time to run to your room really fast if you have something quick to do. I only warn you so that you can get dinner when it's hot, and because sometimes the guys are really hungry and tend to take very large portions. Okay, I think I got most of the important stuff covered."

Lily looks at her phone just as it and everything mechanical begins to vibrate or beep and flashes, "2:00."

"Perfect," Lily says, happy that she finished right on time.

Chapter 8

Nick, Tess, and the girl who I still don't know her name, say goodbye and head out. Sterling stays by us and asks if we are ready.

Lily, Sterling, and I all turn and walk out the back door in our own little group. Apparently, all classes are outside. Earth – my first one – is back in the woods. Air – my second – is in the fields outside the woods. Water – my third class – is on the shore in our bay of Lake Michigan to the right of the woods. Fire – my last class – is in the front of the mansion on a giant paved square that makes up part of the driveway. Lily explained all of this to me at breakfast earlier, drawing a map with her scrambled eggs.

We come outside. A gentle, rolling field begins right in the immediate back yard that stretches to the right and left of the mansion for at least the length and width of two football fields. A dense forest surrounds the edges of the field on all sides except for one side of the outer boundary of the field back and to the right, where the cliffs and lake are located. Lily turns to the left as Sterling and I head straight.

"Strength class is this way so I guess I'll see you at dinner. Good luck!" and she runs off towards the structures that, out in the distance in the far left of the field, look like things you would find on a playground.

Sterling and I continue walking towards the woods. I see other people either heading towards the woods themselves or forming a group in the field, to the right of the imaginary path we are on to the woods.

"That's where you'll go for your air class," Sterling motions towards the group that has formed.

"How far into the woods is the class?" I ask, a little nervous we'll get lost – okay, I'll get lost.

"Just a few minutes, but it's easy to find," he says reassuringly.

I try to make it sound as if I am trying to be funny and hopefully he won't know it is the truth, "What if I'm directionally challenged?" as I like to call it.

"Nah, it's easy even for those people. Plus it's hard to get lost in the woods if you have an earth Gift."

Okay, so I feel a little better…not. I'm not sure how my earth Gift can ever help me. Unless, it can make the trees talk and tell me the way.

"Don't worry."

We reach the woods, and Sterling is right. The path is clearly marked. They have placed stepping stones in the middle of the path and have traced the path with red bricks to make it even easier to see. I can't get lost.

The woods are beautiful at this time of year. Not quite as beautiful as during fall or winter, but that doesn't make it any less beautiful. The sun shines through the top of the tall trees and brilliantly flows down on us. You can hear the birds and squirrels hopping around on the branches, and other little creatures running around the floor of the forest. Today is so clear. I can make out a group up ahead of the path.

"That's the class, right?" I ask, nodding my head towards the group of people we are approaching.

"Yeah. See I told you, you wouldn't get lost," he teases.

We reach the class who are just sort of standing around talking. There are four kids – three girls and one guy – and I can't find the teacher.

"Kira, this is Cammie, Erin, Becca-" Sterling shows me each of the three girls.

Cammie has brown hair and brown eyes and is slightly taller than I am. Becca has red hair with beautiful, navy-blue eyes. Erin has magnificent black hair that flows in the wind and emerald green eyes as if the gem has been placed inside them- "and this is Kaleb." Kaleb is also really tall with brown hair and green eyes not quite as pretty as Erin's. I vaguely remember him from earlier.

It worries me that the instructor isn't here yet, "When does the teacher normally get here?"

"Well, Reese is normally here hiding somewhere, planning her daily grand entry," Erin says, looking around.

I already figured out Reese is the teacher and I was going to ask what Erin meant by "grand entry" but my question is already being answered.

A tree by the head of the group is shifting and twisting apart. The center glows an unnatural white light and then births the mold of a human. The human shape starts to form colors other than brown and features other than rigid bark. Sure enough, Reese, the earth teacher, has molded herself into the tree and now molds herself out. She is more on the short side. Her hair is the most beautiful color brown like deep, velvet chocolate. Her eyes are a hazel of green and brown as if the earth blended together a mixture of its hues and crafted them into her eyes. Her smile is brilliant.

"You rang?" Reese jokes. "Alright," she pauses for a second then turns towards me, "first I heard we have a new student who will only be with us for an hour each day so we have to hurry. There she is. You're Kira," she walks towards me. "I assume the kids have alerted you to what their names are, and I 'assume' that because they probably didn't but I can say I have a little hope in them."

They know she's teasing but they attempt to act offended.

Sterling remarks in a joking matter, "No, you say 'assume' so it *sounds* like you have faith in us when really you think we won't do anything right. Even though we do it – every time."

"Yes and this way you will continue to surprise me every time so there's no need to worry about it every time," Reese continues to tease and the conversation takes on the affect as if they have had it before. "Now we have to move on to the lesson – so sorry. I have no more than an hour to teach it and after Kira leaves I'm going to have you all practice. Oh one more thing before I forget, Kira, you've probably figured out that us adults here don't like being called Mr. or Ms. Well same goes for me. It's Reese, just Reese. Okay?"

"Got it."

"Great! Alrighty now, today we are going to do something pretty easy as an introduction for Kira to the realm of earth. We are going to work on simple defense mechanisms that will prove useful in combat. One is something most of you have probably already taught yourselves, which is using vines as rope-like defenses."

Reese walks over to the tree she had earlier morphed out of and concentrates, closing her eyes and taking deep breaths. She opens her eyes wide and tilts her head towards the tree. After a few seconds, vines begin growing straight out of the ground, entwining and twisting themselves around the tree. They pull so tightly that the tree begins to crack under the pressure. Before the tree can split, Reese must have command the deadly vines to recede back into the ground and leave the tree alone, as the vines are now retreating out of sight.

"Ta-da!" Reese bows at the concurrence of her performance. "Okay now I would like Kira to come up to the front. I want you to try to do what I just did."

Oh great, I wonder what embarrassing thing I'll do.

"Okay," I say reluctantly.

I step towards the tree and stand next to Reese. She moves me so I am squared up with the tree, and she says, "Alright, close your eyes and focus. In your mind control the vines."

From behind me, Sterling tries to help and relax me, "Don't worry. We won't laugh if you accidentally make weeds grow instead of vines."

I laugh quickly to get it out of my system and I begin to concentrate. I close my eyes and take deep breaths similar to Reese. I think, "Vines," and envision what I want them to do. I can feel the dirt around my feet being re-deposited by what I hope are growing vines. I can hear bark crunching as the vines wrap around the tree and I know I have succeeded.

I grow excited, enough to blow my concentration. What happens because of it is disastrous.

At first, I don't think anything is wrong. People are saying, "Wow!" and "Oh my gosh!" most likely because I had actually done it. Someone screams and I hear thrashing as if someone is fighting off someone else. Curious as to what is going on, I throw open my eyes and meet a horrific scene instantly.

It is like Planet of the Vines. Thirty feet tall vines are blooming up, bursting everywhere. They are entwined around everything including the Gifted, hence the screaming. The vines aren't squeezing anyone, but they are restricting movement quite well.

I want to shy away from everyone in embarrassment. Unfortunately, I can't do that because someone has to exterminate the vines and Reese seems to be trying but it isn't doing any good.

I close my eyes and focus again. I call out, "Vines," again in my mind and re-imagine what they should do. I remember that

Reese opened her eyes to watch her progress and still was able to focus, so I open mine, monitoring the development.

Around me, the vines are untwining themselves from the class and the surrounding scene, and slithering back into the earth. The woods are no longer infested with vines, but as the vines disappear so does all of my hopes of having any friends.

The class is rubbing their arms and legs, taking deep breaths now that they can. The class has returned to their normal, calm selves and is beginning to turn towards me.

I can't look at them, too afraid at what I'd see. Would they be mad or scared? Do they feel betrayed that I attacked them – which I didn't, but they may have thought I did. I stare at the ground, biting my lip out of a nervous habit. The long silence proves even more disconcerting. I brace myself and I lift my eyes to see what is happening.

I guess it isn't so bad; no one looks mad or betrayed. Most look serene and stare at me with curious, *supportive* eyes. The ones who aren't looking at me are staring at Reese, laughing. I swing my head and look towards her, wondering what is so funny. I understand when I see.

I guess a vine slid into Reese's hair and, when it had slunk back into the ground, left behind dirt, bits and pieces of leaves, and tangled hair. Now Reese is struggling to pick the rubble out which looks to be difficult since she doesn't have a mirror. She continuously violently shakes her head humorously, attempting to dislodge the remains.

For a moment I forget my current situation and laugh with everyone else.

After a while, though, I decide she needs help.

"Reese, stay still for a second. I've got an idea."

She actually listens and stops shaking her hair.

I close my eyes and concentrate again, only this time summoning the air Gift inside of me. I tell it what to do and let it ride. I open my eyes to see if it is working.

The wind is blowing all of the pieces of dirt and wood out of her hair, but leaving behind a mess of knotted, wild brown hair. Perfect! Everyone, including me, starts laughing at Reese's new problem.

"Great, just great. I bet I'll just have to cut it now," she grumbles.

We all stand here laughing for a while. Slowly we start to return to normal, and my discouraging situation returns to the front of my mind. A moment before I had been smiling, now with one thought, my face instantly darkens with despair.

Meanwhile Reese made a hair tie out of a stem and uses her newly made hair tie to pull her hair out of her face.

"That'll have to do for now, I suppose," she concludes this little episode. "Back to work. Where were we…?"

Oh no, here it comes.

"Oh, right, Kira," my insides curl up, tensing, "you did excellent wrapping the tree, just next time wait until after the vines have safely receded into the ground before you get excited," Reese finishes, lightly joking at the end.

That was all? I had nearly squeezed half of them to death – on accident. She even has started to move on with her discussion.

I awkwardly walk back to the group, sill avoiding eyes. Sterling, who is standing next to me, whispers into my ear, "Stop worrying about it. When I was new here, I nearly took off several peoples' heads with a very large stick while trying to get it to draw a message in the ground. All Reese told me afterwards was 'Put more control in the back end.' Not to mention, you wrapped that tree almost as well as Reese did, which is incredibly advanced for most beginners, let alone first-day beginners."

I guess you could say his words help a little. They help me to stop worrying whether people are mad I nearly killed them. I still don't understand what the proper reaction to what happened is, and so I'm not sure how to feel myself.

The stress continues to mount for the rest of the hour because, apparently, on your first day of class you're automatically the volunteer. I continue to show almost perfect attempts, only being a fraction of lesser quality as compared to Reese. I'm not able to tell whether there really is a giant, green, envious monster emerging from all the students, and if this monster threatens to swallow me whole; it could just in my head. Let's be honest, it's probably just in my head.

Finally, mine and Reese's phones vibrate and beep, "3:00," relieving my growing fear at the chance of having another mishap.

148

"Okay Kira, if you can, try and practice some of the things we discussed. I understand that with all four classes you won't have much time, but the weekend starts tomorrow. Sterling, why don't you walk Kira out to the field, just to make sure she doesn't get lost? We'll see you Monday, Kira."

Reese waves goodbye and continues instructing the class.

Sterling and I start down the path. I didn't think I would get lost by myself, but I guess the buddy system is always a good precaution.

Sterling breaks the silence, "You did really well today, which probably shouldn't be a surprise since you're-"

He cuts off, most likely not wanting to make me feel uncomfortable. Honestly I'm still not sure how to react. I mean, it seems as if breaking Kasten's prediction and the four Gifts are becoming the ghosts of my past, following me everywhere. I'm not sure how to take it.

I nod to acknowledge that I heard him and that he hasn't offended me and, well, I don't know what else to say.

"What do you have now – what class, I mean?" he asks, eager to move on to a new subject.

"Air, then water, and last fire."

"Do you know how to get to all of them?"

"Yep."

We reach the end of the woods and I can see the air class to the left in the field.

"Do you think you'll get there okay?" he teases.

"Well I doubt I'd get lost in a foot high field, but you never know," I pause and giggle. "No, I'll be fine. Are you going to Zac and Lily's movie night tonight?"

"Yeah."

"I guess I'll see you then."

"Yeah, and at dinner," he smiles.

"Oh right. Duh," hello, I'm a blonde. "Alright I better get going."

"Me too. See you later."

He turns around and I continue on a diagonal from our parting spot, heading off into the thick tallgrass.

Chapter 9

I arrive and the instructor introduces himself as Chris. He is tall, with light brown hair and brown eyes. He looks to be in his young thirties. He introduces me to the class.

The entire class consists of five other people. I know Jamie, but he is the only one.

"Kira, this is Lesley," Chris points to the only other guy, who has shaggy blonde hair and teal-blue eyes, "Brooke-" a short girl with long, brown hair and green eyes, "Lindsey-" a tall, red head with sapphire-blue eyes, "and Tori-" a medium-sized girl with beautiful black hair and her brown eyes are on the verge of red.

Jamie is the first to say hello.

"Hey," I return and we both smile at one another.

The rest of the class politely says hi. I begin to associate some of the names with the faces and hopefully begin to really remember them.

Chris continues on, "Now Kira, since you come in the second half of the class, what we're going to do is this: the hour you're gone I'm going to go ahead and teach the rest of the class. Then, when you come here at three, they will practice whatever I taught them while I catch you up. Hopefully, I can teach you faster, since you're the only one, and then you can join back in with the class."

He now instructs everyone else to move towards the middle of the back yard, directly behind the house, while he and I remain where we are. They form a large circle and I can see each of them begin to concentrate. All of a sudden, I see the wind picking up in and around their circle as the tallgrass and their hair are whipping around. The invisible wind begins to pick up little particles of dirt and leaves, establishing an outline of the movement of the wind. The wind jumps right into their circle and it starts to spin and spin. It gathers more objects from the grass and swells and enlarges. It is now raging around, forming a large, consuming vortex of wind. I'm not quite sure if you would call it a tornado. It would be as frightening as a tornado if it was free to do as it pleased without being controlled by the class.

I want to watch them longer but Chris redirects my attention.

"As you can see, today I showed them how you can work together and create something big and powerful. Of course, you can create a vortex by yourself but it won't be as turbulent, unless you're a very powerful Gifted. Today's lesson is also connected with Monday's because the classes are going to combine and you'll learn how to work together with other Gifts and create things like cyclones, tornados, and dust bowls."

"Why is their creation not a tornado?"

"Because a tornado is a storm cell, produced by hot and cool air colliding and is fueled by the storm. Therefore, you need weather for the storm. So theirs is just a vortex.

"This activity can be complicated if you don't understand the process, so don't be afraid to ask questions. First, I'm going to

152

try and fully explain the best way I can what you will need to do in a second. I know it's your first time so I don't except you to be perfect."

I nod. If this goes anything like my earth class went, we'd be producing a full on vortex pretty soon that – naturally – will go completely out of control.

Chris continues, "Okay since there are only two of us, we are going to stand across from of each other. Normally, when there are more people you make a circle."

We move about twenty feet apart and the class is about fifty feet to the left of the space in between Chris and me.

"Now close your eyes and concentrate on the wind, and I'll do the same."

I close my eyes and focus on the air portion of my Gift.

"I'm ready," I announce, and I am.

"Good! Still keep your eyes closed but now try and mentally find my presence here – if that makes sense – and hold it. I want to warn you first, though; I'm going to do the same so you'll start to feel a distant pressure in your mind as if someone's trying to break in. It'll just be me. It is what you're supposed to feel when you connect Gifts. Now try it."

I feel kind of dumb but I try what he asks. I imagine myself in the field we are in and now I picture Chris across from me. I imagine my hand reaching out as if I am in an introduction, and his is reaching towards mine. We finally connect and hold; his grasp is firm, but gentle. If that's possible.

That's when I feel the pressure inside my mind, as if a second party has lodged itself inside. I panic only a moment before remembering it is just Chris. The imaginary Chris and I are no longer hand in hand, but are connected by a faint, light blue circle. I feel a strand of humming energy in the bond and I can tell it is the connection between his mind and mine.

"Very good, Kira! That in itself was advanced for a beginner. I'm sure in your earth class you figured out how to use your Gifts when Reese made you the permanent volunteer, so you should know how to command your Gifts – well enough anyways. I want you to tell your air Gift to come forward and tell it to fly around the two of us in the circle you see connecting us in your mind."

I do what he says and speak in my mind which I guess is really just thinking, "Wind, come and blow around us in a circle-" I imagine the picture of the hovering, blue circle again, "-in this circle."

I feel the gentle, calm breeze that had been blowing unnoticeably around me, pick up into a fierce wind, whipping my hair out of my face. My eyes are still closed but I am almost positive the wind is beginning to enter the circle I have created and is not only flowing from me but also Chris.

"Kira, open your eyes – but still keep your focus."

I slowly open my eyes, and at first I am frightened. I remember the huge, swirling mass spinning inside the invisible circle is under control and I relax. I can barely make out Chris on the other side, his short hair blowing around like crazy. Our vortex is about twice the size of the class's, although theirs is nowhere to be seen. Probably because they are all gaping at ours and couldn't concentrate enough to keep it going.

My hair is thrashing in every direction, slapping across my face. You'd think being so close to a large, fierce vortex, you'd be sucked in or at least have to restrain yourself from being sucked in. The only part of me that feels a tug from the spinning is my hair.

Chris yells over the raging wind, "This is excellent, Kira! Let's see if we can walk and move it at the same time. You can put your arms out wide at 180-degree angle like you're trying to hug the vortex. It's not necessary but it might help you to stream more direction into its movement."

I need all the help I can get so out go my arms and so do Chris's. The most amazing thing happens. The imaginary blue circle inside my head forms a real, visible circle – well more like two semicircles. Each semicircle begins with a hand, mine or his; it is interchangeable. The light bends around the vortex and connects with the other hand. The circle isn't solid but pure light. It wavers and dips but still remains; it almost looks like the Northern Lights although it doesn't change color.

In my peripheral vision, I can see the surprised and amazed faces of the class as if they are watching the coolest thing in the world. Chris even looks slightly amazed himself, but he soon regains focus.

"Super Kira! Now begin walking slowly towards the class."

Oh, great! Here comes the difficult part. I take a deep breath and with my eyes open, I slowly begin to walk to the left. Chris maintains an even pace with me, not taking a step until I do, and the vortex moves with us. Occasionally, it gets a little behind or ahead and runs into the blue light. The light acts somewhat like an electric fence, zapping the vortex back into the center.

We finally get the space between us and the class down to about twenty feet when Chris tells me not to walk any farther.

"Lesley, walk about thirty feet away from the class in the direction I am facing," Chris instructs and a guy, Lesley, does as he says, moving thirty feet towards the house.

I wonder why he did that.

"Now Kira, without walking towards the class, follow the circle towards your right and walk to the back center of the vortex."

We both begin moving in towards the back of the vortex. As we do, the semicircle protruding from my left hand and his right expands just as the opposite semicircle condenses. Chris and I come a mere five feet apart with the semicircle from my right hand and his left only a foot long, creating more of a giant oval-shaped light circle.

"Good. Next turn and face the class, but keep your arms out until I say," he is still yelling but not quite as loud.

Both Chris and I do as he says and the oval-circle remains intact.

"Now we're going to try and move the vortex towards and around the class – but not around Lesley – without moving ourselves. You're going to have to focus a lot, but you have to keep your eyes open. We're also going to have to release the circle so it can move without us and not get zapped, but don't do anything until I say. First, concentrate on what you want the vortex to do."

I turn my head towards the class so I can focus. I take several deep breaths and command the vortex in my mind on what I want it to do. I even form a blueprint of where it needs to go. Finally there is nothing else to do to prepare myself.

"I'm ready," I say, sounding (shockingly) confident.

We are facing the class so I can barely make out Chris's nod in the corner of my eye.

"You may slowly lower your arms to your sides, but you have to focus strongly on what the vortex must do; otherwise it will go out of control."

I slowly lower my arms like he had said until eventually they are at my sides and the magnificent circle of light is gone. If this was the earth class, here would be the point when things go haywire. I am highly focused this time though, not letting anything waver my concentration.

"Ready?"

"Ready."

In my mind, I push the vortex forward and soon it seems as if my mind – and my Gift of air *are* the forces moving the vortex –

which I guess they are. It seems too surreal to have the power to control such a powerful thing though.

Gradually, the vortex crawls its way to the class. I think at some point they figured out they need to huddle together and very carefully Chris and I ease the vortex over them, trapping them inside.

You'd think the vortex would jostle the class a little and yet it doesn't. Just like how it had only tousled my hair.

"Wonderful! Now Lesley can you find a rock or something?" Chris yells over to Lesley.

I can see Lesley searching around the yard and finally he picks up a giant rock.

"Now I want you to throw it as hard as you can into the vortex," Chris directs.

You would think that the rock would pass through and either lose momentum and crash in the center or fly through the other side of the vortex and still fall and crash. However, it does neither. The rock soars through the sky and smashes into the side of the vortex as if it flew into a brick wall and shatters into a million, different pieces.

"See? The vortex is supposed to act as protection, not allowing in anything unwanted. That's why it's a useful defensive technique to know," Chris yells.

I am still shocked at the destruction the vortex caused; in fact, I don't see how a tornado could be any more powerful. Yes it was only a rock, but what if a bird accidentally flies into it? Will it be blown to pieces, too?

Of course, my shock causes my chain of misfortune to catch up with me. I'm no longer completely focusing like I should be and in fact I'm a little zoned out when it all goes wrong.

Apparently, the water Gift inside of me got bored doing nothing, so it decides to take advantage of my lack of concentration. It takes a few screams and a tap by Chris for me to notice that something is wrong.

I refocus in on the vortex and the class and I am stunned at what I find.

Remember when I said my water Gift went a little erratic when I zoned out? Now I am watching what it has done.

It combined with my air Gift in the vortex creation, but it can't be called a vortex any longer since it is consumed of water, creating a cyclone.

The cyclone, unlike the vortex, has disturbed the class, seeing as they are completely drenched from head to toe. They are bending over, gasping for as much air as possible with water everywhere. Once in a while, I catch a glimpse of their faces and see utter and complete horror as their lives are slowly being choked out of them.

"Let go Kira," Chris commands calmly.

I look at him, not only with horror but also with newfound confusion.

"I'm not connected anymore. You're the only one powering it."

I really look at him now. He is standing with his hands raised up as if he is approaching something that calls for extreme caution. I gaze back at the cyclone that should be smaller now that it is just powered by me, but it isn't. It is still overwhelming and immense. The class isn't choking on gulps of water anymore and therefore aren't as scared.

But I am. I have really buried myself this time. At least before in the woods, no one looked as if they were about to die. Sure they didn't die – then or now – but this time if the water would have continued like it did, they probably would have lost consciousness. Even if they aren't mad at me, how can they ever have a normal conversation with me without wondering if next time there will be a "too-late"?

I have to at least prove to them that it was an accident, and I'm not a murderous lunatic.

I close my eyes like before and focus. I continue the air Gift but withdraw the water. Now adding the fire Gift, but making sure not to make it an inferno, I attempt to dry their clothes and warm them.

When I am sure they are dry and warm, I release the Gifts that are powering the vortex. There is a rush of wind blowing against me, as if the collected winds are dispersing again to their normal cycles. Now there is nothing.

Without the continuous release of energy, there is nothing shoving the drain I feel to the back of my mind. It is overwhelming; my mind is in a hazy lull. I open my eyes to see Jamie walking towards me, but I'm not completely sure it is him as my eyes are beginning to roll and I shut them again. My legs start to wobble and my knees buckle until finally they give out. I slink to the ground, but someone catches me before my head slams down on the ground.

My mind is swimming and I can't process a clear thought; yet, I never lose consciousness like the last time this happened.

I'm not sure how long I lay here, in whosever arms are still holding my head. It is a while, though. Eventually my head stops swimming and my eyes stop rolling around inside my head. The devastating exhaustion and grogginess wear off and I decide to try and open my eyes. Bad idea.

My eyes are pierced with the blindness of day, but it isn't even pure sunlight that stabs my eyes. My eyes feel as if little bolts of electricity are passing through them. I keep opening and shutting them and eventually they become used to the light. I finally open them completely without pain and look around.

Chris and the class are off in the middle of the field. He is working with them on something, probably so they won't swarm around me. I was right when I said I saw Jamie walking towards me as he is the one holding my head and lightly playing with my hair.

He notices I am starting to open my eyes and move around.

161

He asks, "How do you feel?"

"Wiped out," I groan.

"You maintained the vortex for twenty-five minutes with Chris, and then the cyclone for five minutes by yourself. Of course you're wiped out," he smiles, and I'll admit it does make me feel a *little* better.

I remember what that cyclone caused, and a dark wave of guilt spreads through me. Suddenly, I long for comfort as fear and panic rush in, for caring arms to hold me tight *like my mom's*. But that is gone forever, and Nikki is unavailable, and I am alone. Yet, I still feel as if I am about to flood inside with a devastating amount of misery. I can't seem to push it aside and hold it in. I feel a panic attack rising.

Jamie is already so close to me, sort of holding me up as I am too weak to do it myself. I turn and lean into him, wrapping my arms around his neck. His body heat swells around me and seeps into my skin, bundling inside me, creating pressure against the hurt. I need support too much now to care how insane I must seem to him. His arms are no longer needed to hold my head, but instead of just letting his arms drop he wraps them around me, holding me as tight as I am holding him. Because of this, I know it is okay to unleash the flow of guilt and embarrassment that has been locked inside me.

Now please don't think this is how I normally am. Normally, when I feel something coming, I lock it away and become determined not to let it out until I'm alone in a remote,

162

dark corner. I never cry in front of anyone who's not family. God, I feel like a cry baby now, allowing everyone to see how I feel and how distraught and confused and utterly lost I am. I *never* let that show and I *never* lose it like I am and I *never* get to the point of being the blubbering idiot I'm being now. It's like giving up, giving in.

Meanwhile, as I'm babbling in my head and tears are rushing out, Jamie calmly speaks, "Hey, don't cry. It's okay. Sshh."

The problem is that it all feels so familiar, so practiced, tempting me to continue bawling. I'd only met Jamie this morning. How is it possible that he is now patting my hair and gently trying to quiet me as if he has known me longer than a few hours? He probably is thinking I am some emotional, dramatic freak – which at this moment I am.

I actually smile from calling myself an emotional freak.

I have truly lost my mind, I think.

Slowly my smile turns into a giggle which grows into a laugh and soon I am crying from laughing so hard. Proof I really have lost it. *Will sanity ever return? Find out in the next segment of The Emotional Lunatic.*

As I pull away from Jamie, I expect him to look at me as if I am a complete psychopath which is exactly what I would have done in a similar situation. But he isn't looking at me like that; he is smiling at me, as strange as it is.

My lunatic happiness doesn't last for long. I'm not able to hold back all the mixed feelings I have. One feeling slips through, darkening everything inside and outside of me in an instant.

Jamie, continuing to surprise me and not treat me as a stranger, sees the change in me, and this time he is the one to pull me in.

"Hey, it's okay. Don't worry about earlier. Nearly everyone almost kills someone on their first day; everyone's used to it by now. Besides, they're too curious about you creating that cyclone to be mad at you."

"But you didn't see your faces. It didn't look like you guys were used to it. It looked like you guys were terrified out of your minds." There it is. What really has been glued inside my mind and tormenting me: the terrorized faces of the kids I *almost* killed.

"Well yeah, we were scared and fighting for air, but everyone expected it – or something – to happen. That still doesn't make us less afraid when it does happen, but deep down inside we all know there's no real need to overly worry. The teachers would never allow something to get so out of control that someone would die. Did it get that far? No. So don't worry, okay?"

"I don't know. It doesn't seem like it will be all right," I whisper into his shoulder.

"Yeah, I kind of remember feeling like that my first day, but look at me now."

I pull back and look at him. He doesn't look unsure or sad or hurt like I probably do. Jamie looks confident and normal, well like the nothing's-wrong kind of normal. He starts smiling at me, and it isn't a smile clouded by insecurity and depression. He really does look just fine.

I breathe calmly and return his smile with one of my own.

"Do you mind me asking what you did your first day?"

"No I don't mind," I think he is starting to blush – if it's possible for guys to do that, "Chris did a pretty basic lesson, simple really: construction of air currents. Well he made me guinea pig like all teachers do to the new student, and of course it didn't go well. I created the current perfectly, but I blew it a bit too close to Lesley. I had so much energy in it that it actually picked him up – and that threw both of us off.

"So you've probably figured out by now, when you don't have total concentration, your Gift takes advantage of you when you're inexperienced. Well, the air current holding Lesley decided it was going to change the direction of flow…to up. Lesley flew up about fifty feet in the air. I freaked out and released my air Gift. Luckily, Chris had a fast enough reflex to slow down Lesley when he fell so he only broke a *few* bones.

We are both laughing, my memories of sadness completely washed away by how genuine his laugh is, with no hint of regret or remorse. Maybe it isn't a big deal. I am still glad that my next classes won't have any other kids around for me to *almost* kill.

Speaking of the devil, mine and Jamie's phones begin vibrating violently and I think I even hear a "4:00." We both stand,

I a little stiffly, and we make our way to Chris and the group to be dismissed.

"So she is up," Chris jokes. "That was quite something Ms. Kira. I was just telling the group that the cyclone you created is an example of what the water class and air class can combine to create on Monday. I expect you all to act well when all of us come together. Kira, you won't be having your extra classes; you'll just meet with earth then you all will come out here. All the classes will mix, and then at four o'clock you'll be dismissed with everyone else.

"Alright, you all did very well today. You may go."

Everyone, except me of course and *Jamie*, turns and starts walking towards the mansion. I don't know what Jamie plans on doing, but I turn and start heading the opposite direction as everyone else, towards the lake.

"I know it's pretty obvious and all, but do you mind if I walk with you there?" Jamie asks, shyly.

"Come on," I say with a smile.

Chapter 10

There seems to be a constant flow of people around us, all heading back at the end of *their* "school day." I blur them out. Once I do that, the walk is peaceful. Crying earlier leaves me filled with an overall self-happiness (however long it will last), and walking with the silence that currently hangs over us, is serene enough for me. In the tranquil calm that protects us from the deafening river of people, I am able to think about things – not dangerous things, not things my mind wouldn't dare to wonder to, not here, not now. Instead I think how maybe after a while, Jamie and I will become friends – good friends. I mean, he's already shown me an overwhelming amount of compassion and sympathy. It would have otherwise been impossible to show that if he didn't, maybe, well, care at least a little.

What am I saying? I just met Jamie last night. How can he possibly know enough about me (even if I am *the one*) to know that something is there between us?

Okay, wow! I really just need to stop thinking because I'm pretty sure the-lack-of-sufficient-oxygen is starting to seep into my brain, causing delusional thoughts.

Luckily, Jamie interrupts my delusional thoughts, "So you have earth first, right? And then air. I'm guessing – since we're heading towards the lake – you have water now. That means you have fire last?" He looks at me questioningly.

"100-percent," I say jokingly.

He doesn't understand it though, "Huh?"

"That's what you got on your pop quiz," I tease him some more.

He doesn't say anything but smiles instead.

"You'll love Kelsey and Beth. I'm sure you loved Reese."

"Yeah, she was definitely a bit different, but in a good way. Who are Kelsey and Beth though?"

"Kelsey is the water instructor and Beth is the fire instructor. Beth is married to Chris; they and Trey and Nikki are the only ones 'together.' Although, there have been rumors of maybe Reese and Max – the cook – as a thing, but nothing's been confirmed."

I can't tell if he is joking or not about Reese and Max.

I begin to see our cove of the lake. If you've ever seen Lake Michigan on a windy day you'll know what I mean when I say the waves are huge today. Rolling and thundering and casting away anything in their wake. With the clouds overhead blocking the sun, the lake's waters look so blue, they are almost black. Yet, the lake still finds a way to shimmer as its waves crash and roll, white caps foaming miles off the coast. The only thing separating me from the beautiful water is a seventy-five foot cliff.

Down and to the left, as the border between the woods and the lake there is a single white shore where a single person stands. From the shore on both sides, the land rises up and up to form high rocky cliffs that level out at the top with the ground on which we stand, leaving the shore in the valley below. There is a stone step pathway that leads down to the shore, but before I begin the decent, I stride over to the edge of the cliff.

They have put up rails probably so people won't, well, fall off and die. There are a few painted-white benches placed here and there.

I lean against the rail that is closest to me, looking out over the murderous sea. Even though it probably would kill you if you allow the lake's hands to grasp you, it is still beautiful, in a dark kind of way, menacing and yet magnificent.

You'd think I'd be used to its strange beauty since the only time I haven't live in Wisconsin was the first six years of my life when my family and I lived in a large-small town (if that makes sense) in Georgia. I can't remember one year that I've lived here that we haven't driven up to the part of Kenosha that's on the shore line to visit my cousins or farther up to Michigan to my aunt and uncle's lake house for Thanksgiving. Lake Michigan still continues to amaze me with its dark beauty.

"Be careful. If you fall in, I don't care how special you are, I am *not* jumping in after you and I highly doubt your water Gift will stand a chance against that angry mess," Jamie says teasingly.

"You be careful because I might *push* you over and I definitely won't save you," I tease him back, shoving him slightly to the side with my elbow. Smiling now, I say, "The first time I saw Lake Michigan, I was six. It looked sort of how it looks today; as if it was pulled from a black and white movie. Being six and all, I thought the black and white water was a portal to a black and

169

white world. Of course it wasn't though. Anyways, my family and I were at a shoreline restaurant with a few tables outside on a wooden patio that was literally built on platforms over the lake. The restaurant gave us some pieces of bread to throw down into the rocks next to the patio where some seagulls were. I had finished throwing my bread before my parents and sister and wandered over to the back which was where you could look out over the Lake. It enthralled me – the water I mean.

"The wind picked up and blew my hair, adding to my delusions that it was a highly magical place. Somehow unnoticed, I climbed the railing and jumped. I remember falling, falling, thinking that the portal was working, transporting me into my black and white world, and then I smashed into the water and an icy numbness completely consumed me, trapping and paralyzing me. I was a little fish when I was young, so I knew not to swallow water and to hold my breath. I could even swim a little. You would think I would have been scared, but strangely I wasn't – well, that is until I realized I hadn't traveled to nor was I going to my black and white world anytime soon.

"I began to fight the icy water, the best I could at least. But on top of the numbness that had held me, the giant waves above had a dominant current below that pushed and pulled me every which way. I was six so it wouldn't have been that hard to do. I was almost out of breath and energy so I had no choice but to stop fighting and just sink and let the current hopefully guide me to the surface."

"Where were your parents or the police or someone?" Jamie asks shaken.

"It was too dangerous for my parents to jump in. They hadn't seen me jump so they couldn't have known where I had gone or what direction I had jumped. There weren't any police or firefighters around. I was on my own."

"How are you here then if no one knew what was really happening?"

"I don't know," I say honestly. "I lost consciousness one moment and then remember waking up on the little bit of sandy shore by the rocks where the birds had been eating our bread. Everyone said that the giant waves had just pushed me in, but-" I am shaking my head, "but underwater there wasn't just one force pushing one way; there were many."

"Maybe once you lost consciousness it changed?"

For some reason, I just *know* that wasn't it, but I don't know what it was so I shrug, "Yeah, maybe."

"So how can you have gone through that and not be afraid or resentful of the lake?" Jamie looks...*haunted*.

"Maybe it's because of my water Gift. It's kind of hard to hate water if it's a part of you," I am looking at him closely. "Jamie, what's wrong?"

He isn't looking at me anymore; instead he is staring out over the lake, "I guess it is kind of beautiful."

"Jamie? Are you okay?" I am concerned. He looks as if he isn't here all the way anymore, as if part of him is off somewhere down memory lane. "What happened?"

"I didn't even realize it either."

"What are you talking about?"

"Seven years ago, the day I discovered my mark, my family and I were on our boat on Lake Michigan. I was ten. The Gift – when it recognizes itself – is very unpredictable. I didn't even feel the slow drain of power. My air Gift was pushing us forward at a high speed. We thought we were going fifty-five because the boat's motor said that was how fast we were going, but later I found out the boats we were passing were at least going seventy.

"We were going so fast and the boat was so big, we thought it was just a little bottle or something in the water, but it wasn't. For some reason there was a buoy all the way out where we were. My dad saw it and tried to turn the boat, but it wouldn't turn."

"The air Gift wouldn't let him?"

He nods, "So when the boat wouldn't turn, my dad tried to slow the boat down, but my Gift had our path locked in, and it didn't include avoiding what was quickly approaching," he pauses for a second – Are there tears building in his eyes? "It wasn't a big buoy but at the speed we hit it, there was no way."

"Jamie?" How can he not be crying? I am even crying.

"Everything slowed down. We all flew up about thirty feet in the air along with about a million pieces of the boat. I can *feel* the air rushing past me even now. My Gift protected me – only me.

172

It slowed me down when I fell and blew things away from me. We all had life jackets on; I mean, it was Lake Michigan, but it was also Lake Michigan with ten foot waves and black-abyss waters."

"Jamie?"

"There was no way. They didn't have a greater power helping them. My sister was only five-"

It had been tears that were building in his eyes and now a single sparkling one spills over.

"I'm so sorry, Jamie."

Because of my Gifts, my parents won't remember me; his are gone forever. Did they forget him when they died? Would the forget-me rule change in the afterlife, where ever we all go – heaven or hell – hopefully heaven.

"You'd think I'd resent my Gift, yet it's the lake I hate."

"Kira, is that you?" A woman's voice calls, sounding distant.

I look around and back at the mansion, but I don't see anyone. Jamie lazily gazes over my shoulder, down towards the shore. It reminds me I have a class to go to and that's probably where the voice is coming from.

"I-I-" Why am I stuttering?

"Yeah I know; you gotta go. I'll see you later," he tries to smile but fails miserably.

"Okay."

I am about to turn and walk down to Kelsey the water instructor, but I feel as if there is still something I need to say.

"Jamie, it wasn't your fault," I tell him firmly. Walking away from him, I can barely hear his whispered response.

"Maybe."

Chapter 11

I take my time walking down the stairs, making sure I don't trip and fall and die. Once I reach the shore, I quickly make my way over to the woman.

"Are you Kelsey?" I ask hesitantly

"Jamie must have told you. That is him up there isn't it?"

I know it is, but I turn around because I thought he'd have left by now. There he is still staring out over the lake.

"Yeah," I turn back to my teacher. "I'm sorry if I'm a little late. I wasn't trying to skip or anything."

"Oh, you're just ten minutes late, but I don't mind being alone out here. It's peaceful – rejuvenating even, being alone with your Gift's element – in your case, your Gifts's elements. Or is it Gifts'?"

"Gifts'," I say smiling.

"There's a reason I'm here teaching water and not teaching grammar at some school."

She doesn't look like she belongs in a classroom all day anyways. She isn't tall, but she isn't very short either. Her hair is wild and untamed, brilliant blonde wisps flying around everywhere, and yet, it couldn't be any more beautiful. Her sea green eyes are alive with the non-existent sunshine from above. Her brilliant smile captures the purest color white and appears so natural, so permanent. Something seems to radiate off her; a warmth, a amiable, comfortable glow.

"I suppose we better get started," she sighs and gives one more longing look over the lake. "I want to start off by asking you if you had anything to do with the giant *cyclone* my class and I saw in the air field?" She smiles slyly.

I feel my cheeks redden, slightly embarrassed. "I might have had *something* to do with it… or maybe all of it."

"I take it, it was an accident."

"Well, I wasn't *purposely* trying to drown them."

She isn't angry; she is laughing.

"Maybe I should be glad it's just you and me for this class. Today we are working on tidal waves. The objective is to create, well, a giant wave *without* crashing it into us, but it can go around us. This isn't a complicated process like I'm sure Chris made the vortex. Oh I'm sorry; I didn't mean anything towards him. It's just that he probably instructed you step by step what to do."

It is as if she had been there.

She continues on, "However, unless it's something complicated, that's not how I do things. Most times water just needs a little instruction – but that doesn't mean it can't go out of control," she smile, as if she knows how my past two classes have gone, which she does happen to know one, apparently. "Normally it's a pretty easy flow, however. Why don't you try it now?"

"The giant tidal wave?"

"No! The mini tsunami!" she laughs, "Of course the tidal wave!"

"Right now?"

"No. tomorrow!" She smiles.

"With no directions? All by myself?"

She nods.

"Okay then, if you say so." This isn't going to go very well, so to begin, all I do is focus on protecting Kelsey and I and remind myself to *try* to not destroy anything.

I close my eyes again, concentrating. I find the new part of me that decided to take advantage of me earlier, now actually calling it to participate. This time, instead of imagining a tidal wave and what it should do, I silently speak the actual command to my water Gift. I start to feel a drain; it startles me momentarily because I'm not used to feeling it so quickly.

I open my eyes and begin to hear through my ears again after blocking everything out in an attempt to think. Far off in the lake, I am able to see an average size wave rolling towards us. At first I don't realize the wave only looks average because it is so far away, but it rolls closer and closer until it is still a distance away and yet is looming over us. It has to be at least the two-thirds the size of the cliffs that also loom over us on the beach.

I realize that if I really don't focus and protect us from the wave when it reaches us, we will be crushed and drowned within seconds. I think of a plan of action so that when the wave meets us, it will avoid us and still hit the beach. Finally, it is here; at least sixty feet high and twenty feet wide, it has arrived into our little bay. This is the moment, for the first time today, that I actually fear for *my* life.

Kelsey, however, is less than concerned.

"Miraculous!" She seems awestruck and blown away. Has no one else today produced a wave this big?

In the short time I notice Kelsey, the wave has crossed the distance between us. I keep the command of what it will do now planted firmly in my mind, although less confident after beholding how terrifying the wave is.

Nevertheless, right before it crashes into us, the wave does exactly what I have told it to do. The wave splits in two; each part of the wave sweeps past us on either side. To split the wave, each side rolls over closer to its prospective cliff, and now the farther parts of the wave beat against the cliffs. I see the wave is just barely smaller than the cliff, but the impact against the cliffs shoots the water the remaining distance up the cliff. The water flows over the top before rushing back down to its home, dropping, falling, cascading back down.

The parts of the wave that don't hit the cliff roll right past us and smash into the trees. Luckily, none fall but the waves pick up and carry some bramble and leaves on the forest floor. I see the waves start to spread out over the woods and thin out. Now, similar to the tide reaching its high point, the waves race back to merge with the rest of the lake. For a while, the waves in our bay are a bit more chaotic than they have been today, but even that fades back to normal.

"Wonderful! And see? No problems this time," Kelsey smiles brightly.

"There's a first for everything," I say, heavy on the cheese-factor.

She smiles at my cliché and continues, "I want you to try something, if you don't mind." She pauses for a moment, probably checking if I have any objections. I would never object to a teacher. My par-*they*-taught me better. Sensing that I'm not going to deny her request, she continues, "For right now, just think. Picture this in your mind: the giant tidal wave you just created is rushing towards you again, only it's not under your control – let's say Bret and Tessa's. You know who they are, correct? Imagine yourself pulling water from the lake and encircling it around you."

In my head, I now have a circle of water around her and myself.

"Now feed it. Give it more water to completely enclose us in a dome of water. Give it strength to protect us and shield us from the incoming wave."

In my head, there is an ever-rotating flow of water in the shape of a dome around us; there is also a giant enemy-wave rolling towards us. As my determination and concentration harden, so does the dome's strength and determination to protect us.

"Hurry Kira, open your eyes but keep the image you have going."

In the real world, my image has slipped out and there is a water dome like the one in my head surrounding us and everything on the other side of it wavers and seems to drip with the water of the dome. As my eyes pass over a spot of movement outside, I stare more closely at it.

"It's a tidal wave I am producing. I want to see how strong your encirclement is," Kelsey updates me.

I see the wave is rapidly growing and approaching us. For the second time today in this class, I fear my dome will collapse and we will be crushed by the wave – if that's possible since Kelsey is its source. So maybe I would just die then. This fear causes my determination not to fail but to grow stronger, the dome's strength doubling along with it. The wave has reached us.

The second it makes contact with my dome, I feel an immediate depletion of energy, almost enough to knock me off my feet. However, the water explosions that the two water creations fabricate are able to keep me going.

The wave does a complete loopty-loop, rolling and bending up the side of the dome and now falling backwards towards the direction it came. Water rushes up into the sky, spraying mist. What makes it so beautiful is looking at it through the dome-water on water. The double-refraction of light.

Once the last wave crashes and Kelsey informs me it is okay, I allow my concentration and summoning of water to fade, and with it leaves the stunning water dome. Without anything distracting me from my dangerously low level of energy and with the knowledge that I no longer need to continue giving energy to anything, I fall to the ground. The sand is a soft, squishy, welcoming pillow beneath my head.

My eyes become fuzzy as if I have looked straight into the sun for a while, and eventually my vision blacks out. My entire body feels as if it has participated in a triathlon; my bones and muscles are mush. Lying here, the only movement being the rise and fall of my chest as I breathe deeply, feels like that one relieving moment when you are finally able to lie down and go to sleep after a long, tiring day. My mind goes blank, too exhausted to think a complete thought. I fall asleep; a peaceful, rejuvenating sleep.

I awake sleepy, but revitalized to find Kelsey using her Gift to make shapes with the black water.

"Do you feel better?" She hasn't been facing me and yet she knows I'm awake.

"Much," I respond, stretching out my arms, legs, and back (probably looking similar to a cat).

"You should. You slept for about thirty minutes," she teases.

I jolt up quickly, alarmed at how long I have slept. Standing up so fast turns out to not be a good idea as, immediately, my head begins to swim and I have to lie back down.

"It's okay. I knew when I asked you to do the dome you would finish like this. At least with the group, they do it together, sharing the impact. It's not as bad when it's dispersed. You, on the other hand, received all of it since you were doing it by yourself, 'ya know?"

I nod instead of actually speaking, to save energy.

Kelsey switches topics, "When there are more people powering it *theoretically* the dome will be even stronger. However let me tell you, yours was probably more powerful than the class's."

I narrate to Kelsey about earlier, during my air class when Chris and my vortex was larger than the class's, and how it was still as big when only I was fueling the cyclone.

She looks at me wonderingly. It's probably about the hundredth time I've seen that look expressed towards me today.

"It seems as if you continue to show us just how special you really are."

I sit silently. Well, how do you respond to that humbly and graciously? Because what I really think I feel is frustration. Okay maybe not frustration, but awkwardness. I mean, they would think I'm special just because I'd have broken Kasten's prophecy even if I am the clumsiest, laziest, worst Gifted in the world. The things I've been doing in my classes might not actually be that miraculous but the teachers could be biased.

Anyways, Kelsey pulls out her cell phone and checks the time.

"It's 4:55. We should get you up and over to Beth. I'll help you since you still seem a little unstable," Kelsey smiles, holding my arm and carefully helping me slowly to my feet.

Getting up slowly and with a little help this time, my head doesn't swim and my legs don't waver.

"Thanks. I think I can manage now from here, but would you mind walking behind me?"

"Sure."

With her close behind me, I slowly begin climbing up the cliff.

I hope she doesn't think I'm an annoying, slow snail – which I am, but – okay maybe it wouldn't be so outrageous to think that, I think to myself.

By the time I reach the top, I am gasping for air, and I move to sit on a bench for a second.

"I'm glad you're stopping; you need a break. Those stairs really are too steep, and this is almost your forth class of nonstop usage of your Gifts," Kelsey smiles. "Hopefully, Beth won't make you do anything as advanced as I just did. In fact, I'll walk with you to meet her. For one thing, to make sure you don't pass out or fall down," she teases, "and another thing, I'll talk to Beth and see if she'll do something easy with you today. I'll promise on Monday then, not to do something this drastic, and hopefully she'll do the harder activity then – if she doesn't mind."

Kelsey has walked over and taken a seat next to me.

Hearing her talk about Monday leaves me with the nagging feeling like I have something to do then. I remember, "Aren't all the classes combining on Monday?"

"Oh right, thank you for reminding me. I'll ask her about Tuesday then. How did you know that, unless I mentioned it and would now be suffering memory loss?"

This makes me laugh for some reason.

"No, you haven't said anything to me. Chris did."

She smiles, "I should have known."

All of a sudden, both our phones begin vibrating violently and beeping, "5:00, 5:00!"

"Come on. We better get you to Beth," she wraps her arm around mine and gently hoists me up.

"Okay," I say dejectedly as my body aches with the movement.

Chapter 12

Now that I'm not climbing steep, slippery stairs, I'm able to walk a little faster. We stay silent most of the walk. I'm trying to save energy; Kelsey is probably thinking. I guess you could say I am feeling better, not quite *wonderful*, but almost back to normal.

In the five seconds I process all of this, Kelsey has gotten a little ahead of me and I quicken me pace to catch up with her. She is heading towards the center of the driveway where a woman is standing.

This woman, Beth I'm assuming, is tall and almost frighteningly skinny. She has brown hair that barely falls past her shoulders and her eyes seem to burn with fire – not possessed fire, a playful, flickering fire. If pushed too far though, the fire would turn on you. Her eyes almost remind me of Nikki's. Beth (we're just going to say it's her) is smiling brightly.

"Kelsey, Kelsey, Kelsey," Beth is shaking her head but smiling, "you just couldn't save some energy for me, could 'ya?"

"Hi, old friend," Kelsey says giving Beth a hug. "I had to teach her too and there was nothing else to do."

Beth smiles.

Kelsey continues, "I came here to see if you wouldn't mind doing something easy today, and on Tuesday I *promise* to save you energy?"

"So you didn't just come here to see me?" Beth appears to be hurt – a false pretense, of course. Soon the smile has returned, "Oh, I suppose I can *allow* Kira to have an easy first day."

"Thank you, and I really do promise to do something easy with her Tuesday and you can have all the fun," Kelsey smiles and begins backing away.

"You better," Beth replies, still relentless in her smiling.

I am grinning brilliantly at the two of them. They seem to have known each other a long time. Maybe if it's possible they knew each other before this new life of ours. How could that work, though? Nikki made it seem like you're normal until you're taken (like me) or your mark recognizes itself. One of them (Kelsey or Beth) had to become Gifted first; therefore the other would completely forget their friendship. Unless, maybe the memory-erasing doesn't work on us at all even if we're still "normal," or maybe once the other also becomes Gifted, they remember. Either way, I think I'll ask one of them someday.

By now, Beth has turned her attention to me, "I'm sorry about that. We must seem a little crazy to you." She's *still* smiling.

"No, not really. My sis-…sister," after faltering once, I force the word out, "has-…had a best friend that was really special to her. I mean, they were completely ridiculous whenever they were together. They even told people they were long-lost twins and came up with a joint last name – combining her last name and my sister's." I smile at the memory of Haley and Elizabeth – her best friend, and really mine too.

"Yeah, that sounds quite a lot like Kelsey and I when we were younger."

I ask her, "Did you guys know each other before you were Gifted then?"

"Strange enough, we did. When Kelsey became Gifted, I completely forgot her," for the first time, the smile disappears from her face and a grim shadow crosses over. "But it didn't feel like everything was normal. I was depressed, as if all of a sudden someone was missing from my life – someone I really loved, but everyone I'd ever known or loved was there.

"About two years later, I became Gifted and came here. One of the first days I was here, I ran into her, but I still hadn't remembered her. Of course, she never forgot me so she was crazy-happy and started hugging me and jumping up and down." Her face darkens, "It was sad to see her disappointed face when I just stared at her with confusion. Then she started rambling like 'of course you don't remember me yet; I mean you were *just* Gifted.' I asked her 'what are you talking about?' but she never told me.

"Over the next week, little tid-bits of memories started flitting through my mind the more I saw Kelsey. It was weird. I still had the new memories of what I thought my life had been for the past sixteen years – the memories I received when Kelsey became Gifted.

"Then the memories with Kelsey started coming back. I had never seen them before and yet I remembered what had happened in each one perfectly, and still, I perfectly remembered the life I had had without her. It's like I had been living two lives simultaneously.

"Finally, I was able to talk to the people you guys would think of as like Nikki and Trey, about these memories of Kelsey. They told me probably what Nikki and Trey told you about 'normal' people forgetting us. After that, it all started to make more sense. I was no longer getting tid-bits, but full, real memories of my life with Kelsey. I eventually learned that my illogical depression had resulted from Kelsey leaving. Of course, Kelsey was so happy when I came to her to tell her I remembered everything and I was so happy to realize that the hole I had during my depression was filled."

That look of sadness she had is gone and the shadow is hardly noticeable.

"Still to this day though, I feel like I lived two lives – one with Kelsey, one without. Which, I guess maybe I did or maybe I didn't. Maybe the life without her was just made up, fake: something to fill the gap of time that she had been in my life. No one was ever able to explain it to me – well at least understandably. Those 'fake' memories feel so real; I can pick out one and remember what happened that day like it was yesterday. Those memories feel as real as the ones with Kelsey."

"Does it work that way for everyone that knew another Gifted before the mark recognizes itself?" I ask curiously.

"Yes, you can ask Zac and Lily about it, too – I think I saw you talking to them earlier."

I nod, "Yeah, I've been with them the most since I got here."

"I think Zac became Gifted first, but it shattered them both. It tends to do that to the Gifted twins, and for some unfortunate reason, there tends to be a lot of twins. Sometimes, I wonder if the mark is more prone to that kind of gene. It sucks too, because it's harder for them during that period when only one is Gifted. It's especially hard if only one has the gene; then only one will ever be Gifted. I mean, I'm sure you've heard twins – some twins, at least – have a special, close relationship with one another. Now imagine that dependency and support of one another suddenly ripped apart, as if a part of them is also ripped away.

"Lily was in a condition worse than I was," Beth's eyes have grown sorrowful and sad long by now. "We knew she also had the mark, but we were afraid she wouldn't make it through the wait."

"What do you mean 'make it through'? Was she sick?"

"Think of extremes, when people have been so depressed, they have found all and any part of life meaningless, no reason to get up in the morning, nothing to look forward to. They won't talk to anyone. They stay by themselves all the time, alone; rejecting any form of life or love. What do those people normally end up doing?"

A sparkling gloss covers her eyes; one, I'm sure, is forming in mine at the realization of what she meant. Lily must have been at that extreme, that loss of life. She is so alive and animated and warm now. She seems whole.

Maybe *that* is the key; she hadn't been whole then. She was missing a very large part of her being. Now, she has become whole again and has found that reason for life.

"Couldn't you have 'taken' her to force the mark to recognize itself?"

"No, it only works like that if the Scorned take her. We would have caused her family to forget her, but she still wouldn't remember Zac…Don't worry! Your family – they won't be like Lily. We know none of them have the mark."

I haven't thought of *them* in depth since this morning – and for good reasons. Now, I can't help but think of them as Beth must have thought they were already on my mind. I start to think if one of them were to become so depressed. None of them have my spiral birthmark; they would never become Gifted and remember me. Their hole would never be filled.

A new horror befalls me. *There is no hole.* They have lost who I am without a slight remembrance of my existence, without a hole, plain and simple. I guess that's maybe a good thing; maybe this is the way it's supposed to be. I resolve that it is good there is no pining hole.

I lock away that resolution now and move on, eager to distract myself.

"Is there something easy you want us to do today?"

She examines me closely, debating if I am still upset. I smile vibrantly. She seems satisfied.

"Now I'm positive Kelsey has pretty much wiped you out so what I've thought of is pretty low-key."

"She did, but I'm feeling much better now."

"Ah, you think that until you try and do too much; you'll see what I mean when you do this activity."

I really do feel better. Energized, but I don't protest.

"Okay, first I want to tell you that the only reason we are going to do something this easy, is because you're at your lower end of energy. I want to make sure you understand I don't think you're slow or weak or *dumb*."

I nod encouragingly.

She lingers one more moment, studying me. Then, "You probably already know by now that you have to concentrate intently. With fire, it requires double the concentration; fire burns with one touch and is very dangerous when out of control," she looks at me, taking on a more solemn expression. "Now there's two ways you can create the situation in your head. If you want, you can imagine you are trying to protect us from something. The other option is we are the enemy and you are trying to trap us. What I want you to do is this: physically create a ring of fire, plain and simple."

She hadn't been kidding when she said "something easy." Well, this was easy compared to what else I've done today.

"Okay," I reply, a new confidence surging through me.

"Don't get too arrogant," she says slowly, a smile creeping onto her face, "because then you don't concentrate and it doesn't go as easily as it should."

The uneasiness doesn't return. I grow more somber and nod my head. I re-enter myself into the isolated world of concentration. I feel how tired I am now that I have to actually *do* something and *process thoughts*. The weariness isn't a heavy weight though. It is manageable and I push it to the back of my mind.

Focusing now, I use the situation that I am trying to protect Beth and me from something in order to instruct the fire. I can feel my cheeks redden and my body being heated by a warm glow that feels like the summer sun. Beth notifies me to open my eyes which I also take as a sign that I have succeeded in forming the ring of fire.

There in a circle around us, is a red hot, flickering fire. It is taller than both Beth and I, and its circumference is big enough not burn us by proximity but small enough not to leave the area of the paved driveway. It looks dangerous and mean; its orange flames alive as if burning energy in the air. Yet, its harmful fingers do not yearn to touch us but, instead, reach towards the nonexistent *something* that I imagined was a danger to us in order to create the image in my mind.

What does reach us is the scorching current of heat that radiates everywhere. If my face looks anything like Beth's, then it is beet red as if it has been burned badly by the sun.

"Very good! You can extinguish the fire now," Beth instructs me.

I withdraw my fire Gift, sucking it back into me, filling me with a strange but serene warmth and peace. This little extra burst keeps me on my feet as I am otherwise exhausted. Even with the energy burst, I'm not able to stay on my feet for long. Beth was right when she said even this would leave me fatigued.

"Do you think we could sit for a little?" I ask sheepishly.

"I told you the fire would be more tiring than you would think," she grins, obviously having picked up on my reluctance earlier to believe such an easy thing would even be exhausting.

We both sit down and relax comfortably.

By now, the cool, July, northern breeze has flushed away the redness and heat of our faces, replacing it with a pale whiteness from the quick change of temperature. It is comfortable and refreshing. The heat isn't overwhelming any longer and the cold isn't cutting. I take a deep breath of the cool sea air, letting it fill my lungs with a more pure air.

"Do you mind me asking you something?" Beth asks quizzically.

Alarm first springs to my mind, but it soon subsides and I let her know to continue.

"I should probably wait to ask this question until later on in your training, when you've had more of a chance to experience it – if you're going to – if it's possible…Your Gifts are central to who you are, in a way, and your Gifts are composed of earth, air, water, and fire; so many opposites are found within that: water/fire, earth/air. Do you ever feel those disparities battling inside you, one trying to come out over the other?"

To be honest, I really don't understand what she means exactly. Yes, I understand my Gifts are all opposites, all very different and powerful, but they're all under *my* control. *Most of the time*. Right? How can they fight?

Beth continues, seeing my silence as confusion.

"No, you probably wouldn't understand yet, would you? You were only Gifted two nights ago. You wouldn't have any idea what I'm talking about – that is, *if* what I'm talking about is even possible. But," she pauses for a moment, "if you ever do understand or experience what I'm saying, would you come tell me? I'm interested in how so many opposites can co-inside as one."

"Of course, but do you mind me asking," I wait for her to give me the approval that I can continue, "you and Kelsey are best friends and you're a fire Gift and she has a water Gift. What is the difference between your two opposites and my four?" I ask, hoping to better understand what she had been talking about.

Her smile has returned, "From the teacher that I probably shouldn't be, good observation – and good question. The difference is, Kelsey and I are *two, separate* people; our Gifts are separate. Yours, however, are very much together, all inside of you. How else to explain it? Um…okay, Kelsey and I, yes, are opposites, but we are two people, with only *one* element that

194

defines each of us as who we are. You, on the other hand, have four elements that define your character and they are all opposites, all different. *I* believe that could cause internal fighting between them when you have all those unique elements as a part of you. As you can see, it's complicated, and I'm not doing a very good job of explaining it. We'll just have to wait to talk about it more, when maybe you have experienced it."

"I think I sort of know what you're saying about you and Kelsey and me. It's natural for two different people to be opposites; their personalities and make-up of who they are makes them unique and therefore different. What you're saying about me is that it's not natural for one person to have four completely different elements that fashion them."

"Exactly."

"I thought our Gifts are just…'powers,' not factors that influence us?"

"No…and yes. Yes our Gifts are 'powers' – in your words – but they also give us a certain quality, or qualities. They can sometimes define what choices we make. For instance, fire may give someone a fierce, wild, untamed personality and may cause them to make spontaneous, risky decisions. When we say your Gift is a part of you, we mean it literally; they are a gene that defines your traits from the moment your mark is formed."

"When I was in that warehouse with everyone fighting, I was looking around, and one of the first things I noticed was people's eyes. Some looked fierce- like you said – or vicious, or playful, or sweet."

She nods, "Yes, our eyes – what we feel when we look in depth at them – are normally one of the traits identified by our Gifts, but then again sometimes a trait you'd think belongs with one Gift shows up in a different one's eyes."

Now we've reached into something I actually understand, partially because I have actually experienced what she's talking about, "You mean how Bret's green eyes resembled dangerous, green electricity, something more suited for weather Gifts, and yet wasn't he an extreme strength Gift?"

"Yes, yes exactly!" her smile reaches full potential. "You're very smart to have recognized those traits when there was so much chaos going on and to understand it now more in depth."

"I always did get straight A's," I say, smiling at her joy that I wasn't a complete hopeless case in learning any of this.

Catching me off guard, our phones begin buzzing intensely, "6:00, 6:00," and I jump about five feet in the air.

"It's six o'clock, already?" I ask puzzled.

"Yes. Well, it took you and Kelsey about ten minutes to get here. Then it took us a while to get going and after that…" she shrugs her shoulders and smiles, "I guess time flies when you're having fun – or something like that."

I grin at *her* cliché.

We stand up and walk down the path, up the stairs and through the beautiful front doors. Indoors is just as modern and flashy and gorgeous now as it was earlier. The entry room is filled with the golden light of a setting sun. There are several groups of people flowing steadily down the spiral staircase and making their way down the hall in the direction of the kitchen. Beth and I easily slip in with everyone else.

As we reach the kitchen doors, Beth turns to me before she walks away and says that I did very well today and that she'd see me Tuesday and we'd do something a little more challenging.

And now there is one, in a sea of people...

Chapter 13

Alone now, I walk to the back where the food is waiting. It looks like pizza – thin crust, extra cheese – is on the menu tonight. I must be late to arrive because I am the only one back here; everyone else is sitting down eating. Everyone other than one man who, at the moment, is tossing pizza dough into the air. He stops for a second to say hi.

"Hello Kira, nice to see you again!" Max tells me what each pizza is and adds, "they're not as good as my Philly cheese steaks, but they're not bad if I do say so myself."

Well of course they aren't bad. You're a gourmet chef, I think to myself.

He returns to his pizza throwing.

Hhm, pepperoni or supreme? Supreme.

I grab two pieces and a mountain dew from the fridge. Now for the hard part: where to sit? I gaze around the dining room. No completely empty tables.

All of a sudden, Lily – *you gotta love her* – starts waving at me, "Kira, over here."

Whew, thank you Lily. Awkward situation avoided.

It seems to be Lily, Zac, Jamie, and another girl sitting at a table. I think her name is Kyllie.

"Hey," I say to everyone, setting my plate down and sitting down myself.

They all return my hello politely before continuing the conversation I interrupted about tonight's Movie Night.

"We've already watched *Push* about five-hundred times; not that *again*," Zac complains.

"Do you not like it?" I ask.

"No, I like it; it's just we've watched is so many times that I *need* a break from it."

"Okay, so *Push* is out. What about... *The Avengers*?" Lily asks.

"I guess it'd be better than *Push*. We haven't watched *The Avengers* nearly as many times," Zac agrees, along with everyone else.

"I'll go and find it in the store room after dinner. Who's taking care of popcorn and drinks this time?" Lily asks, appearing to be the organized individual of the group.

"I think it's me," Jamie says.

"And me," the girl I'm almost positive is Kyllie adds.

"Okay, and Zac...what am I leaving out?" Lily acquires an annoyed look on her face.

"Clean up duty," Zac replies, sounding a little disinclined to fork out the information – probably because he is the one stuck doing it.

"Oh right, and that's yours isn't it?"

He nods reluctantly.

I feel odd going to the movie night and not helping with any of it.

"I can help clean up," I volunteer, even though I really hate cleaning.

"Okay, thanks," Lily smiles at me.

"Don't worry it won't take us *that* long since there's two people cleaning now," Zac seems happier now that he is sharing the work.

I don't say much more during dinner, partially because I don't always know what they are talking about and partially because I'm not a very talkative person. I finish eating before everyone else, but I wait for the rest of them to finish. Slowly, everyone else in the room clears out, rinsing their plates and putting them in one of the many dishwashers. Our tables are one of the last ones remaining.

Lily takes out her phone and checks the time, "6:45. Should we start getting ready?"

"We can probably start to start getting ready," Jamie says.

"Start to start?" I ask, teasing him and giggling,

He smiles, "Yeah, you know, start getting up so we can actually start getting ready at 7:00."

"Yeah, I know," I smile.

We all stand up, wash our dishes, and try to find space for the dishes in one of the already-packed dishwashers. Now we all head into the hallway. As we pass the hallway I think that leads to the movie theater, I ask confused, "Where are we going? I thought the movie theater was that way?"

"It is, but we have to go to the storage room first," Lily explains.

"And where is that?"

They hadn't shown me a storage room earlier.

"It's in the lounge, in the corner across from the staircase on the same wall as the entrance to this hallway. You'll see in a second," Zac answers me this time.

Sure enough, the hallway opens up into the lounge and on the right next to the hallway entrance, is the wooden door that leads into the storage closet. You wouldn't think that a storage closet could be big enough for all five of us; however there is plenty of space left. In fact, we probably wouldn't have any problems fitting fifteen people in here.

The storage closet isn't really a closet; it's more like a room unto itself. All of the walls are lined with shelves and shelves of random items. The middle of the room is the same as the walls – row after row of stuff. A library of junk.

Jamie and Kyllie head to the back wall where I can see boxes of popcorn (oh yum, movie theater butter), one of those popcorn kernel popping machines, oil (the peanut kind) for the machine, two-liter bottles of sodas, and cups. Pretty much all the concessions Jamie and Kyllie could need.

While they hover in that direction, Lily moves to the middle region of rows of shelves where it looks like all the movies are kept (and boy, are there a lot). I don't know what their organization system is, but I think Lily is going to need more help than Jamie and Kyllie. Zac seems to have the same idea as he is going over to help Lily. Once I see how their shelving system works, I realize Lily didn't need much help either.

They shelve everything in ABC order (leaving out the word 'the') and they have a marker sticking up when a new letter starts. All Lily has to do is go to the very beginning, find "A" (which she has already done) and then scan through it to find *The Avengers*. Before I even reach "A" (somehow I managed to start in "U"), Lily has *The Avengers* out and is walking over to the clipboard next to the door to sign out the movie.

"Hey Lily, sign out the popcorn machine, will 'ya?" Jamie requests, sliding the popcorn popping machine off the shelf and carrying it while Kyllie carries everything else.

"Sure, but I'm putting it under my name so I'll have to come back with you to sign it back in," she says while she fills in another column.

"Did you make sure to get napkins this time?" Zac asks.

Somehow, with all that stuff piled in her arms, Kyllie manages to hold up the napkins.

It takes us a while to walk to the movie-theater room as Kyllie keeps dropping something here or there like she is attempting to leave a trail of breadcrumbs. Each time we have to stop and someone goes back to pick it up as Kyllie really can't. Eventually, I come up with the bright idea that Zac, Lily, and I can help carry some of the stuff, which after that shortens the trip.

The theater room is as big as a real movie theater: fifty-foot screen (or however large they are), stadium seating, projector room at the top. To the right of the door we enter through, is a long table where they place all of the concessions. To the left of the door,

202

begins the stairs leading up to the higher rows of comfortable seats and the room where the projector is that shoots the movie onto the screen.

"Ever seen how a movie projector works?" Lily asks, mischievously.

"Nope," but I get the feeling it is a good idea to follow her and find out.

     *   *   *   *   *   *   *

"That was cool," I say as we start walking down the stairs.

By now, the smell of popcorn and butter has filled the air and the sound of an endless amount of popcorn kernels popping has long become annoying. Jamie has probably popped fifty cups of popcorn. Kyllie has gone to get ice and is now scooping it into the same amount of cups as there are of popcorn. I wonder why we need so many but I remember this place has over fifty residents that could all very well show up tonight, then what if they all want two cups of popcorn?

"The movie's in and ready. How are we doing on popcorn and drinks?" Lily asks.

"Good, we both have gotten fifty cups," Jamie says, leaning against the table, waiting for the popcorn to be done.

"Kyllie can stop then. Normally people reuse their drink cups. Jamie, you should-"

"Yeah, yeah, I know; keep going," Jamie says, rolling his eyes.

"It's only 7:30, so you have plenty of time. The ice in the cups might melt before it's eight o'clock, though."

An idea pops in my head.

"I can help with that maybe."

Zac, who has been sitting in one of the many seats texting, now waltzes over.

Concentrating on the ice, I summon fire, and I manipulate it to lower the ice's temperature but sucking away the heat. Immediately the ice can be seen shrinking and condensing as the ice's particles are so cold. Some kind of steam seems to cast off of the blocks as the room-temperature air hits them.

"That should hold for a while," I say, proudly. "What do we do until the movie?"

"Well someone over here is still not done popping popcorn," Jamie says, a little sarcastically.

"Oh, just keep popping," Lily says smiling. "Normally, we hang out. People start coming around 7:55, so it won't be too long now. How did you like all your teachers?"

"I like them alot. Reese seems a little crazy. Kelsey and Beth are fun, especially when they're both around each other."

"Yeah, they are pretty awesome. What about Chris?"

"Yeah, he's nice. I'm just not sure how he feels about me practically killing the entire class," I say, adding a little humor to my voice. Hopefully the humor clouds the worry I feel.

"Are you kidding? He loved it – the cyclone – not all of us almost dying. He's not mad at you; it's normal to have near death experiences on your first day," Jamie says, jumping into the conversation because, really, he is the only one who can talk about earlier in class.

"Yeah, it wouldn't be your first day without them," Lily adds. She begins laughing, "On my first day, I was partnered with Liv. I don't know if you know her or not…Anyways, one person had to get the wind knocked out of them and the other used their healing Gift to put it back in. Clearly I would be the first to do it – the healing – and I guess I put so much air in her that her lungs almost exploded."

"How is that possible?" I ask grinning.

"I have no idea," she says beaming.

Almost at the same time Lily speaks, Zac remarks flatly, "It's not."

"Not according to Kayla."

Purposefully interrupting their fight, I ask, "Who is Kayla?"

"She's the physical strength and healing teacher."

"Oh. Who's your teacher Zac?"

"Kyle."

I nod.

"I know Nikki teaches the telekinetic people, but what about Trey?"

"Trey teaches the psychic people; that way there's a teacher for every Gift," Zac says.

"Well what happens if a new Gift is created?"

"No other Gifts can be created – at least, it's highly unlikely if not impossible. There has never been a new Gift since the Gifted were first created, but if there ever is, they'd probably have to go to the class that's a closest match to their Gift, and then hopefully they'd stay here and wait for any others that are like them. That first individual would become the first teacher. But like I said, it hasn't happened yet to our knowledge," Zac says.

Slowly people start to trickle in, grabbing a popcorn and drink, forming groups and taking a seat. As Jamie finishes the last of the popcorn, we also grab some snacks and sit down in the smack-dab-center of the movie theater. I save Lily a seat on the end as she has to go hit play. I had asked her if *she* wanted to sit next to Zac, but she said she didn't want me to sit alone on the end. Turns out, Lily and I are both stubborn people, and even after I told her I didn't mind and she should sit next to her brother since that's why this whole event had started, she still insisted that she should sit on the end.

The theater has filled up and almost every row has a group occupying it. Now I can see why so many popcorn packages were needed; the movie hasn't even started and we are already down by three-quarters.

"So have you seen *The Avengers* before?" Zac, who is sitting next to me, asks.

"Yeah, I thought it was great," I reply.

"Oh, if you've seen *The Avengers* already, you should have said something. We would have showed a movie you hadn't seen."

"Nah, I've wanted to watch it again lately. It's been a while since I've seen it."

Suddenly the lights dim (like in a real theater) and the screen turns the lime green of the parental rating. Lily flops down next to me.

"Here we go," she says as she picks up her popcorn from the drink holder it was sitting in.

Chapter 14

"That was a lot of fun," I say to Zac, as we are still sitting in our seats, waiting for everyone to leave so we can clean up.

"Yeah, that's pretty much why we've stuck to it."

"Don't forget to shut off the lights when you're done," Lily calls back. Lily and Jamie leave, carrying the popcorn popping machine and *The Avengers* back to the storeroom, while Kyllie rolls two garbage cans into the theater and leaves too. The cans have a broom and dust pan in each.

"We should get started," Zac says, walking down to the concession table to start throwing the popcorn bags and empty cups away. Apparently everyone puts their trash on the table once the movie is over and the clean-up people throw it away. I would have trash cans waiting at the end so everyone could throw away their *own* trash, but I don't say anything. Yet.

Crunch...crunch...crunch. Popcorn crumbs crunch under my feet as I walk down to help Zac.

This is going to take forever, I groan to myself, looking at all the crumbs on the floor that I am pretty sure are consistently dispersed on every row. *Too bad we can't just blow it away. Oh, duh – I'm so dumb.*

"Hey, Zac? Are we allowed to take *shortcuts* cleaning this up?" I ask, throwing away some of the cups that had rolled to the ground, into the trash.

"I don't see why not. It's not supposed to be some kind of punishment; so yeah, we could."

"Good, because I have an idea. Could you stand by the door for a second?"

He moves into a safer place than where he had been and I start to focus. I throw my hand over the table, beginning on the left and shifting to the right towards the trash can as if trying to push all the trash in the same direction as my hand. An air current forms and moves along with my hand, doing exactly what I want it to do: sweep the trash into the bin.

Table: done.

"Well that was easy," Zac attempts to move again, but I stop him. I'm not done yet.

I call back air, raising my hands as if lifting something. With my hands, rise about a million pieces of popcorn crumbs, being held by an invisible, hovering air current. I compile it all into two large popcorn spheres – one for my left hand to control and one for my right. I swivel in place until I am facing the trash cans and each of the popcorn spheres are positioned over each of the two cans. Unfortunately, the popcorn balls are bigger than the trash cans, so I can't drop them in. I close my fists and clench. As I do so, each sphere slowly crumples smaller and smaller in size; the pieces that are breaking off fall into the bins. Finally, the popcorn balls are small enough to comfortably fit into the trash cans.

"Done," I say triumphantly. "And, since I'm sure you feel so guilty about not doing *anything*, you won't mind taking care of these, will you?" I roll the trash bins over to him, teasingly.

"Has anyone ever told you, you are a very smart girl?" he asks, staring blankly.

"Maybe once or twice. Tell you what? I'll help you, anyways."

I take one trash can, Zac takes the other, and we roll them out. We pause a moment so he can turn off the lights and shut the door before we start down the hallway.

"There's a giant dumpster on the left side of the house – well the side opposite as the garage and driveway," Zac explains.

"How does it not stink up the place?" I ask grimacing at the possible smells we'll find waiting for us.

"I'm not really sure; probably something Trey and Nikki set up with the air Gifts."

We reach the back door where we have to separate the garbage bags from the bins and carry them.

"I'll take yours if you want," he offers.

"That's okay. I used to have to take the garbage out at h-home, so I'm used to it. What do we do with the cans?"

"We just leave them here. They're used to clean up after meals. That's why we have to have everyone put their trash on the table until one of us can go get them; normally at the beginning of the movie, whoever has kitchen duty is still using them."

"Now it makes sense. What's kitchen duty?"

"One of the few chores dished out around here. Just a few final clean up duties to make sure the kitchen and dining room are nice, neat, and spotless at the end of the day."

We turn the corner and a worksite trash dump comes into view. Surprisingly, an awful, rotten smell never reaches us. I don't linger longer than I have to so as not to wait for the smell to arrive. We throw our trash bags into the pile and race back to the house.

"That was probably the fastest clean up time ever – thanks to you," Zac says, appraisingly.

"I bet it would take a while to pick up every one of those crumbs – especially when there was only one person doing it. I mean, what I did was completely necessary if we didn't want to be stuck there all night," I say, trying to avoid the normal, boring "thank you." (Did it work? Was it creative – but still got the message across? These are the questions I ask myself.)

"Well, all I know is that you have no idea how much I owe you," he smiles.

"Don't worry about it," I say, returning the smile. (It seems to be becoming a habit with him: the smiling. I'm sorry, I mean the times when he's not sarcastic or grumpy.)

We start climbing the endless staircase.

"It's only 10:30. Did you girls get those boxes out of your closet and all of them unpacked?"

"Yeah, I did. Lily got all of the boxes out quickly and I got all the stuff put away in about two hours."

"Oh, cool. Anything else you need to do that you would need me for or is there anything you want to do?"

"I think I'm pretty much all moved in, so no problems there. I'm actually kind of tired, so I was maybe going to go to sleep," I frown.

"Oh, okay."

Does he sound a teensy bit…disappointed?

"Unless you want to hang out or do something?" I ask tentatively, unsure if I want him to say yes or no.

"No, I'm pretty tired myself," he says nonchalantly, but it still sounds like a lie.

We come to a stop on the third floor landing.

He is smiling again, "Do you think you can find your room from here or will you get lost?"

"I don't know…it's kind of tricky to follow a staircase and then walk down a hallway," I say, lightly sarcastically.

"Okay, I'll see you tomorrow then."

He turns and walks down the hall as I turn and continue up the stairs.

*   *   *   *   *   *   *

The shower's hot water feels good on my abnormally cold skin; the warm, steaming water relaxes it, un-tenses all the knots. It feels good to wash away any dirt and to smell like fruity soap bubbles.

I step out of the shower and throw on a pair of pajamas and a T-shirt. My new sense of cleanliness and the pajamas' comfortable feeling brings me back to a lot of nights at-.

I turn off the light in my room and crawl into bed. That depressing feeling that settled on me last night doesn't return so strongly now. It is still heavy and sudden, but there isn't any panic behind it. Only sadness. Holding the blankets close to my face, I allow the tears to spill; what would become a nightly routine at this rate – at least until the moments of grief go away.

After crying for a while, the pain begins to dull and fade away – until tomorrow night it would seem. My mind is racing but my body is nearly asleep and it drags my mind down with it, unaware of the nearing storm clouds.

Chapter 15

Nikki's eyes flash open wide.

"Sound the alarm!" she gasps, rushing out of bed. She throws on a loose sweatshirt over her tank top, leaving on her fuzzy, plaid pajama bottoms. Only now does she realize Trey isn't here.

"Trey? Trey?" she whispers frantically. "Oh God, where could he have gone, and now as we are about to be attacked?" She thinks aloud, on the point of hysteria.

Suddenly, the emergency lights begin to flash, illuminating their room every few seconds with a piercing red light. She eventually discerns in the flashing lights that the door is open, meaning Trey had left – also meaning he probably set off the alarm that is now sounding. Nikki bets he had foreseen the Scorned coming. Unfortunately, she can't worry about him for long; the situation doesn't allow it and he can handle himself. She hurries out of the room into the second floor hallway. She slows down for five milliseconds at every door she comes to on her left and right to pound several times in order to hopefully wake up anyone who hasn't already woken.

Her heart lightens a fraction as behind her she hears doors opening. The adults are officially up and moving into attack-phase. Nikki is approaching the second floor landing, preparing to climb some stairs as she slams into Trey.

Her lead heart is alleviated with only the attack to worry about now that Trey's whereabouts are no longer unknown.

214

"Oh thank God, Trey," Nikki remarks, taking a several-second pause to tightly hold Trey as she relinquishes her worry.

"I'm sorry. I should have woken you, but we had little time already, and I knew you'd want me to set off the alarm first. I'm sorry; I'm so sorry," Trey whispers into her hair.

"No, you did the right thing. It was more important to get everyone up than wake me up to the point when I could have actually comprehended what you were saying," she rambles on anxiously, wiping a tear out of her eye.

"They're almost here. They're coming from all directions: sky, woods, lake, and vehicle – or driveway as most would say. We need to make sure everyone's up and ready, and we need to get Kira out of here somehow," Trey says, gasping for a breath by the end.

Nikki almost looks frightened. Of course she is on the inside, but she never has showed it before – she has to be strong. She caught a glimpse, though, of the feeling of the approaching enemy.

"What is it?" Trey asks. He has never seen his wife look as scared as she does right now.

"They are so angry. They want revenge; they want to kill us. They aren't leaving until their anger is satisfied...and until they have Kira."

Trey and Nikki stare at one another for what seems like awhile when it really is only a few seconds. It is enough time for

Trey to grasp the seriousness of the situation and why Nikki – who always appears so brave – is so afraid. His own attitude sobers.

"I already locked the back and front doors, but that won't slow them down much."

They start to climb the stairs as Trey continues, "I'll make sure the boys get ready; you take care of the girls and protect Kira."

They reach the third floor landing in no time, but before Nikki continues on up, Trey grabs her and holds her in his arms.

"I love you," she whispers into his shoulder, sounding so small, insignificant.

"I love you, too," Trey says into her hair. "Be safe."

Nikki begins climbing as Trey heads down the hallway. She is switching into emergency drive; the nerves in her brain re-wiring to survival mode. She feels the shift in her veins, the adrenaline beginning to course through.

*   *   *   *   *   *   *

"Nikki?" Zac and Jamie yell up to her, taking two steps at a time to catch up to her.

"They're coming from all directions – including the sky. Didn't you see Trey?" she asks them, assuming they are here to ask her about it.

"Yeah, we saw him knocking on doors and shouting. We were already on our way to come up here to get Lily when we saw you heading up, and here we are," Zac fills Nikki in on what they were doing.

216

"Oh."

They all reach the fourth floor and start running, "You guys take the left side."

Zac and Jamie pound on all the doors they come to on the left as Nikki does the same on the right. With two doors left: Kira's and Lily's, Nikki freezes, her face paling.

"They're out there, grouping up, and Matt's Minding me – they need more help barricading the doors. You two: get Lily, get Kira, and once the outside's clear – or clear enough – get her out of here," she tells the two boys strictly, a little louder than necessary even with all the noise in this situation. As soon as she finishes speaking, she takes off running at top speed towards the stairs.

As the guys turn back to the only two closed doors, the one on the right opens, leaving the door on the left, the only one that remains closed – probably in the entire house.

Chapter 16

What are all these flashes? I think, hardly coherently. *This is the strangest dream.*

It is as if I am watching a slideshow of pictures that never stop, all forming one blur of colors. I can't understand anything that is going on, and somehow even asleep, it is making me dizzy.

"*Kira?*" A deep voice I have never heard before enters my dream. It is menacing, outlined in evil, sending a dark chill down my spine.

"*Kira?*" It whispers again, but in a dream, I don't have the control to answer.

"*Kira?*" It whispers once again.

I want to make it stop; it is creeping me out.

"Kira?" Now a different voice – one that I recognize – speaks my name urgently, followed by a hard, fast pounding on something.

Stop, stop! Stop it! I think, groaning in my head at the loud noise.

The sinister voice returns, but fainter, "*Kira?*"

How can I feel the hairs on the back of my neck rising and yet still feel like I'm dreaming? I think and I attempt to shut up the wicked voice in my head, but find I can't speak. I am still asleep.

Yet, I hear Zac say, as if I am wide awake, "Oh, screw the door rule."

"Kira? Kira?" the nice voices – Zac's, Lily's, and Jamie's – are right next to me, shaking my arm and rubbing my shoulder, pleading with me to wake up.

I want to; I am tired of this in-between, and their voices sound worried and critical.

The evil voice gives one more faint whisper of a "*Kira?*" and it is gone, along with everything else: no blurring images, no voices, no one shaking my arms and shoulders to wake me up. Just darkness.

Now everything flies back; Zac, Jamie, and Lily frantically calling my name – Lily sounding the most desperate, and the gentle jerking of my limbs. At last my eyes open; no more dreaming. They open, however, to meet a very confusing sight. A red light is flashing: *off... on... off... on... off...on.*

Question number one: why doesn't someone put on an actual light? In the flashing light, I finally distinguish the worried, pale faces of Zac, Lily, and Jamie. Lily's is tear-streaked.

"Oh thank God! You wouldn't wake up," she shrieks, wrapping her arms around me the best she can, wiping away the tears.

"What's going on?" I ask, confusion spreading across my face. You know that way it does, when you just wake up and someone wants to know what the square root of pi is or even what you're having for breakfast.

"The Scorned. They're here; they're getting ready to attack," Jamie says, trying to hide the fear that I can so easily see across all of their faces.

A loud boom rumbles through the house, followed by a thunderous splintering of sound. The room shakes as if an earthquake is passing through; dust and pieces of ceiling rain down.

"They're attacking," Zac's face drops five shades of color faster than the room requires to settle again. "Hurry Lily; help her get changed. Jamie and I will guard the door and see what's going on out there, and keep an eye on things," he says, and both guys are out of the door.

Yes, yes, I know it is dumb – very dumb – of me to sit here for a few seconds *dumb*struck, but I can't process it all. Unfortunately, now isn't the time to process it. Lily is already fishing through my dresser.

"Here," she hands me a T-shirt, jeans, and a loose sweatshirt, along with tennis shoes and socks, "these are perfect. Put them on – quickly!" Now she is out the door, too, and I am alone once again.

I must now take the time to brag about how fast I can change (lucky for them), because I had those pajamas off and the new clothes on faster than 'one, two, three.' I ran to the closet to retrieve a hair tie, since last night – while searching for my phone charger, tripping on my own two feet, and falling into the boxes – I managed to find the box with my hair ties in it. I left the box there when I unpacked. I pull my hair back once I've managed to untangle one tie away from the rest.

I am opening my bedroom door as it is suddenly pushed back at me and Zac slips past me into my room. I can hear a loud, rustling wind howling against my window. Zac runs over to it and throws open the curtains. There, about ten feet from my window, are three or four Scorned; it is difficult to see in the dark how many there are. The rustling wind has been the Scorned trying to blow out my window.

"I need help!" Zac shouts back at me. The shouting is necessary because the wind has become so loud.

I rush over, "How are they doing that?" referring to the flying Scorned.

"Air Gifts. We're going to use it against them. They're suspended by air currents, but you're more powerful than they are. If I strike lightning at them as a distraction, it'll then make it easier for you to blow them down. But-but you have to slam them down, hard – really hard – against the ground – or house. I'm sorry. Are you getting it, not getting it?"

He expects me to think? Now? But the gears do start to turn and I catch on. I try to keep my eyes from widening in horror, because I know he doesn't like it either but I have to do this, and I also know he is right. If I don't take them out, they would only come back after me, or worse, go kill one of us. I nod, signaling him to go ahead with it.

Zac hesitates a moment to say, "I really am sorry you have to do this, so soon especially," before he continues on.

We both begin to concentrate. We give one another one more look. I turn and stare out the window. All of a sudden, a bright white light flashes before my eyes, almost blinding me. Along with it comes a loud, very deafening roar of thunder, and almost simultaneously, the wind on my window pulls away.

Now it is my turn. I close my eyes to focus.

Air, I call, the command already in my mind.

I feel a substantial drain of energy and I stumble into Zac. I open my eyes to see no Scorned outside my window, but if you look close and hard four stories below and wait for the blinking lights from inside the house to light the outside, you can see three dead bodies lying there. I stand – well lean, staring, with pain and hurt and guilt consuming me entirely momentarily.

I just *killed* three people *on purpose.* This is different from last time – the night I became Gifted, because last time I had no idea what was going on. This time, I consciously caused death, and it kills *me* to know this.

"Kira?" Zac asks, and there seems to be pain in his own voice. He sounds almost distant to me, but his voice is coming closer. "Kira? Come on. We have to go," he says, sounding almost ashamed.

I finally pull my gaze away from the three bodies and instead, bury my face into Zac's shoulder, taking strength from him, not just for the reasons that include my lack of energy.

His arms slowly come around me. I am too stunned to cry, but I can't leave this room and be around people. I can't leave this room where, for now, the dark hides me in a tight blanket. Finally I have it together enough to do that – to leave, and I pull away first.

Suddenly, a flash of foreign anger sears through me – anger that isn't mine. It's almost as if I can feel someone else's presence, and his or her frustration is blinding. It only lasts an instant, replaced by a crippling headache. I clutch at my head, like they tell you to apply pressure to a wound to stop the bleeding. *The pain!* It's unbearable! I cry out, sinking to my knees. It's as if someone is electrifying my brain, driving red hot coals through it, and beating it useless.

I completely forget about the outside world, the fighting downstairs, or even Zac, who is now crouching right beside me, begging me to tell him what is going on. All I can think is *pain*; all I can do is *scream*. Tears swell in my eyes, blocking my vision; though I doubt I would be able to see anyways because of the burning pain. I am crying, begging God to make it stop. Distantly, I feel arms around me, leaning me forward into a chest. His hands rub circles in my arms and back. He murmurs to me, comforting words, rocking me. Anything he believes could help. It relieves my mental state, but it doesn't affect the pain. It only lasts a couple minutes, but in those minutes the pain makes it feel like hours.

By the time the headache finally disappears, it leaves behind a dull ache in my head, like being hit leaves you sore. I am gasping and trying to stop crying and calm down. At last I become aware of the world around me and find I am practically sitting in Zac's lap. I scoot an appropriate space away from him. His shirt is wrinkled, creased, and damp from where I buried my head in it. Then there is Zac, looking at me. Zac's wide frightened eyes bearing into mine.

"Kira?" he asks in a small voice. "What just happened?"

Do you know what I should say? Because I certainly don't; I have no idea what that was. I just sit here, staring wide-eyed, and frankly terrified, looking into his oh-so-wonderful eyes. Those beautiful blue eyes…My eyes continue to stare into Zac's, and his analytically, into mine. The intensity of them frightens me and makes my insides squirm.

Breaking the silence that has settled over us, however not my gaze, he asks again in a *little* bigger voice this time, "Kira?"

He sounds worried about me; then again, maybe *I* should be worried about me too. It is now that I realize maybe Tess and Becca were right; maybe I like Zac or could like him – or I could have a little crush on him at least…

See? I'm not one of those girls that can't admit her feelings about something to herself. Now admitting them out loud is a completely different story.

I am not thinking rationally. I don't even think I am connected to reality in this moment. I feel sudden joy that the pain in my head is gone. I feel sudden fear at the overwhelming possibilities stacked up against us with the Scorned's invasion. I suddenly feel fearless.

Maybe that reasonably explains why I do exactly what I do.

Without giving it another thought, regret, or chance to change my mind, I lean over and kiss him. At first I feel him just sitting there – probably shocked – but an instant later he relaxes into the kiss, and starts to return it.

I may not have done it for any of the right reasons – or any reason at all, but I will gladly remember this kiss, whether or not anything moves past this moment or we end up screaming at each other next thing you know. He holds me close. I wouldn't say we are making out or kissing – oh I don't know – *passionately*. It isn't exactly one of those cute, innocent kisses you see on commercials between two children, that's a quick peck on the lips either. *I'm rambling aren't I?*

It's over.

"We have to go," I say, not looking at him, a bit of embarrassment creeping into my voice. I stand and refuse to look at him, afraid that after that he'll start being cranky again or push me away. He doesn't say anything though, and I don't think he is looking at me either.

Out of the corner of my eye, I catch him nod.

I move in the direction of the door.

"Let me go out the door first," Zac says, slipping past me as if nothing happened, and now I follow.

Oh, my God. It's as if Hell has broken loose. It is *terrible*. There is fighting *everywhere*. The emergency lights are still flashing, there are alternating screams every thirty seconds, and worst of all, the Scorned's triumphant shrieks as their opponents – the Gifted – are struck down, creates a horrific feeling in the pit of my stomach. Lily is over to the left of me, kicking some major butt, and Jamie is about five feet from the door, battling with another air Gift.

Surprisingly, Zac is a foot in front of me in *hand to hand* combat. Ope, nope, he just knocked the other guy out.

"Come on," he says and takes my hand. He starts pulling me down the hall.

"Wait," Jamie calls, kicking his opponent in the gut who then proceeds to fall hard against the wall – head first. "Nikki said to wait until the sky is clear. I think she wanted us to fly her out."

"Yeah, except Lily and I can't do that, and Bret and Tessa are probably expecting us to go that way."

"Nikki knows that, but she still wanted us to go that way, and Kira and I could support all four of us long enough to get out of here."

If steam starts to come out of their ears and nose I warned you first.

"Okay, okay," I say looking at both of them, "Jamie and Lily will go out the window, while Zac and I go whatever way he wants-"

"A diversion," both guys say at the same time, smiling and completely forgetting about the past minute's argument.

"Yes, but go out Lily's window," I tell Jamie.

"Why?"

I lost them.

"Like we said, they'll be watching *my* window, so it'll *hopefully* take them a little longer to realize you're going out Lily's. That way, it'll take them longer to realize I'm not with you, which gives us more time to get downstairs and outside. If we're really lucky, it'll line up perfectly that as they're going out back to get you, we'll be going out the front."

Congratulations, light bulbs are going off; we are making progress.

"Which only leaves: where should we meet? I don't know this area well enough to make any decision on that," I add, looking to the two of them for answers.

"When you and I get out of the house we should grab a car. Jamie can carefully lower Lily down to the side of the car and you can help her in from there. It probably wouldn't be a bad idea for Jamie to come down too – save energy and all. It's up to you, though," Zac suggests, looking over at Jamie. "But once we're on the road, we shouldn't stop – you know that whole 'you can run but you can't hide' thing. There's nowhere completely safe we can go anyways."

We all nod in agreement.

"You should circle a little, try to hide in the trees and watch for us to come out. Meet up with us farther down the driveway, out of view of the house."

There is nothing else to say; no other pre-planning to be done, but we continue to stand still, staring at one another, a little

227

scared. Well, at least I am scared. I can't speak for them, though; they've probably been through things like this before – just the other night in fact, but their eyes hold a glimmer of fear in them still.

Lily trots up to us, interrupting our stare fest, and now it really is time.

Not quite fully looking at her, Zac informs Lily, "We're going to split up. You and Jamie are going out your window – he'll support you up in the air. Kira and I are going out the front door."

Like ours, her face isn't scared, but sad. Zac's own face soon becomes similar, and they quickly draw in to hug one another solemnly, their arms tight around each other. They hug as long as they can be allowed in a situation such as this. I finally look away, feeling as if I am invading something too intimate that doesn't pertain to me. My eyes fall to Jamie.

Has he been staring at me this whole time?

My eyes meet his then fall away, "I want to thank you – and apologize – about earlier. I'm not usually like that – the whole breakdown during class, and I'm sure it was a lot to handle."

I rapidly steal a look up at him.

He is *smiling*.

"Come 'ere you," he says, pulling me into a big bear hug. "When are you going to learn you're *not* an annoyance to the world?"

You can almost *hear* him smiling.

228

"Maybe I'm not to you," I mumble, smiling a little sadly to myself.

"I hope you know, you're going to be okay. It's all going to be okay."

"I hope so."

I don't know; maybe it is Zac and Lily's goodbye to each other, or the completely disturbing chaos going on around us (yes, the emergency light is still blaring), or my goodbye (for now) to Jamie, but I manage to only allow one tear to drop.

Almost synchronized, all four of us pull apart and switch partners, so to speak.

Zac comes over to Jamie and I walk over to Lily. We hug goodbye. She was already trying hard not to cry after letting go of Zac, and now she is trying even harder.

"Take care of him," she says, muffled by tears, and yet I hear the hint of a smile in her voice. "Who knows what stupid things he'll do in the next ten minutes?"

She pulls away and sure enough, mixed in with all the tears is one of her bright smiles. Even in the midst of all this, I let myself smile back, my eyes probably shining with tears.

Meanwhile, the guys are doing that weird kind of hug when they hug then try and play High-Five with the other's back. (Can someone *please* explain that to me?) Just as soon, they give up "back-high fives" and hug each other seriously.

Hey! Don't make fun of the bro-bonding.

I swear! I hear Zac mutter, "Take care of her for me, please." Just as quick is Jamie's response, "As long as you do the same for me." Then again, I could be hallucinating – it has been a very *weird* day.

It is time – the three scariest words I will probably ever use.

We each turn; Zac and I facing down the hall, Jamie and Lily heading towards her room. Zac takes my hand once again; his feels strong and calming in mine. Together we start down the hall to whatever nightmare awaits us on our path.

Chapter 17

We have to move fast, swerving around fights, hopping over... *bodies*. We take a second stairwell down; well, at least to the boys' floor where we run into a major obstacle. Two telekinesis are fighting *on the stairs* just below the third floor landing. The problem is they are using the broken pieces of the stairs and railing to throw at each other.

The third floor is no better than the fourth; in fact, it is a mirror image. We are half way to the spiral staircase when, right in front of us, a fight goes terribly wrong for the *Gifted* fighter. There are two earth Gifts; I finally recognize in this awful lighting that it is Sterling. He is attempting to squeeze his opponent to death with vines like I had done earlier to him. His opponent, purple in the face, as his last attempt to live, makes one of the lights fly off the ceiling and-

Oh my God!

Sterling's face looks stunned and pained; blood trickles down his face. He falls, and the vines around the Scorned-person loosen. That is, until I see the smug grin on the Scorned's face as Sterling is slowly dying. I quickly re-strengthen and squeeze the vines tightly; it takes less than a minute for the Scorned to go limp.

After the anger subsides, and I realize what I have done, I am overwhelmed with guilt – stomach jerking, head twisting guilt, for killing someone. I can't worry about that now as someone I consider to be one of my new friends, slowly dies right in front of my eyes.

231

Zac and I kneel beside Sterling, hoping *maybe* there'll be something we can do for him, something to make him okay. Sterling can barely keep his eyes open. There is a dark red, sticky clump of hair on the top of his head that a thin stream of blood flows down from on the side of his face. Neither one of us is a healer. Sterling's eyes eventually give up and close and slowly his chest will stop moving up and down.

The worst part is I feel so helpless, watching him die, sitting here doing nothing. Earlier in earth class, he helped me and tried to cheer me up; he was *nice* to me. Now it feels as if I am *letting* him die. I can't just sit here. Ideas – not very thought out ones, might I add, start to form in my mind.

"What if we quickly find a Healer?" I ask urgently, hoping, praying, maybe, *possibly* we can do something and that it isn't too late.

Zac shakes his head somberly.

"Well there's got to be something we can do?" I will proudly admit to crying at this point – and why shouldn't I? Someone is dying or… *will die.*

He shakes his head again, defeated, "It's too late."

"How do you know? How do *you* know he is – or anyone is …*dead*?"

"Their light goes out," he says, surprisingly serious.

"They're not Tinkerbell, Zac!" I say hysterically.

"The light of their Gift! The spiral! The spiral goes out!"

In case you have forgotten, let me remind you that from the time we become Gifted, we all have a faint glow emitting from our spirals that eventually you get used to. Sure enough, Sterling's is gone; it has dimmed to the point that it has faded away.

I know we don't have a lot of time, but someone – a kid – just died, and there are probably more dying right now. An innocent, protecting life has been taken because some people are mad-eyed, revenge-crazy. And people continue to die. Nothing changes. The world doesn't stop, and no one has the time to mourn the deaths. *Someone* needs to.

Well I do – at least for a few moments. Zac reminds me we need to go, starting to pull me up from the ground. I reluctantly stand and follow him, giving one last grief-stricken look back at the still, pale face.

I am distracted while we are running with objects flying everywhere. As you can guess, that isn't a good combination.

"Kira!" Zac, who has gotten several feet in front of me in my haze, shouts as he is running fast towards me. The world seems so slow for a second. "Kira!" seems to hang in the air. The flashing red light seems to switch unevenly, leaving us in darkness an instant longer than light. That is, until Zac collides with me, and the world catches up to me.

We hit the ground just as some kind of fireball flies over Zac. Despite the shock that that flaming *thing* would have hit *me*, I also have the *wonderful* feeling of the air being knocked out of me

– hard. I must say, though, that momentarily not being able to breathe is much preferred over not breathing at all – ever again.

Apparently, the Scorned-person wasn't even trying to kill me, but was aiming for someone else. No more fireballs are flying our way.

"Sorry. You okay?" Zac asks, gently helping me up.

"You mean now that I can breathe." I try to make it obvious I am only teasing, but I continue more seriously, "yeah, I think so and don't be sorry. You saved me."

With my head fully out of the clouds, we rush on and finally start down the spiral staircase.

I try not to pay too much attention to any of the fights we pass – which are practically everywhere – and I only look back a few times to make sure we aren't being followed but everyone is occupied fighting the other.

Zac peeks down around the corner at the second floor landing before we pass it and make our way down to the bottom floor. We pick up the pace until we are out of view of those on the second floor and moving down towards the ground floor and exit.

"Oh my God," Zac says, sounding *devastated*.

I worry about what could be waiting for us, but I see now.

The beautiful, breathtaking entryway is completely destroyed. There is weak smoke rising off of the wreckage of tables, the couch, chairs, and that magnificent, glass front door. The windows are smashed, the glass shattered all over the blackened and scratched hard wood floors. It feels so *wrong* that something so beautiful has been destroyed like this; tears are creeping sting my eyes. Not to mention, this is only one section of the house. The more I look around, the more disheartened I am.

"Okay, either your diversion plan is working or something's definitely wrong because I do not see Bret or Tessa. We should still hurry though," Zac says as he begins hopping around the wreckage of furniture and crumbled wall. I can hear glass and other fragments crunching under his feet.

I try to follow in his path the best I can, but I take one wrong step, almost tripping on a broken picture frame. I pull myself together and follow Zac out what used to be those beautiful glass doors that now stand ajar and broken.

As we hurry through the demolished doors, a faint, agitating whisper is tickling my ear. It is unrecognizable; a blur of whispers. I finally understand one: "*Kira*." All Hell blows up.

The ground in front of us explodes as if a bomb went off. There is an eruption of fire and heat and flames and smoke, tearing the earth and grabbing at us. The impact sends us flying; I land on something softer than the hard ground but it isn't a stack of pillows. By the disgruntled snort I'm guessing my landing pad is Zac.

"Sorry," I mutter smirking.

"Not your fault," he grumbles as we basically use each as a crutch to get up.

Suddenly another fireball flies by my ear just barely missing me. I am really beginning to think someone is trying to hit us. It kinda pisses me off too. I look around, seeing the guy who is

235

using us for target practice as Zac suddenly pushes me back to the ground.

"Watch out!" Zac yells.

What is he talking about? Nothing is heading towards us. Suddenly, a fiery object flies above our heads like a fire cracker and explodes on the far side of us. My eyes widen with fear, realizing what Zac had seen coming and saved us – again.

"Thanks," I breathe.

"Sure. Now you're sincere, *after* I save your life," he smirks for just a moment.

Off in the distance I hear an angry, shrill voice screech, *"Don't kill her you idiot.* Do whatever you want to do to the boy – *after* the girl is far away from him."

Tessa. I internally groan. I'm really starting to strongly dislike this woman.

"We have to hurry," Zac whispers in my ear, as close to me as earlier when we kissed. My mind drifts back to that moment and I blush but nod my head. "Wait until I tell you, but when I say so, run as fast as you can to the garage. Got it?" he looks at me; he almost looks scared. Even though I don't care for him bossing me around, I nod my head. He leans in closely again, his lips brush my ear, "You know…what I'm about to do is pretty stupid. I could die. If you wanted the chance to kiss me again, now would be it."

I roll my eyes but decide to throw his sarcasm right back at him. I look at him as if I am about to kiss him when I press my lips to his cheek and move in closely to his ear as he did to me, "Your just being stupid and reckless, not going off to war."

"Nicely played," he grins, standing up then pulling me up into him. Literally. He presses us together. He kisses me, hard and confident.

Zac pulls away and smirks, "But I seriously wanted that kiss."

He is still smirking when he turns his head and suddenly his arrogance disappears. He mumbles something but I can't understand him.

"What did you say?" I ask, leaning closer.

"Run!" Zac shouts, pushing me behind him and giving a little shove.

The Scorned guy is coming closer with Tessa and Bret flanking him. He begins to form another fireball as lightning flashes through the sky, striking down from the heavens as brilliant and defined as a full moon when it is closest to the Earth. Its light is fierce and pierces the darkness like a knife. It is Zac, and the shock of the harshness is like a zap that sends me running to the garage.

I pick a normal-sized, black car with tinted windows. I pull out of the garage and bring the car to a halt, prepared to take off down the driveway. I look back at Zac. He is handling himself well seeing as it's three against one. Well, Bret isn't very useful other than he is snatching massive pieces of debris and propelling them at Zac. Zac is starting to tire though and is falling behind as the Scorned push forward. I pop out of the car and rush up next to Zac.

He looks over at me and shouts, "What do you think you're doing? Go back to the car!" He throws another lightning strike at the random Scorned. He dodges it but stumbles back; he shrieks with rage then springs forward. The three of the Scorned re-form and attack with a greater ferocity but at least they now have two targets.

"You need help!" I jump into the fight, battling Bret and Tessa as it seems the Scorned guy has some deep revenge to settle with Zac and likewise Zac seems to want to tear Scorned Guy's head off.

"No! It's too dangerous!" Zac shouts protectively as he spins around to avoid a fireball.

"That's a little hypocritical coming from the guy that likes to take on three people at a time, with no concern about his own personal safety and refuses help."

Tessa is destroying the mansion in order to either throw new things at me or pancake me under falling rubble.

"Yeah well, I get to be reckless. People aren't dying for me are they?" His voice sounds harsh and frank. He doesn't mean it. He is attempting to get me to go back to the car so he can be the hero...Right? I mean, people *are* dying for me, but he doesn't have to be one that has to die. I'm here; I can help him.

"You don't have to be a martyr Zac," I say evenly. "Or is your motto 'anything for the cause' as long as you get the attention?" I ask, sarcasm rolling off my tongue.

"Kira – go back to the car," he speaks firmly, as if he is my father directing me to go back to bed.

"No."

"Kira-" Zac isn't allowed to finish his sentence though. Seeing as we are both distracted – by each other and our individual battles – neither of us has noticed Bret has disengaged himself from the fight. He has snuck up on Zac and as Zac has been trying to convince me to return to the car, Bret swings and hits Zac in the jaw. It's a hard punch since Bret has Gifted strength and it knocks Zac to the ground.

That was low though; I mean, I know they don't have a sense of right or wrong or fair – but really? Zac is attempting to stand back up, rubbing his jaw, as Bret kicks him in the side.

Zac falls over on his back and groans, wincing and looking ill. Bret prepares to attack again, but I finally remember I'm not a far-off on-looker; I am here and *this* is exactly why I wouldn't go back to the car.

"Don't you dare," I scream and Bret stops and stares at me smugly before bracing to kick again – seeming to aim at Zac's head.

I can feel my adrenaline rising. With a shriek, I send a whirlwind of vines at Bret. They race through the earth, poking and cracking it here and there. They spring out of the ground like springs and wrap his limbs and body and pull tightly.

Tessa tries to aid her husband by flinging a large piece of fragmented glass from the foyer's window at me. I throw up my hand as if that could block me. As if I have formed a solid rock wall, the glass shatters into pieces and slivers that shimmer like pixie dust in the moonlight, before even reaching me. Unharmed by the glass, I push my hand forward and the glass reverses its direction, back towards Tessa. She panics and crumples into a ball when the shards make impact. She screams as the sharply cut edges of the glass slice her skin, but none impale themselves or are fatal. As she drops to the ground clutching her wounds, blood begins to drip down her torn and scissored body.

I turn to the last remaining guy who has slipped closer to Zac, looking as if he wants to gloat. He realizes I am watching him and he freezes. Suddenly, a baseball-sized fireball appears in his hand. He pitches it at me, as if we are playing a game of baseball. My water Gift douses the fireball before it can manage to get within a harmful distance. I swish my hand in a semi-circle around me. A ring of fire forms around the Scorned. He looks around him, terror in his eyes for the first time. The flames lick at him. He cries out in fear and I realize how inhumane I am being. The fire extinguishes in a cloud of vapor, replaced by a swirling wind of water.

His oxygen supply is being severed and he tries to move through the cyclone but it won't allow him to escape. I can see he is struggling to breathe but I'm not going to kill him; only render him unconscious. The guy is sinking to his knees and he passes out. I stop sucking out the oxygen, and I fix it so he can't escape.

I gaze over at Bret who is still entangled in vines; Tessa is...*nowhere in sight*. Crap. Suddenly I see a shadow, created by something behind me. I spin around and there is a bloodied Tessa, with a wild look about her; one eye is open wide while the other is narrowed. It would be funny if I wasn't worried she is going to kill me.

"You're an annoying little girl, did you know that?" she shrieks. "A right brat! You couldn't just be a good girl and go with us could you? Well now it won't be so easy now," she laughs at what she must think is some sick joke.

Enough of this; I have things to do. I attempt to trap her with another cyclone but she resists it, as if she is using her Gift to bend the water away from her.

"How dare you!" she screeches.

Tessa's eyes flash behind me, in the direction of the front porch. I turn my head to see what her attention has flashed to. In the next moment, the front doors are rapidly zooming towards me and will reach their target in a matter of seconds if I don't do something. I push an air current at the doors I loved so much, pushing them away. I struggle with it intensively; you can see tremors in the air where the two forces are colliding. Fine. If the doors want to go forward, I'll allow them. When you play tug of war and both sides are pulling hard and suddenly one side lets go, the other side normally falls back on their butts. I am counting on this principle now.

I fight the doors one last time with more force than I had before and now I relinquish my Gift and duck. As predicted, the doors immediately fly forward, zooming straight over me. I close my eyes before I see the moment the doors collide with Tessa who has been standing behind me. I hear a thump and look up.

The doors and a lump are lying on the grass of the yard. The lump is clearly Tessa, who isn't dead but I highly doubt she'll be causing much harm anytime soon. She is tucked in a ball moaning. To make sure she will be occupied for a while, I not only wrap the earth around her like a blanket but I also secure her in a vortex. This will take her some time to break out of after she recovers.

I rush over to Zac. He has lost consciousness at some point and it worries me. I brush his hair out of his face and lean in close to his nose and mouth to observe if he is breathing. Thank God he is.

"Zac," I mumble, my voice cracking, needing water. I swallow and say again, more firmly, "Zac, wake up."

I don't really expect him to hear me so I am left with one option.

"Sorry about this," I murmur apologetically but it doesn't matter at this moment.

I summon forward my water Gift, condensate some water in the air, and splash it in Zac's face, like throwing a glass of water. His eyes flash open immediately and his body jolts forward in his return to reality. He is breathing heavily and looks disoriented for a moment before his eyes start to clear and he can see me.

"Are you okay?" he asks, a frown on his face.

"Are you joking? You're asking me if I'm okay when you're the one who's been passed out? I was about to ask if you are okay."

"I thought we already talked about this? You are more important than I am," he rolls his eyes.

"Well then maybe I should have left you for the Scorned guy to rip your head off after I had gone. Would that better fit your sacrifice?"

"Actually that might have been a good idea. I've been needing to get things settled between him and I for quite a while now."

"What happened between you two? What did you do to make him *so* angry?"

He looks down guiltily, "I'll tell you the story sometime, but we should be going now."

I sigh, "Yeah, you're right."

I try to help him up the best I can – I'm not the strongest or most coordinated person, you know. He doesn't need much support though; he is doing fine on his own.

"You driving or am I?" I ask.

"I'll drive. It'll be easier for you to help get Jamie and Lily into the car, with your air Gift."

"Oh, right. I wonder if they're doing okay. I hope they're resting in a tree somewhere; this would have been an awfully long time for Jamie to keep them both suspended in the air."

"Jamie's pretty smart. He knows his limitations. He'll do what he needs to do."

Zac is getting into the car. I take one more look behind me to check my three hostages are still securely captured and to ensure no one else has snuck out. There doesn't seem to be anyone else following us so I slip into the backseat to better help Lily in. Zac starts driving as soon as my door is closed.

"Keep an eye out for them. I don't know how easy of a time we're going to have seeing them."

There was nothing to worry about. As soon as they see us, they come out from their hiding spot and are hovering right in front of us. Zac presses a button and the sun roof of the car opens. He comes to a stop right under them.

"Um, question: why don't we just let them get in the normal way? We're not exactly on some high profile speed chase right now."

"This way is more fun, but *fine* we'll do it your way since it will probably take less time," he grumbles. Clearly he likes doing stupid, reckless stunts like lowering people down through sun roofs.

I stand up and stick my head out of the sun roof. Jamie is holding Lily in his arms, supporting their mass together. He is getting as close to me as he can and is about to transfer Lily.

"Wait! It's okay. You can just set her down on the ground. You guys can get in the normal way."

"Oh thank goodness," Lily tosses her head back with relief.

Jamie pouts, "But I wanted to do it the dangerous way."

"Hey, if we all get through this, we'll practice it some other day. Hurry up though before the Couple from Hell start coming after us," I smirk, amused by the guys' disappointed reactions.

"Okay, okay."

They land by Zac's door. Lily is a little weak-kneed and Jamie is shaking. I open the left hand door and get out to help. I quickly usher Lily into the car. I wrap an arm around an exhausted Jamie. He is trembling and feels clammy; his breathing is ragged.

"Are you going to be okay?" I ask worriedly under my breath as we circle the car.

"I'll be fine. That's not the easiest trick to do and I've only ever practiced it once or twice. I just need to rest. Hopefully I'll fall asleep once we start driving."

"Why don't you sit in the back with Lily then? It would probably be more comfortable," I offer genuinely.

"Are you sure you don't mind?"

"Come on, let's hurry and get you in the back."

I open the door for him and he lowers himself into the backseat while I hop into the front seat. Our doors slam close at

245

about the same time and a fraction of a second later the car is moving.

The car is quiet – peaceful. We are all relaxed it seems; the tensions from the past hour seem to have been shut out of the car. I'm pretty sure Jamie is sleeping already. Lily is awake and staring out the window. Zac is slumped casually in the driver's seat one hand on the wheel, the other stretches over the center consol. I sit here, looking around, and out the windshield.

"Any idea where to go?" Lily breaks the silence.

I look at Zac, but he doesn't say anything. Instead, his free hand starts messing with something stuck between the driver's seat and the console. His attention flirts between the road and whatever he is trying to pull out. He is making me nervous; mostly because I don't trust other drivers nearly as much as I trust myself.

"Let me," I say politely, reaching over to help pull it out.

"I've got it," he yanks it out right as I reach for it. "Here, take it," he holds the giant book towards me.

It is a United States map, rumpled and clearly used.

"What do you want me to do?" I ask bewildered.

"Oh I was thinking you could count how many states there are. What do you think?" he rolls his eyes. "Figure out what place we should head towards."

"I don't know," I say bemused.

"That's why I gave you the map Sherlock."

"Well what kind of place are you looking for? Crowded or rural? City or town? North, south, east, or west?" At this point I think of any question I can ask to annoy him for basically calling me stupid.

"Oh for the love of-!" he snatches the map out of my hands.

"Hey!" I yelp defensively.

"Lily, you take it," he flops the map back towards her.

She huffs but sits forward to grab it.

"The two of you, I swear."

I pout and stare daggers at Zac. He rolls his eyes and glares at the road.

"Alright, let's see," I hear Lily mumble. "We're heading north. Hm, what to head for? We could head for the city of Milwaukee. By the time we get there, we'll need to load up on gas and either come back or keep driving."

"Sounds fine. You're going to have to give me directions."

"Okay," she mutters, sounding reluctant.

"You know Lily, if you're tired, you can just give the map to me. I'm pretty sure I know how to get to Milwaukee once we get on the highway anyways," I suggest helpfully. I've been to Milwaukee several times; I know the exits. I need help to get us away from the back roads.

"I don't know…You might kill Zac or he'll kill all of us by crashing."

"I'm just telling him when to turn; no funny business. Plus, if you give me the map, you can go to sleep. You are looking kind of tired."

"You know I was going to give it to you anyways. You didn't have to try so hard to convince me," she smiles and passes the map forwards.

Once it is safely in my hands, I turn to Zac and gloat, "Ha!" I pipe triumphantly.

"Yeah, yeah, just tell me when to turn," he says, gruffly.

I giggle while starting to flip through the pages.

"Go ahead. Laugh it up fuzz ball."

I stick my tongue out at him and smile.

"Oh, very mature," he says pointedly.

"I know I am. You could use some lessons though."

"Wow."

"You two," Lily mumbles from the back seat. "Shut up," she barks like a mom telling her two kids to settle down.

We give each other one more silent look and return to our own realities.

Soon enough Lily is sleeping in the back, forehead pressed to the window. We have been driving for about thirty minutes. Zac turned on the radio about fifteen minutes ago but nothing really good is on. The volume is turned down low but it is still the loudest sound in the car. We have been sitting in silence. Every once and a while, I sneak a peek at Zac, thinking about our kiss from earlier. It seems so ridiculous now. I barely know the guy and what I do know is he can be an arrogant, sarcastic jerk. Sometimes he has been kind though, and nice, and funny, and...*oh lord listen to me*! The real question is where does it go from here? Where do I

248

want it to go; where does *he* want it to go? Maybe because of that second kiss, he might actually be interested. Am I?

"Did Lily fall asleep?" His voice propels me out of my mental breakdown but I am so disoriented it takes me a minute to respond properly.

"Huh? Oh, uh, yeah she's sleeping."

"You okay? You're not hurt are you? Evan didn't hit you with a fireball did he? If you haven't said anything until now, then I might zap you with lightning."

Aside from threatening me, Zac sounds genuinely worried.

"No, *Evan* didn't even lay a scratch on me. I'm fine actually, getting a little tired maybe. Speaking of that Scorned guy, what's the deal with you two?" It probably isn't my place to ask but a little voice reminds me that whatever the answer is nearly killed me twice tonight.

Zac drops his head away from me, not wanting to look in my direction.

"It's a long story," he sighs.

"We have plenty of time. If it's the privacy you're worried about, Jamie won't wake up for at least another forty-five minutes, and Lily has to already knows," I say comfortingly.

"No one knows the exact details. Lily knows something happened, but she doesn't even know all of it. I think it's the only secret I've ever kept from her."

I don't know if it's because it is past two a.m. and he is tired, but Zac's eyes are hollowed out and deep, dark. He looks so tired and glum as if he has been building this sadness inside him for years.

Maybe it isn't my business, "You don't have to tell me. This is obviously something you don't want to talk about; otherwise you would have at least told Lily by now." A small smile of understanding draws across my face.

He shakes his head, "It happened years ago. It wasn't like I did anything wrong. I should have told her by now, or told someone. I guess I'll just have to settle for you," he smirks, a flash of the Zac I have seen the past two days. The smirk fades to a grin, and his right hand drifts down to hold my left.

Kira, you're moving too fast! You just met this boy; your first impression about him could be totally wrong. You should NOT have butterflies in your stomach right now, that little voice of reason shouts at me in my mind, only increasing the fluttering in my stomach. *Well what did you expect? You did kiss him first,* the voice of logic argues.

Even if I'm not sure how I feel at the moment, I don't break the hand holding, not wanting to reject him. Meanwhile his eyes have gone from me back to the road. There his amusement falls, replaced by what appears like guilt.

"It was two years ago, a little after Lily was Gifted. She was new to it all, but I convinced Nikki to let her come on a mission with us for some practice. More to shadow the fights, get a feel for how it works, but I didn't plan on her ever being in any danger. Well, we miscalculated their numbers and she ended up having to fight so it wouldn't be a lost cause. She didn't do badly for her first real fight," Zac smiles faintly. "She knocked a couple people out quickly, but then she ran into a more experienced Gifted strength. Evan's sister.

"Lily wasn't ready for someone like that. She hadn't learned enough yet...Maybe it is my fault...I'm the one that brought Lily there; I'm the one that-" His voice catches.

I lay my other hand on his and trace my thumb across his skin.

Zac clears his throat and continues, "Lily was getting her butt kicked – and I don't mean that lightly at all. She didn't ask for help; I knew she wouldn't either. She was losing ground fast though, crying out as Evan's sister aimed at spots that already had bruises. I had to do something – didn't I?" He stops and looks at me doubtfully.

I nod, tracing calming patterns on his hand.

"I'll admit I panicked a little too much, but I didn't do the worst I could have. I over-exerted myself to fight off my two attackers and then I ran at Evan's sister, hoping to catch her by surprise. Luckily I did, otherwise something horribly wrong could have happened to me or Lily. I rammed into Evan's sister, holding onto her, and pushing her backwards. I had so much momentum that I couldn't freely stop and I lost my footing along the way so we were gliding along uncontrollably.

"Nothing bad would have happened if the concrete wall hadn't stopped our fall. I was fine because she was my cushion, but

251

her head got smashed into the wall." Zac's line of sight is distant and empty, haunted. "I hadn't meant to kill her. Honestly. I just wanted to get her away from my sister, knock her out even. Evan must have watched us crash into the wall as a second later, hands were ripping me up and throwing me to the side, out of the way so he could see her.

"She is the first person I have ever killed," as he speaks I feel unspeakably sad. I feel as if his child-like innocence has been stolen from him with that sentence. His face even appears to have lost its youth for a moment, drawn out with regret and guilt. "I couldn't help but sit strewn out where Evan had thrown me, and gape at the girl's mangled body. There was blood pooling on the floor. By the time Evan's grief turned into rage, the battle was almost over and Lily and Nikki were pulling me up and dragging me off. He never got a chance to hurt me for what I did to his sister, but he's held a grudge since then and snatches every chance he can get to try and kill me – or Lily – as you can see from earlier."

"Do you think he'll ever give up?" I ask.

Zac shakes his head, "No. He won't stop until one of us is dead. Partly because of the Scorned blood in him, but with that aside, I think I would feel the same way. I think I would hunt for retribution just as long if he had killed *my* sister. I think about the fact that I killed *his Lily* and I feel awful. I took away someone so important and significant in his life; not for a day would I wish that on someone."

"You were just trying to protect your sister Zac. You know you did not intend to kill Evan's sister. You know you are not a bad person. What if you hadn't done anything and just continued fighting your own battles? Lily might not be with us today; I might never have gotten the chance to meet her and you would be the one swallowed with grief."

I want nothing more than to relieve some of his guilt. It has been two years. He needs to stop killing himself over this as I can see the affect it has as it tugs at his features, dragging them down, creating deep shadows in his face.

"I know!" he whimpers desperately, now more firmly, "I know. It's just every time I see him, it all comes back: the guilt, the pain, the remorse, like his anger and grief come."

"I promise you'll get past this one day. Evan might have to either forgive and forget or be killed, but this won't last forever."

"It'll have to be the second option. The Scorned don't 'forgive' – it's not in their nature. I can't wish him dead either; I'm the one who started this really."

"It was an accident."

"Accident or not, someone still died."

"You said it yourself earlier: 'you really didn't do anything wrong,'" I quote him.

"For the record I'd like to correct that statement. I hadn't *meant* to do anything wrong," he scoffs grimly.

"That's what counts-"

"Do you think that matters a shit to Evan who had his sister forcibly taken away from him forever?" Zac is fuming; his eyebrows are bent rhetorically. I know this is a sore subject for him; I was just trying to help. He shouldn't be so angry with me. I'm fighting with my features to control them and not let the hurt I feel show. Zac must notice it though because his face softens and he relaxes once again – deflates.

"I'm sorry. I know you're trying to help, but I don't think anything will help me get through this until it's all over."

I don't say anything else; I nod and continue to trace invisible lines on his hand. The silence and relaxing purr of the car makes me drowsy and I feel my head losing the will to stay up. It probably isn't the greatest idea but I shift to lean over and rest my head on Zac's arm. Closing my eyes, I feel the hand I am holding shift and I move one of my hands away so that he is once again holding mine as opposed to the other way around. I have nearly drifted off when I hear him mumble.

"Thank you."

"What?" I ask groggily, twisting my head to the side to try and look at him without sitting up.

I see him smile faintly for the first time since he started telling the story about Evan.

"Thank you for not hating me for it."

"Well for one, I think that would be hypocritical of me; and secondly, there would be no reason to hate you for that. Your personality – maybe, your attitude – definitely a reason to hate you," I wink at him, but then frown, "I think you hate yourself enough for it that you don't need anyone else to badger you about it."

He stares at me a moment curiously, "You have the same uncanny ability as Lily to be too wise for your own good sometimes."

I smile shyly, "I'm a smart girl. What else can I say? Besides, you're not that hard to figure out. You're like chocolate covered ice cream: crunchy and messy on the outside, a total softy on the inside."

He chuckles, "Okay go back to sleep now. You're either delusional from lack of sleep or you're hungry and we can only fix one of those problems."

Don't ask me why but I give him a peck on the cheek before resting on his arm again.

Chapter 18

I don't know how long I sleep for, but suddenly I feel myself returning to the little black car – possibly because I catch a wift of coffee.

"When did you get that?" I ask sleepily.

"About fifteen minutes after *you* fell asleep on me and I was the only one awake. I got off on an exit we came to and stopped at a McDonald's. Not the best coffee in the world but it's kept me up so far."

"Do you want me to drive?"

"Um does *someone* even have her driver's license on her -"

" – Like it matters -"

" – *and* I've already drank half the coffee so I'll be wired for a while now. We should be getting to Milwaukee soon, and we'll call Nikki and see how it is going if we haven't heard from her."

"I feel bad you've been driving this whole time and it's so late. Then again you were the one who *insisted* you should drive."

"It is okay," he huffs, "I'm always the one to get the short stick...*Don't* – say anything."

I stifle back a giggle. I'm not the only one who giggles though. I turn my head to gaze back at the two other passengers.

Lily hasn't opened her eyes but she smiles and two seconds later she voices, "That's what she said."

Zac, of course, attempts to play it off, "Oh nice one Lily," he says sarcastically, "*real* funny Sis. Ha," he adds for good measure.

Lily cracks herself up, laughing. She happily mutters, "I try."

"Yeah, and *I'm* the cocky one. *Right*," he rolls his eyes.

"Relax. I'm going back to sleep; don't get your panties in a wad."

I look over Zac's seat to see her smirking and shifting her position. Her eyes are still closed. She doesn't say anything else.

I laugh out loud for the first time during this whole exchange. Zac turns and stares at me.

"Hush! Quit encouraging her."

"Ha! I hope it does encourage her. Someone needs to do that to you more often. It helps with the ego," I sit upright, reaching my free hand for the coffee.

"Hey! Hey! Hey!" he pipes, using his arm to blockade the coffee, "Just what do you think you're doing, huh?"

"Well Zac – you see – there's this thing called *taking a drink*," I emphasize sarcastically.

"Not of *my* coffee you don't."

"I'm going to take one sip, not drink the whole thing."

"Nope."

"Selfish much?"

"Unsanitary much."

"What? Are you afraid of getting the common cold from me? You should have thought of that one before you kissed me."

"No I am not worried about getting sick, and to the contrary, I believe *you* kissed *me, first*," he says pointedly, smirking.

"Okay fine, so why can't I take a sip of your coffee?"

He shrugs, "Because I say so."

"Only moms are allowed to say that."

"Then I guess - ..." he abruptly shuts up, his jaw snaps closed grudgingly and his eyes narrow. I realize why.

My eyebrows lift with mock innocence, "I'm sorry. What was that Zac? What were you going to say? I think you should finish that sentence," I smirk. This is too much fun.

"I was going to say," he says slowly, "that I guess that I can't say that then. Instead, I'll make you a deal. If you promise to shut up, you can have a sip."

"No talking – at all? What am I supposed to do then? Besides, aren't you going to miss my lovely conversations?" I ask, feigning offense.

"Hardly," he snorts.

"Fine, I'll take the deal. I don't want to talk to you anyways," I mumble. Well there is nothing he can do about my speaking *after* I have the coffee. Might as well play along until then.

It is warm still, but a little too bitter for me. The smell is amazing though.

"Alright alright! That's enough," he says seeming rather grouchy.

I open my mouth to say, "Okay, I'm putting it down," when he stops me immediately.

"Stop. Remember our deal? You can't talk," he sneers triumphantly, a little too sassy for my liking.

Here is where my brilliant battle strategies come into play.

"Oh yeah? What exactly are you going to do about it now?" I smirk.

Suddenly, there is a shock of static electricity that sparks my hand.

Surprised, I yelp, "Ow!" My hand flies away from his, and I hold it in shock.

What was that? I think, rather confused.

"Wait a minute!" I gasp. "Did you just shock me – on purpose?"

"You asked me what I was going to do about it. *That's* what I did," he laughs, finding himself *so* funny.

"Really? Because you think going around *shocking* people is just so *amusing*? That's a great idea you got there Zac." Noted sarcasm.

"Ah, did I hurt your hand?" he pouts, as if he is genuinely concerned. "I'm sorry."

No he isn't and just to rub it in, he goes back to holding my hand as if he is trying to comfort me.

He is so irritating sometimes, I shriek in my mind, *but he does make revenge so temptingly easy...*

I huff, pretending as if to give up and leave the argument there, but inconspicuously I focus my mind on my fire Gift. I wait for the ball to be put in motion. A minute later, I start to notice my hand getting warm, but it doesn't hurt or burn. I watch Zac out of the corner of my eye and see his eyebrows furrow, bewildered. In a flash, he jerks his hand away from mine and mumbles a mixed stream of profanities and interjections. He waves his hand around like a fan, probably to cool it down. He reaches around to anything that could be cold, pressing his hand to it, sucking out the chill before moving on to the next item.

"You. Stupid. **$%#@. Crazy. $@#*^.* Geez!"

"You started it," I grin.

"I barely zapped your hand, besides everyone gets shocked once and a while. You freaking burned the crap out of my hand."

"You're such a *baby*. There aren't even any blisters," I roll my eyes.

"You little -!" he snaps, his voice rising. "You know what?"

"What? – Ow!"

Zac takes his burnt hand and pokes me, shooting a zap of prickly static electricity into my arm. He does it again in a different spot. And again. It is a more deadly form of tickling.

"Ow! Zac! Ow," I squeak.

"Yeah! Who doesn't like it now?" He asks through clenched teeth, starting to smile.

I stop resisting and quickly call forward my fire Gift, heating myself to a fireball. Hint: I'm not actually on fire. This time, when he pokes me he yelps like cartoons shriek, "Yow!" His finger is bright red. I start giggling.

"What were you saying?" I ask slyly, slowly moving my hand towards his arm, barely grazing it. He swears from that small contact and moves as far away as he can in this car. I wonder how hot my skin feels. "Is there a problem Zac?" *Maybe you can't take what you dish out?*

He mumbles something incoherently and I ask him to repeat it; I couldn't hear him.

"*I said…*" he sulks before continuing, "Truce?"

I smile, "I don't know. I'm having fun with this."

"Can I point out that I *am* still *driving*? Do you think it's really a good idea that you are *burning* me as I am going seventy miles per hour on the highway and it is three a.m.?"

"Fine, I guess you have a point. Truce – *for now*," I wink.

"Oh, is that a threat?" he quirks an eyebrow teasingly.

"It's a promise."

"How about, I won't start anything if you won't?" he smiles.

"I don't know if I can trust you…" I narrow my eyes inquisitively, smiling.

"What? Me? Come on now, who saved your life – *twice* – earlier? That's right. This guy."

"Okay, okay, calm down. I surrender. I surrender," I smile.

"Finally," he grunts.

"That's attractive," I comment sarcastically.

"I know you think I am," he says suggestively, wagging his eyebrows.

"Shut up," I mutter, rolling my eyes.

"Admit it," he says, his smile turning into a flat out toothy, grin, "Admit that you like me, even when you act like you hate my existence."

"Whatever – and I don't act like I hate your existence. Way to blow that out of proportion."

"Say it."

"Not a chance."

"Just say it. I already know you like me."

"I have no idea what you're talking about."

"Say the words Kira."

"Zac-" I warn, annoyed because I do like him – or could like him, given some time – but stating that would be admitting defeat and his ego would grow two sizes and *that* I don't like.

Kira?

I freeze, a vise grip on Zac's hand. My knuckles are turning white.

I hear him say, "Wow, okay I get it. I'll stop. Take it easy there," as he tries to wiggle my hand looser.

Kira...

"Kira!...Kira? Hey are you okay? What's wrong?"

I can barely hear Zac anymore, asking me what is wrong, saying my name. The creepy voice overpowers his, and soon Zac's is completely gone.

Kira? It asks tauntingly.

What? I snap, trying to hide my fear.

Sorry about the lounge. Bret and Tessa always were a little explosive-prone, It says, sneering.

Who are you? I ask, trying to sound brave and *not* terrified...I don't think it is working.

You'll see soon enough, but right now we have a more important matter to discuss. I'm sure you feel so guilty about all these innocent lives being taken-"

Why? They *attacked* us.

Kira, you know the reason they came was not just to kill all of you – that was an advantage for them. You know *that they are at the Gifted mansion for you; killing everyone is their 'bright side.' You know your friend dying was* your *fault, even if it was indirectly. You know it.*

A heavy weight is beginning to collapse on my chest and a gripping fear is freezing my thoughts and constricting my breaths at the knowledge that deep, deep – we're talking Earth's crust-deep, he is right. I'll never ever *ever* let him know that; even though he is probably hearing me thinking about it this very

263

moment. I quickly hide that thought in a box where he hopefully won't find it, and I focus on a different point.

How did you know about Sterling dying? I ask icily. He isn't about to take Sterling's death, laugh at it, and then throw it in my face without any bitterness from me – even if all of this is my fault.

Kira, I'm in your head. I can go anywhere you go, talk to you whenever I want, he says smugly.

Well I'd appreciate it if you wouldn't, and I try to push him out, but the stupid presence comes back.

Now, now Kira; no need to be hostile. I have a very important task to discuss with you, and I know you will agree to it.

Wanna bet? Why would I do anything you tell me?

First of all, for the reason we have already discussed: to save your friends. You wouldn't want the guilt of their deaths on your hands because you were too proud – too selfish – to put yourself before others.

I've really got to stop listening to him, I think grumpily to myself. Did he just laugh at me?

Sneering, he continues, *And for another very key reason. Do* they *look familiar?*

Unwillingly, a picture flashes into my mind. Ah, shit.

Chapter 19

Fear, horror, anxiety, sadness, disbelief, frustration, longing, and a lot more fear and anger are pretty much all I can feel a*nd think*. It's *them*, the people I have tried so hard to forget. My family – my *old* family. Mom, Dad, Haley; their faces are full of terror – and courage that is trying so desperately to take charge.

It looks as if they have been taken hostage. They are all huddled together in a corner of a stone building; their hands and feet are bound. Haley appears the most afraid; Mom and Dad are attempting to show bravery to comfort and soothe her. It isn't working very well.

There is a woman standing over them, guarding them. Her shirt is an off-the-shoulder; I can barely make out her red spiral, the mark of the Scorned.

Who are you? Real ice seethes through my thoughts to him, because I *know* beyond a doubt that, whoever he is, he isn't on my side.

Now don't get ahead of yourself; we're not quite there yet. First let's discuss these people. You know them and don't try to deny it. They're your family – well they were *your family.*

The Scorned woman in the scene in my head slaps Haley across the face. Haley tries not to cry out but tears are jetting down her face. Her cheek is cherry red, and it looks like her lip is split and bleeding. The Scorned woman isn't done. After she slaps Haley, she hits my mother in the stomach. Mom's face twists in agony as the wind is knocked out of her. The Scorned woman kicks my father flat in the chest with more strength then I thought she could be capable of, and my dad is pretty built. He flies backwards against the wall with a very loud thud; his face fills with pain.

Nothing, *nothing* has ever felt so terrible; I feel sick. Like my Mom, I can't breathe. I can feel my face is hot with wet tears, but they aren't helping to cloud my vision of this upsetting scene that is occurring all in my head.

What terrifies me the most is I realize whatever this mysterious voice wants with me is the reason it has my parents and sister. It wants me to do whatever it desires, and it has found its guarantee I will do it.

Oh, so you are smart. Good, the voice remarks on my thoughts smugly.

Don't hurt them, I say sternly, and yes I know it sounds all oh-so-dramatic, but I *really* don't care at the moment.

I'd actually really love to, but unfortunately I am a man of my word and I promise you to let them go if you *take their place."*

Of course – because that's totally *original* and I *totally* didn't see *that one* coming.

Where? I don't feel my response needs more than that.

A picture of *me* now forms. It is as if I am looking at the car from the outside in. I can see Zac, Lily, and even Jamie. It flashes into my mind like I am looking down on myself from an omniscient point of view, and now the scene is off, darting away at a blinding speed, down a road. A left turn here, right turn there, a few more here and there; now nothing for a while, just trees and ground and road, rushing past me. Just barely in my peripheral vision is the first sign I've seen – a street name. Hadrian Road. Huh, suiting since Hadrian means "dark one." How I know that? Not really sure.

Right beyond the sign is a gravel driveway barely visible, shrouded by overgrown bushes and low-hanging branches covered with dark green leaves. The picture starts jetting down the driveway but fades away, never presenting me with an actual destination. I figure it must be basic navigation after that. Whatever is at the end of that path must be what I am looking for.

The scene suddenly returns, only in a hallway now, and it makes a point to show me three doors before finally, the picture really does disappear.

If you must, bring your friends along. After all, I'm sure the kids wouldn't mind a few more heads to roll around, he sneers. I swallow the bile that is creepy up the back of my throat. *I look forward to seeing you,* the voice says smugly and I feel its presence *finally* slipping away.

Control flows through me, taking over my senses and setting them back on track. When the voice was talking, I could see but none of it made sense. I couldn't hear or feel anything, otherwise I would have noticed Zac's pleading voice to "snap out of it" and him bewilderedly shaking me, trying to physically shake me out of it. I begin to notice now though, as I unthaw. I know I am ultimately free when an energized jolt quakes through me, awakening every inch. Immediately I am alive and aware of everything, including Zac's wide frightened eyes, bearing into mine. He must have pulled over at some point, because we are stopped on the side of the road. Somehow neither Jamie nor Lily has woken up.

"Kira?" he asks in a child-like voice, so much like earlier. "What just happened?"

For some reason, his question catches me off guard – and tongue tied. Silence choking my ability to speak, I sit staring wide-eyed and frankly terrified, looking into his beautiful blue eyes.

I know in an instant; I am going alone. Otherwise, it will be like switching him, Jamie, and Lily for my parents and sister. Unfortunately this means I'll have to somehow convince them to stay behind.

"Zac."

"Kira."

"We have a problem."

Chapter 20

Zac is frozen, spaced out with fear.

"Zac?...Hey, I'm sure it will be fine," I try to say convincingly. Then again, I don't think it will be fine for whole different reasons.

"The fight is *still* going on?" he asks, looking rather precarious.

"Yes." Lie. "Nikki said both sides are super-exhausted, but the Scorned refuse to retreat." Lie again. I take a deep breath. I don't like lying, but I can't tell them who really Minded me. For one, I don't know exactly who it was.

"Maybe all of us shouldn't have gone with you," he looks around the car guiltily.

"Hey! One, maybe two, extra fighters would not help them that much. Besides, Nikki said no one has seen Bret or Tessa in a while. She figured they came after us." That technically might not be a lie; they probably did start coming after us as soon as they were able to break free and recover. "If they catch up to us, just two people might not be enough to get rid of them."

"They definitely won't stand a chance against the four of us," Zac says grimly.

I nod, rather dazed.

"Are you okay?" he asks concerned. It seems to be becoming a pattern.

"I just hope everything will be alright. I don't want anyone else to die."

"It'll be alright. The Gifted have been around for centuries, and I don't think we'll be going anywhere any time soon," he tries his best to smile but the seriousness of the situation is starting to get to him too. "It'll be fine," he mutters, as if trying to convince himself more than me.

Zac starts the car again and pulls back onto the highway.

"Shoot. We need to stop for gas."

"You should probably get off at the next exit then."

"Right."

Sounds start coming from the backseat; bodies shifting, yawns, all those noises involved with waking up. I swivel around to see both Jamie and Lily beginning to sit up, stretch, scratch their heads, and yawn.

"Well good morning *sleepy heads*. How nice of you to join us!" Zac says, sounding overly fake, seeming to have suppressed the serious heaviness from a moment ago. I elbow him (too nicely) to get him to be nice before I turn back to the other two passengers.

"Well I hope you guys slept well for how long you've been out," I smirk.

Jamie speaks through a yawn, "I feel great."

Like contagious chicken pox, once Jamie starts to yawn so does Lily.

Lily says, "I don't know about that, but I could kick some Scorned butt right now if I need to."

Zac and I exchange a very brief, secret look; a simple flashing of the eyes, before we continue as if there is nothing wrong.

"We're getting off the highway? Are we turning around?" Lily asks, talking through another yawn.

"No, we're just stopping for gas," Zac replies, rather evenly, focusing on the road and not giving any sign of emotion.

"Oh."

"Yeah, so everyone go to the bathroom now and get all your business taken care of because we are not stopping again until breakfast," Zac jokes. I think of car trips with my family. *My family…*

We all laugh at him.

"We know *Mom*," Lily teases, clearly traveling down the same memory lane I had gone down.

In this moment I know what I have to do so they don't follow me, but I can't imagine they are going to like a second of it. They'll forgive me eventually, or maybe they won't, but I don't really think they will be *that* mad and upset. I'm rambling again…

As I am planning through this in my mind, we pull into the gas station that is practically abandoned other than one employee. Lily and Jamie are hopping – stiffly – out of the car and limping off into the gas station. Zac is gazing at me warily. He doesn't ask me what is wrong; his eyes do it for him. I try my best to smile; I try my best to convince him not to worry. My eyes continue to stare into Zac's, and his delving into mine. The intensity of them

271

frightens me (or that could just be the guilt) and makes my insides squirm as if his gaze can see the truth and knows what I am up to. But of course he can't. He has a weather Gift, not a Gifted mind. He doesn't have the ability to see into my mind and read my thoughts. Thank God.

Stupid, wonderful blue eyes making me use God's name in vain, and getting all distracted.

Yet, neither of us looks away, like we are frozen here for eternity.

"Kira?"

Aw, he is worried about me. Well, I should probably be worried about me, too. Except I have two families to worry about instead, and both are currently being threatened by an evil, cruel mastermind – a.k.a. the voice. I suddenly feel as if I am stuck in a melodramatic movie and the plot line is now instructing me down a perilous path that leads to ultimate doom. I feel as if there are so many things building up inside me in this moment, knowing that in the next moment I will be leaving them, that I can't help but to lean over and kiss Zac again. Call me a stupid, emotional girl if you want.

Zac doesn't hesitate this time; he immediately responds, holding my face in his hands. The sensation of kissing him is becoming more familiar, more comfortable and in that it becomes more satisfying.

I pull away – back into the *real* world and suddenly I feel guilty although Zac's smile *almost* clears away my troubles. My stomach remains in a knot, worryingly.

He grins, "Come on, let's go see how Jamie and Lily are doing and fill up on gas."

I nod, blushing and looking down. We each begin to step out of the car. I am about to close the door when he stops me.

"Oh, can you get some money out of the glove compartment?" he shrugs apologetically.

"Sure," I reply politely.

"We keep it in there in case of emergencies like this. It should be in a white envelope."

It is, lying right on top, and I quickly have it in my hand and am closing the door. The next minute changes the course of this early morning.

A strong gust of wind comes up and swipes the envelope out of my hand and carries it towards the line of trees at the back of the station. I notice later on that the funny thing is there was no wind blowing in that moment.

"Crap," I swear – well that kind of language is swearing for me. I start jogging after the envelope.

"Well way ta' go butterfingers," Zac remarks sarcastically and rather rudely.

"Shut up and come help me," I call back behind me.

I hear him sigh, "Fine. I'm coming."

The envelope drifted to the edge of the tree line, nearly completely out of view of the gas station. Some of the money has blown out of the envelope and is scattered around in the grass. We collect it all quickly and together stuff it back into the envelope. I impulsively decide this is the time; now is the only time. When I come to terms with this, panic from the guilt of betrayal hits me.

"I-I'm sorry," I stutter out.

He stares at me with confusion before he rolls his eyes.

"Don't be. It's fine."

Oh, God, here it comes.

I shake my head apologetically, "No. No – I'm sorry."

The last stronghold is gone as his smile disappears in bafflement, and almost....*hurt*.

My luck seems to be getting worst. Almost like a sign, Jamie and Lily walk out of the gas station looking for us. They approach us casually. I think it is them at least, with the cover of night still over us. I slide away from Zac; our hands getting space from one another.

It is time. I feel the steady pull of energy leaving me as I slowly and inconspicuously put more and more distance between the three of them and me.

Lily tries to hide the awkwardness she probably feels when she purposefully coughs twice then says, "Well sorry to interrupt...*this*, but I really think we should get out of here before one of the creepy, red-freaks pops out of nowhere."

"About that..." Guilt can be clearly heard in my voice.

"*What do we have here...*No, no, she's right Kira. *You* really should be going."

The voice that still brings chills to my arms and legs with that arrogant sneer just walked out of the sea of trees, seeming to appear from the darkness itself, with her steroid-addicted husband beside her.

"If you think she's going anywhere with you, then you *really* have lost your (insert word of choice) mind," Zac says defensively.

"No need to resort to vulgarity, Mr. Railey, and besides, we weren't referring to that. Were we Kira?"

I imagine their three heads swiveling around to look at me, betrayal in their eyes; as if they know what she is talking about. Instead they stand their ground, believing Tessa is only speaking in threats.

"If you think you can come to the Gifted mansion, hurt our family, and then try and guilt-trip Kira into coming with you then you really need to stop sniffing whatever crap makes your hair do *that*!" Jamie interjects, jerking his hand towards her hair.

"Watch it boy," speaks Bret in defense of his wife.

"Why? What could you-"

Well folks, the atomic bomb just dropped on little helpless Japan and the chaos is beginning to set in.

Jamie tried to walk/step/bump towards Bret as if to try and "get up in his grill;" I don't know – I don't pretend to understand guys and their testosterone-fueled, budding-heads arguments.

Anyways, he tried to walk forward and ran right into the invisible wall I built around him, Lily, and Zac with the Gift of air. He stumbles backwards and falls into Lily, who, of course, stumbles into the other side and bounces forward – kind of like a pinball game.

For a second, fear flashes across their faces as they realize they are somehow trapped in an invisible bubble. Predictably, their strong, confident faces return, only this time they are a lie, but their anger isn't.

"Neat Tessa. Cool trick," Jamie raises his voice with frustration, practically screaming it at her. "Bet this hurts though," he rams shoulder first into the wall, barreling into it with all his weight.

The air ripples but holds strong despite how it feels like someone has lightly punched me in the gut.

"Does it look like it hurt me?" Tessa sneers.

Is she playing along just to goad them or is she trying to hint to them that it isn't her trapping them?

Either way, it further pisses Jamie off, so he continues ramming into the wall like a football player attempting to tackle a receiver with the ball. He does it so many times that Zac finally grabs him by the arm and stops him before he passes out from too much trauma.

I grow weaker and weaker from every hit until I collapse to my knees.

"Kira!" Lily shouts and begins to come towards me – mistakenly thinking I am in the bubble with them.

Wham!

Zac and Jamie begin to notice what is happening behind them, racing towards me to see if they too are thrown back…

Wham! and two tenths of a second later…*Wham!*

"What the hell is going on?" Jamie yells. I' m assuming they've pieced together that I'm not in the circle with them, and quite possibly that I have something to do with it.

I sadly gaze at each of them, allowing the guilt to surface on my face.

"I'm sorry," I say slowly, tears running down my cheeks.

Hurt is the one clear emotion on their faces, along with hints of betrayal, anger, and denial. To worsen the matter, I'm not done. Vines grow out of the earth, wrapping around them, trapping them here. They fight and pull against the vines. Zac tries zapping them which fries those, but new ones grow back. Lily is the most energy consuming to restrain because of her super strength; however it doesn't take nearly as much energy as Jamie's football practice had required. I still need something stronger than the dome to keep them in and others out.

I think of something, something I can maintain long enough for me to put enough distance between us. I know I have the ability to withhold Jamie, Zac, and Lily for the minute I need to remove the dome to do it.

As the dome mixes back into the air, its energy returns to me, but quickly departs once again as blended water-air wisps spiral around and around my friends. Once it fills in, my friends are completely surrounded by a smaller version of the cyclone I formed much earlier today. I figure there is no point in devising more inconspicuous methods of containment since anyone (who's normal) who happens to see anything supernatural happen will forget it afterwards anyways.

Something flickers in the corner of my eye; Bret and Tessa snickering. I don't understand where all the anger comes from in this moment but here it is, and I blame it for my actions. It's as if I believe they are two feet from me and my arm swings out to push them. Of course I'd never actually reach them, but I feel a gush of energy rush from my arm. That force reaches Bret and Tessa, slamming Tessa against a thick, rock-solid tree. Bret, however, is about 240 lbs. (totally guessing) and so he barely stumbles. Tessa looks to be out cold.

The fact that Bret is still standing angers me further. Oops, not anymore.

Wham!

He's down.

I don't look at my friends – or who I hope will still be my friends. I turn and walk back to the car. I try to put in as much gas as I can, convincing myself that Zac, Lily, and Jamie or Bret and Tessa aren't going anywhere any time soon, but the paranoia gets to me after about fifteen dollars-worth. Hopefully that'll be enough for me to make it to wherever I'm going – or at least far enough away from here that I can stop later on again if I run out. As I pull out of the gas station and start driving up the road to the highway, I pretend not to hear the screams that are pleading with me to not leave, to come back. Sadly, that isn't an option. I pretend not to hear Zac, Lily, and Jamie shouting and screaming at me, "Why would you do this?" or "What's going on?" or "We trusted you," so I don't have to answer them.

I hate the utter silence in the car, but music will distract me from the many things I need to think about – like remembering the directions to wherever I am going. Just like that, the directions run through my mind: the left and right turns adapting to the course I now have to take, and then Hadrian Road. You'd think that'd be creepy that it just automatically comes back into my mind the second I think of it…

Am I extremely nervous about what is to come? Check. Do I completely want to turn around and forget everything? Somewhat, but I can't and I won't. Am I one-hundred percent angry? Hell yes. Well maybe it is determination, but whatever. I am focused.

Is that…? Already? Hadrian road. There's the brush that hides the driveway. I sweep it away with my Gift and start down the gravel path. I don't think about the fact that I might not come back out of this alive; I don't think about the fact that this could be an even bigger trap than I already think it is.

Chapter 21

I can see the building, I'm guessing, is the Scorned headquarters. Incredibly – and creepily – it is the exact same design of the Gifted's, but this one is more…sinister, darker. The shadows that fall down along the house seem to be blacker than the night sky, as if trying to shroud a grotesque monster that hides in its veil. Every feature that contributes to the beauty of the Gifted house, makes this one more brooding. The beautiful entry way of the Gifted mansion is the exact same door here, but this one appears to be unwelcoming as if anyone who enters through it will be consumed into nothing but an empty darkness.

Of course, *that* is the way I have to go, that is the path I am on. Yeah, I have about *zero* luck.

I turn off the car but leave the keys in the ignition as I don't really have a place to store them, and I get out of the car.

I do not want to do this; I *really* do not want to do this. Oh sure, I seemed so confident and, well, not scared *before*, but let me tell you, it is a lot easier to say something is easy *before* you're actually staring it in the face, having to do it, because *now*…It is very frightening.

Breathe Kira…breathe…ok go. Just like that I slowly begin to inch forward and I do mean at the pace of a slug. As I climb the stairs, my heart is beating fast, and loudly; I feel light headed. The more I move, though, the more stable I become. Well, isn't that ironic?

Since they already know I am coming, I figure there really is no reason to try and sneak in, so I throw open the doors as if I am walking into my own house.

Remember how I said the outside was like a sinister replica of the Gifted house? The inside is much worse. The furniture is all dark colors – well, black. The night causes it to look haunted and ghostly; the shadows descend in certain spots, making it seem old and abandoned. The entire scene gives me the creeps.

Paranoid, fear drives me to run towards the hallway and start to scan all the doors on my right. I need the third one I come to.

It looks like any other door; same white wood, same brass doorknob, but I know it is nothing like the others. Somewhere beyond this door is my family in more trouble than they deserve to be in. Along with them, is a man who is un-doubtfully evil and twisted, who deserves everything I am going to unleash on him.

Because my family won't remember this anyways, I decide why not show up with a bang. As quickly as possible, I creak open the door to get a look at my "stage." However, what is viewable ends eight steps down where there is a landing and the stairs flip around the wall. Perfect! I'll make it down to the landing, come out in view of everyone downstairs and then set all Hell loose.

Only one problem with my plan: when I reach said landing and I am about to set said Hell loose…there is a door in my way. Actually…I can work with this.

Boom! The door flies off into whatever lay beyond it, blowing bits and pieces of the wall around it everywhere. I hear screams but I don't know if it is because someone was hurt or it scared them.

Objective 1: Locate Mom, Dad, and Haley.

Objective 2: Remove whoever the hell is in my way.

A foreign energy is surging through me. Yes it's most likely very strong adrenaline, but it's as if I am high off of something – and *no*, I don't know how that *actually* feels but I can guess it's something close to what I feel now. I feel as if I can jump to the moon, or at least complete what I set out to do *on a rampage*. (Just what they want: a pissed-off, revenge seeking, adrenaline-controlled, hormonal teenage girl on a rampage. *This is going to be fun*.) You'd think I have an army backing me up; nope, just good ole' me and my Gifts.

I step down the stairs and into the basement. If this was a movie, right about now the intense, action-y, blood pumping background music would get really loud as a bunch of flips, kicks, and punches are thrown. Except, in my case it is wind, water, earth, and fire.

To my complete utter disappointment, there is only one Scorned person in sight. That is just fine; I recognize her as the girl from the vision earlier. Huddling close together is my family. They have a couple of scrapes and bruises, but otherwise look unharmed; it lifts a huge weight off my shoulders.

I wait for them to look as relieved to see me as I am to see they are okay, or *something* other than fear. Suddenly I remember that they have "never" seen me "before," not to mention will forget me again after this. That really is a depressing thought.

I quickly snap out of my reverie and turn my gaze back to the girl who now has an evil sneer on her face *that really pisses me off.*

Whoosh. Annoying, evil girl is thrown against the hard, stone walls in an instant.

*One point for me...*except I forgot she can fight back. This weird, cloudy dew forms around me and I can't see out of it. The little hairs on my arms and neck lift, along with strands of the hair on my head – as if it has static electricity running through it. I feel as if a zap of lightning shocks my spine as I am sent to the ground, cringing in pain.

That little-! Unfortunately, "that little-" did deserve a point...so we are tied. *Not for long.*

After the crippling pain fades away, before even trying to stand up, I send a tumbling whirlwind of messy Gifts at her, and once I hear the crash of contact, I roll to my feet and throw more. I keep throwing masses of wreckage at her – whatever is the first thing to broach my mind – over and over, relentlessly, growing weaker and weaker. Panting heavily, the anger and adrenaline rushing out, I finally stop to observe a very beaten up, bloody girl as she struggles to move her limbs.

As she is momentarily occupied, I rush over to my parents and sister and that little boy who had been in Walmart with them that I hadn't noticed before, and quickly and with great difficulty untie their bindings, hesitantly only a moment at the sight of the boy.

"I'm sorry, but I don't have time to explain anything. There's a black car parked outside with the keys still in the ignition. Get in it and start driving."

Without giving myself time to look at them and probably burst into tears, I start to turn away. Unfortunately, my mom finds the courage to speak, "Wait! Are you not coming with us?"

"Sorry but I've got some bigger problems to take care of."

"At least tell us your name."

After a moment's hesitation, I do.

"Kira."

"What a lovely name," she says absent mindedly.

Once again, you would think so since you gave it to me, I think to myself.

I want to spend more time with them – hours – but it isn't possible. With lead seeming to weigh down my heart, I hurriedly command them, "Go!" I turn back to a now fully-recovered, very ticked off girl.

With an ear piercing screech, she flies off the ground, but before she hits me with another bolt of lightning, we are interrupted.

"Enough Maggie!"

That voice! The little hairs on my neck and arms rise, little nervous goose bumps forming all over; a tingling sensation runs wherever they form.

He was here! He is here! Well duh, Kira; you knew that. *Maggie* looks just as frightened as I am – *and she is on the same side as him!*

"You may leave now."

"But-"

I'm not looking at him – I can't yet – but in my mind I can picture his eyes flaring and his neck bulging at being questioned. I thought twisted-plotting version of him is scary; angry-fuming version is terrifying.

"Go, Maggie!"

Hearing the warning in his voice, she slightly bows her head – which is weird – and starts up the fragmented stairs. His anger formed a thick cloud of tension in the air, but as soon as Maggie is out of sight, the man – who I have still yet to look at – seems to calm and revert back to his twisted, cunning side.

"Well Kira, I'm *so* glad you could make it," his tone seems to be mocking a polite one. "I see your friends couldn't make it. What a shame..." he speaks as if he is genuinely disappointed. *As if.*

I know I have to look at him soon otherwise his arrogance will grow to be the size of an elephant – if it hasn't already. Swiftly I turn myself to look at him. Somehow, at some point, he has gotten himself to the very back of the basement – and I mean

285

the *back wall*, opposite of the stairs. He had to have had to walk right past me. I never noticed him and there are no other doors down here – especially anywhere near where he has appeared. How had he gotten there?

He is exactly how I pictured him – I don't mean as in actual facial features – I mean he represents the epitome of all evil – *and you think I'm kidding*. It isn't because of his features; he has *average* black hair that is kind of messy, a little bit of unshaven scruff all along his chin. He resembles an Irishman – or maybe it's Scottish – either way. He is *average* height – for a guy (he still towers over me). He isn't built like Bret, with steroid-addicted muscles; he's probably somewhere in his thirties. *He is average.* Yet, something about him *isn't*…Maybe it is the constant sneer he has, or the way his eyes are a little too wide or the vein in his neck seems to bulge as if he is a wild animal always prepared to pounce on its prey.

While I am staring at him, he starts to pace back and forth as if trying to find a new angle to look at me. Maybe he is sizing me up, deciding how much fight I have in me before I give up. My family are fighters. We don't quit. We don't give up. We're stubborn as crap. If he wants a fight, I will do my best to give him one. I can't promise it will be anything remarkable or enduring though. I am new to this.

"I expected as much character out of you; however, violence is only a last resort. There are much more peaceful, easier methods to solve our little problem."

I snort imagining *him* trying to carry out *peaceful* negotiations; he just doesn't seem like that type of person. Suddenly I realize he was in my head again and I find myself annoyed. I am *so sick* of it; it's manipulative, invasive, and underhanded.

"Oh why thank you! You understand me so well," he remarks with a tone perfectly imitating appreciation; no doubt he actually thought those were compliments.

"But they were. I mean, what else could they possibly be other than the beautiful truth?"

With a soft grunt, I scoff and comment what he probably already hears in my head, "Not all truths are beautiful, especially ones involving you."

"Now Kira, that was extremely-"

"Enough!" This excessive bantering is useless. I'm not here to try and prove to him what an evil, conniving (insert choice word here) that he is, which would no doubt be a waste of time.

Instead of being angry that I (God-forbid) interrupted him, he laughs – *laughs!* I watch him with mild shock.

Is this one big drug house and they're all *on something?* I think to myself, happy for once that he probably heard that one. Of *all* things I have said – or thought – this is what finally angers him.

"How dare you insult me in such a way!" His eyes flare and I notice that he has his fists clenched at his sides.

Now it is my chance to smirk, "Oh yeah, you didn't know? It's obvious really. Tessa's clearly smoking something because

287

that's what makes her – and her hair – so insane, and it gives Bret that 'I am man! Now cower in front of me and my abnormally strong muscles' attitude," I do my best to deepen my voice to that of a baritone male's for my Bret/manly impression, "And you, well you seem to think the world is here for your own personal entertainment. I would just like to inform you that one day very soon you're going to wake up to find we're not all your puppets and can happily knock you right into a twisted, drug-crazed coma that also tends to come with a *killer* headache hangover."

Mr. Kool's cool flies at me as I am barely able to dodge it. Instead, it hits the already destroyed doorway, causing more demolition.

"Oh but I thought you said fighting would be a last resort? What? Am I already too much for you?" I'm enjoying this *way* too much.

"Watch it Taylor," he is attempting to keep his arrogant composure with great difficulty, and to not strangle me right here, "you don't want me as an enemy. Neither you nor anyone else has a damn clue what I'm capable of doing."

"Oh, I'm shaking," I state sarcastically. It is fun ticking *him* off for once.

His cool demeanor slips again as he flings another piece of…I can't tell which Gift it is – at me.

"So was that an open invitation for me to fight back at any time?"

"Last chance Kira. Let me bring you to our side – far away from those tree hugging weaklings who somehow have the guts to say they have Gifts – that they never use.

"Come on Kira, you know there's always been a side of you that's wanted power and control; *I* can give it to you. I can teach you so much; I can make you even more powerful than you already are. I can give you your family back," he acts as if he pulled his wild card and for a millisecond I believe him.

"That's not possible. There's nothing you can do to make them remember me again and -"

"I'm not talking about them," he remarkes snidely.

"If you think I'd *ever* prefer the Scorned as a...*family*," I spit out the word, only because in this situation it is being associated with the word Scorned, "then you really should commit yourself for insanity now."

"Hush you *child*! I am not speaking of them either -"

"Then what are you – You know what? It doesn't matter. I don't make deals with the devil, and I sure don't join him," I say.

"So sure of that are you? 'Evil' is just a term of perspective, an opinion. You've only seen things from the Gifted's side. Why don't you view it from the other side of the looking glass and see who you think is 'evil' then?"

In response, I throw a flaming mass at him that is solely created from pure Gift. I know he won't let it hit him, but I wasn't expecting him to just wave his hand a few seconds before it is supposed to hit him, and suddenly the fiery ball is extinguished.

"So does this mean your *peaceful* negotiations have run out yet, or are you still scared to fight?"

"Such a violent girl, aren't you?" he smirks.

"I don't like prolonging the inevitable," I shrug.

"One last chance, Kira. You will find that choosing *my* side would be very beneficial to you."

"Haven't you noticed that in all the fairytales, the *villain* always says that, but it's never really true? Normally, instead, they stab you through the back – which let's face it, no one would really put it past you to do."

"Just remember, you brought the storm upon yourself."

"Yeah, I'm still waiting for that."

Not two seconds later, I duck my head as the battle begins. I am no longer thinking about technique; I do whatever my first reaction is to the assailant that is flung at me. I have yet to recognize what Gift he possesses. I mean, I don't think it's possible, but it seems to be all of them. At times I find myself surrounded by fire, at others submersed in water, then grabbed at by vines with random objects flying at me. I no longer have the time to concentrate immensely; I can no longer take a pause to concentrate. Only two days into this new world, and with *one* day of training, this is how far I've (been forced to) come.

How is it possible? How can your life change so drastically in just forty eight hours? How can there be so many life changing moments that shouldn't even be possible? Yet, here I am controlling the elements, battling against someone who is most likely Satan's incarnate in the flesh.

…Absolutely…amazing.

Immersed in my own thoughts, I fail to realize, that suddenly, the other person in this fight isn't fighting back. Instead, he is regaining his footing after being hit by one of my wind gusts. Fueled by the fact he let himself be hit, he begins to visibly tremble with fury.

Have you ever had one of those moments in life when you think everything is going fine, then all of a sudden your entire world is flipped upside down and it shocks you more than you ever thought you could be shocked? I am having one of those moments right now.

As if out of thin air, vicious cobras appear, slithering towards me, snapping open their jaws at me, revealing their menacing fangs. I screech with absolute fright, jumping back, scrambling to get as far away from them as possible. Realizing I can't move any farther with my back pressed against the wall, I resort to using my Gifts – which I probably should have done from the start. Immediately, they all catch on fire, burning to a crisp in seconds. The fear remains behind even with the cobras gone; my heart still beats rapidly. Replacing the objects of my fear, are scurrying spiders, tiny and black, racing towards me.

Frantically, I squish them with a giant, heavy-looking piece of debris that was lying near me. I stand, practically hyperventilating, waiting anxiously for the next wave of scary creatures, but no new ones come. He begins to laugh.

"Why Kira, you're not afraid of those tiny, innocent creatures are you?"

"How did you do that?"

"I told you. No one knows what I'm capable of doing," he sneers.

"But how is it possible? Shape shifting isn't a Gift. You shouldn't be able – you can't be able to -?" My mind is racing, trying to understand what is happening, how what he did is possible.

"Wish you'd chosen otherwise now?"

He planned this all along, I realize.

"Do you wish you'd thought of a more original trick to play? I mean, really? Isn't that the oldest card in the book?"

"*Wish you'd thought of a more original trick -*" he mimics me.

"Wow! You're cool," I say sarcastically.

"You're right. I am *very* cool," and with that, he sends a rushing, freezing wind at me.

Shivering, with goose bumps forming along my arms and legs, I warm myself with fire like I did...*was it really only yesterday?* The fight is more intense this time. Somehow it is as if he is re-energized and is fighting with a re-vamped speed. It is becoming increasingly harder to keep up. I am rapidly losing energy; my body begins to exhibit a heaviness that constantly makes it harder to move. It probably doesn't help either, that it is about four in the morning and I desperately just want to curl up in a ball and go to sleep.

He keeps advancing, though, as if he has *Monster* pumping through his blood. It is becoming overwhelming and exhausting. I am getting behind, falling back; his eyes only grow wider, crazier, as if being driven by an unknown entity. He is acting like a teenager himself, one filled with so much *anger* that builds up until it bursts and this is him *exploding*. I can't keep up; I can't match his ferocity. He is coming too fast and too hard.

All of a sudden, I am stumbling backwards out of control until I slam into the splintered wall. The air rushes out of me in a heave and I cringe as air has trouble flowing back in and out. Tears sting my eyes, but I bite my bottom lip to attempt to hold them back and to keep from crying out. He is ever still relentless in his attack, and I throw my arms up in front of my face as if it will form some sort of shield. Well my arms won't but my Gifted energy does form some sort of force field of a shield – for a short period of time anyways.

Pound after pound hits my only protection against him, sending a vibrating pulse through me. It becomes more frequent as the beatings increase, to the point that the vibrations feel like a second heartbeat only jolting me more like shockwaves until it becomes violent, painful, and draining. I can feel my shield growing thinner and thinner, caving in on itself. It feels as if a giant-ton weight is pressing down on my chest and head as the shield only barely remains; the force of impact is the pressure trying to smother me.

I am suffocating. My breaths become shallow, my chest is being constricted to the point I have to inhale and exhale twice for the amount of one normal breath. The only reason I'm not dead altogether is the very thin, remaining bilayer of my Gifts that is stopping the fire, water, creatures, and whatever else he sends at me. My eyes are squeezed shut, waiting for the terror to be over, the pain to be gone, and the fear to disappear. It shouldn't be long before it all fades away, either; the last of my strength is slipping out…

Nothing. No rhythmic pulsing, nothing slamming into me. Only silence, an aching all over my body, and the darkness behind my eyelids. Or maybe my world has simply gone dark altogether. Maybe I am *home*.

A menacing laughter pierces my reverie; it echoes in my head. I feel myself pushing into the wall to scramble away from it, my body cringing into a tight ball, trying to find security and solitude again. But the voice won't go away. It is like a dream – no, a *nightmare*. Is this where I will stay for the rest of eternity? In this nightmare?

Wait…I can still feel the wall behind me and the ground below me. The voice isn't in my head; it is in the living world. *I* am in the living world. I'm not dead – well, not yet at least.

"Don't tell me that's all you've got," he remarks so conceitedly that my eyes instinctively snap open.

This room is much brighter than I remember. My eyes have to blink a few times to adjust. There he is, right where he stood the first time I saw him, with the same evil, twisted, slightly insane smug look on his face. "For someone who wanted to fight so badly, you only lasted, what? Five minutes?"

"First of all, it was at least *ten* minutes," I roll my eyes sarcastically. "Secondly, I'm *not* going to complain that you don't play fair," I speak up defiantly, starting to gain my strength back little by little and I slide up the wall, using it to support most of my weight until I'm on my feet, "or that you're an evil, narcissistic, arrogant dirtbag who should shut up more often than not – or one day, someone will make you."

I don't know where it comes from, but with that I lash out with just about all I have. He is pushed, pulled, and hit only a little before he meets me in my rage. Everything is a blur; my thoughts, my vision, even the Gifts I am sending at him. All that I am able to think and do is react, not even caring what comes out first. Wherever this new found energy came from, I am finally matching him in power.

Suddenly there is a splinting tear ripping through me, as if something is attempting to shred me in two. My head is immediately hammering, pounding against my skull, pulsing. I am being wrenched apart from the inside out, organs being pulled different directions in an internal tug of war. The Gifted energies leaving me to attack him are destroying each other. Water is extinguishing fire, fire is destroying anything earthly, air is a mess

295

all unto itself; one air current here, another blowing a whole different direction over there. Together they are creating a ring of chaos around me, each seeming to jerk my body one way than another in an endless circle of insanity. The whole time, I feel a sense of mental struggle. Beth's words from earlier flash into my mind, and instantly, I perfectly understand what she meant and what is going on now. For the first time, my Gifts are solely in control. Each is like a power-hungry, stubborn, aggressive dictator and now they are fighting for dominance.

It feels as if stress is building up in my chest, the tension growing, stretching my insides as it wriggles around, wringing my insides to try and relieve the nervousness. It only worsens the pressure. It is similar to having a panic attack and hyperventilating. I want to vomit as my stomach flips and twists, writhing in anxiety. I fall to my knees, clutching my entire upper body, breathing rapidly and shallowly.

Gifts are exploding or combining to create a mass weapon of destruction: fire and air collaborate to form a cyclone of fire. Its flames lash out and try to touch whatever is near enough to it and its burning fingers. It radiates heat in fiery, invisible waves, rippling through the air with the gusts of wind. How it hasn't destroyed the ceiling – or the entire house, for that matter – is too insignificant an issue at the moment for me to even pretend I care to contemplate it. What I do care about is the fact that it is consuming the last of my energy, and fast.

Even on the ground, on my knees, my head is light-headed and spinning. I am using all of my concentration to keep my eyes from rolling back into my head. The world is blurry and turning on its sides; as I grow weaker, I feel less heat whipping against my singed face and I more or less feel rather than see my deviant Gifts recede. I slump forward, gasping for breath; every inch of my body is depleted. I shake violently because even sitting here requires more energy than my body is willingly able to give. A heavy sweat breaks out on my forehead.

Off in the distance, I hear a slow but steady clapping and I remember that there is an audience. *Maybe he got hit by something at least*...I think with false hope. I raise my head to gaze at the scene that remains after the whirlwind I inadvertently sent through it. In the room with charred walls and floor, debris of various kinds scattered around everywhere, the evil man stands in the spot he hasn't moved from, seemingly unscathed. No singed features, no reddened or blackened face or arms. No cuts, no blood; nothing.

"I didn't realize when I brought you here tonight, I had also paid for a show," he smirks, raising his eyebrows humorously.

With no energy left, I just roll my eyes.

Alright Kira, we have to get up; it's time to get up, I think to myself, attempting to motivate myself...I don't think it is working too well. I am practically dead on the floor.

"I must say, that was really quite entertaining but come now; time to get up." Leave it to him to be sarcastic and demanding.

Don't listen to him. Stand up for yourself, I think calmly but the rest of my body isn't listening to me. It has obeyed my mind and that ended with my mind getting fried. It has its own will now.

"Maybe you just need a little *push*," he mutters sneeringly.

Suddenly, a pointed, very large, very hard object flies into my side and sends me hurtling in the direction of its propagation. With a painful cry, I land on my back and roll over to my side. I can feel a bruise forming and pain spreads through it.

"Get up," he commands with a growing fury as I remain hunched over on the floor. Again, he kicks me and sends me tumbling, but the only life I show is another painful cry.

"*Get up!*" he cries. With a heave, I am forced up with blinding speed and slammed against the wall. My insides cripple and shrivel inwards, trying to peel away from this extended position but his power is too strong. It could almost be nice; to be able to rest upon the wall, needing no energy to hold my arms and legs and head where they lay. It could *almost* be nice if it wasn't for the fact that the force holding me to the wall is applying too much pressure, as if it is beginning to squash me like a pancake.

"*That's better,*" he comments smugly.

Finally finding an inch of energy, I remark dryly, my voice cracking, "You can't stand not being the puppet master, can you?"

Maybe that was a mistake…

Suddenly the force tightens, squeezing me like a hand would. It is as if a thousand-pound weight has abruptly fallen on top of me. It takes the effort of my entire body to breathe. Even then, it isn't enough; I can feel my face turning purple. My heart is hyperventilating, my brain is panicking. Nerve endings keep screaming, "I need oxygen! I need oxygen! I need -"

I can feel it slipping away – no, not my life – the tight, invisible force that is threatening my life. Now it is gone altogether, and I drop to the floor like dead weight, nothing but a bag of bones, coughing.

"You-! Sick-! Mean-!" I splutter in between gasps of air and lung-severing coughs.

"Uh, uh, uh," he tsks, wagging a finger at me, "don't you remember what happened last time?"

"I. Am. Not. *Afraid*. Of you," I state firmly with the most conviction I've used all night. The rush of oxygen flowing – gushing back through me is giving me a (majorly watered-down) adrenaline burst, fueling me just enough to stand. Well, I don't think I'd actually call it standing; it's more so a shaky, hunched over, unsteady slouch.

"Ah, so you finally found your feet. Good -"

For the first time, I witness a new look on his face. Confusion and concentration. He is staring off into space and he keeps tilting his head as if he is attempting to hear something far off. *I know that look...Wait,* where *do I know that look from..?* That's the look of being Minded.

Suddenly, it is as if a bomb has exploded, spewing molten anger. Its shockwave reverberates and ripples out with a fierce speed, violently knocking into me. Once again girl meets wall rather rapidly and painfully. I hear something snap, but I shakily and hesitantly stand again, limping around him to move as far away from him and his fury, as possible. I reach the opposite side of the room where the door still lies shattered, before he snaps out of his reverie. He whirls around with blinding speed, his eyes darting directly to me. His piercing glare fills me with the burning desire to want to run, to hide, *to cower*. As much fear as it causes me, I still stand firm but I can't stop my eyes from betraying my fear.

His eyes narrow and are cemented with the look of insanity; the veins in his neck bulge and seem to pulse. He is stiff; the muscles on his bare arms are clenched tightly. It seems as if it is requiring all his strength to not "destroy the world."

"I thought you were alone!" he screams and it is as if he has gone mad. "Oh! You're very sly, I'll admit that! Thought you could fool me didn't you?" He is trembling, shaking; he is so angry that he probably can't even see straight right now. The ground is rocking, tumbling, rolling, *vibrating*. The walls shake and pieces of the ceiling crumble and fall. The room is unstable; *he* is unstable.

What's he talking about?

My voice quivers and necessitates effort as my throat closes the first time I try to speak, "I -"

"Shut up!" he roars and loses another piece of his control as raging winds erupt in the room.

Powerful and unpredictable, seeming to rip apart the open air, they fill the room, creating a ring of demolition around him. They come after me, brutally pushing me, and then viciously pulling me another way. It is similar to one of those sick games the jerk-jocks play on the nerdy-dorky kids in which the jocks get in a circle and throw a person around in an eighties movie or superhero movie. It isn't a pleasant feeling.

Finally they stop and I stumble into the wall a few times before I regain my balance.

"You sneaky little brat! You know I could have just killed you all! It would have been easier and much simpler!" he yells.

Without thinking, I speak, "You couldn't have killed all of us! Not alone! It would consume all of your energy to the point you would d-!" Well I guess I should be glad I even get this far before he interrupts me.

"Shut up, you ignorant idiot! Have you not already seen that my power doesn't fit your petty rules? When your stupid friends arrive here in five minutes, I'll have no problem killing all of you and never breaking a sweat," he says, reveling in his arrogance.

Mom and Dad wouldn't come back would they? I wonder, a different kind of fear freezing my mind. *No, he would have said my family then...*

"Wha–what are you talking about -?" I ask, hesitantly.

"Don't act like you don't know! You all planned it. You would come here indeed, distract me for a while and later they would swoop in and 'as a team' – aw," he rolls his eyes, "you would kill me!"

"I have no idea what you're talking about!" I shout unevenly. My mind is racing. I hate being yelled at – how it causes people to sound so mean and angry and violent – towards me.

"Shut up! SHUT UP!" He is psychopathic, as if in a second he will begin shouting at no one in particular – to himself even. He is losing a hold of reality, morphing into some kind of inhumanly demon. Similar to when my Gifts were fighting for dominance, his are set loose. Vines spring from the ground, looking for something to squeeze, grabbing at my wrists and legs. I try to fight them off as fires rupture around me, burning the shattered room, filling it with smoke. I begin coughing, frantically trying to rid myself of all the vines so I can move on to extinguishing the fire. The wind picks up again, swooping around me, creating a vortex. It cycles 'round and around, sucking out any of the remaining air. I splutter and desperately attempt to breathe but there is nothing.

Suddenly it all disappears. I bend over, taking large, deep breaths, when a thick cloud starts to form around me. I can only see gray as the hairs on my arms and neck rise. *Oh no...*

A shock of lightning zaps my arm and instantly a burn-blister forms as the pain sears through my arm. Another shock burns through my jeans to my leg, and eventually all my limbs are shocked. It singes a hole in my shirt, leaving blisters on my stomach and some on my back.

The pain is agonizing, unbearable. It feels as if I am on fire – which, in a sense, I am. Each time a new zap hits me, I cry out, stumbling away from the direction it has come, but as long as I stand in the cloud, it can keep electrocuting me. I try running in a direction, but all there is is gray, until I hit a wall and turn a different direction. But all there is is gray. And a shock. Stumble. Shock. Stumble. Shock, shock.

My mind is fuzzy, clouded, and gray itself. All it can process is, *"Run! This way! Now try this way! Get out! Get out! Get out!"* Until I can't anymore; until my body is physically and mentally too beaten down, and I fall to my knees. The moment I give up, the thick fog reseeds; the tiny shocks lessen to the point that they are just little zaps of static electricity and then nothing. I see him now through my teary, blurred eyes, laughing like a mad man in the *same* position and looking ill at ease.

"It's over Kira. In one minute both you and your 'cute' little Gifted friends will die! It's all over and soon the rest of the Gifted will be gone," He continues laughing menacingly, nothing sane left in him.

No. No, they can't be coming. It can't be them!

"No!"

I do something incredibly stupid in the condition I am currently in, something Zac would be very proud of. I shoot up, now standing. If I am going to die – if this is really it, *they* won't. I haven't known them long, and I don't even know them that well,

303

but I cannot let them die. I cannot be responsible for their deaths, and they don't deserve to die.

It is that final moment. I have been climbing a long, endless staircase and now I have reached the final step. It is that last burst of energy you will give even though you're already tired because you know as soon as you give it, you will be finished, free. The work will be over, and you can lie down and rest for eternity.

Everything; every single piece of energy left in me, I structure it into an orb of power that is both organized yet chaotic, both controlled and frenzied. My mark's light explodes with a sudden light and shows brighter than it did when I was Gifted, as the glowing orb leaves me and zooms towards him. Either he isn't expecting it, or believes it will be too weak to install any damage, so he lets it hit him. However, he miscalculated in his thinking.

Math always made sense to me – especially algebra, so I understand perfectly how if you leave out a step, a number, a decimal, your entire answer comes out wrong. He has forgotten that, at times, I can be just as powerful as him. He has forgotten that I am no longer fighting for my life but others'. I threw that energy in desperation, a last resort – a last request. His error seems to have cost him dearly this time.

My Gifts are vicious, merciless towards him like he was to me, yet they won't kill him. He doesn't stand by helplessly for long; he lashes out at them, defending himself. My Gifts are united this time. Their little outburst earlier seems to have rid them of their rebellion and they are now working together harmoniously.

He defends himself well enough, but he can't gain enough leverage to take the offensive.

Meanwhile, I am dealing with my own struggle, the struggle to stand, to keep my eyes open and awake, the struggle to keep breathing. My eyes will roll and start to drift closed as I snap them open. My legs begin to sway. My ears start to ring. My sight is fuzzy. Little dots cloud them until the dots grow into blotches, and finally I am left with a tiny window-hole of sight. My head lolls forward. I hear something off – something that doesn't belong with the scene at hand…*Footsteps*?

I slowly turn my head to look over my shoulder, rather lethargically. Pounding; *thump, thump, thump.* A faded," Kira!" It is probably much louder in reality, but faded to my ears that are shutting down. My head swivels back around, as if a chain was holding it in that position but released it, letting the wrecking ball swing. My knees buckle then bend, my legs waver then fall, and my eyes droop then close. As I fall to the ground I crash into something, something hard but soothing. *Something with arms*, arms that wrap around me as my head lies on what I guess could be a shoulder and chest.

Just above a whisper I hear a soft, careful, gentle…male voice mutter, "I've gotcha."

He slides us to the floor, keeping me securely in his embrace.

"Come on, Kira," he pleads urgently, "hold on, Kira, *hold on*."

My eyes barely slide open to decipher a blurred, indefinite picture of clear, beautiful blue eyes. *I really need to stop giving that boy reasons to catch me.*

My head falls in surrender. My breathing slows. My eyes close again.

If I was looking down on this scene – maybe from Zac's point of view – I would see the light of my mark start to fade before the world goes silent.

Chapter 22

Peaceful serenity. *Dark emptiness.* Silent tranquility. *Burning pain, screaming.* Beautiful. Rest.

As I flirt with consciousness and what lies beyond the deepest dreams, I don't think. I don't speak. I don't dream. *Feel;* I can only *feel* the change, the shift between the two worlds, the two dimensions. In one I find myself consumed with pain, blazing, writhing as it feels as if white hot knives are cutting my skin, stabbing my flesh, piercing my body. Everything is screaming.

"Please stop! Please stop! Please!"

I scream, though if I form coherent words while doing so, I don't know. My head is on fire, as if it has been fried to the core. It feels as if someone strong is wringing it like a wet cloth, squeezing it like molding clay, twisting and stretching my brain. It makes me want to claw out my hair and scratch out my brain – anything to make it go away. All there is to do is sit through it, hoping that this won't last forever.

This is normally when I'll sink back into the other state – into sleep – and fall back into bliss. In this state, it is cool; the air around me is cool. My skin is cool. My mind is soaked in a tub of cool water that extinguishes my mind's screaming flames and heals it. It feels like being immersed in a cool, spring pool; one of those that, hundreds of years ago, people believed to be sacred: a pool designed by God for healing. One that would mend your wounds, un-wind your mind, and fill you with an absolute sense of peace. I have to say I prefer this world much more.

But I never stay here for long, always having to return to the horror and torture of the other. I don't know how long each period lasts or how much time passes in reality. There is only my routine, my going back and forth between what seems Heaven and Hell. It is simple. Unfortunately, the times of pain seem to be getting increasingly longer but with reduced pain; I feel the place of stillness slipping away. Until, one time – the last time I visit the pool, I find a guest waiting for me.

She is here, just standing there. She seems familiar. I have a feeling of déjà vu but my mind can't place why. She smiles warmly, the laugh lines near her eyes creasing. She isn't that old, but she isn't young either. Her shoulders are relaxed. Her arms hang freely at her sides, untroubled. She in herself seems peaceful, so peaceful, in fact, that ever so slightly the soreness in my own shoulders recedes, the kinks in my neck diminish, and my body becomes less tight with stress – as if her peacefulness radiates to me. She speaks, and her voice is like honey, warm and sweet and easily drifts to me but is thick with compassion.

"Kira."

I gaze at her curiously, a smile creeping onto my face. How does she know my name? *Well Kira, you feel like you've seen her before so you probably have and she seems to have at least remembered you,* I think to myself sarcastically. She continues to stare at me, smiling serenely, and it is one of those smiles that you can't help smiling back. *How strange...we're just standing here staring at each other, smiling; me and some lady that seems familiar yet I have no idea why...*

"Do you know who I am?" she asks, almost musically.

Well at least I know she can't read my mind, otherwise she would have already known the answer to that.

"No," I reply, not meaning it to sound rough, but next to her voice, how could anyone's voice not sound a little rough? "But," I add hesitantly, "I feel like I do."

She grins at me, flashing perfect, white, straight teeth.

"That's okay. Trust me; it has nothing to do with you. My name is Artemis; I am the oldest living Gifted – or Scorned. When you were in sixth grade, I used my former name and became your literature teacher: Ms. Morgan."

I open my mouth to say that: no, my sixth grade literature teacher was Mrs. Blakely, but suddenly an unclear puzzle starts to form in my mind. My sixth grade classroom; everything looks the same as all my other memories of it. The desks, the boards, the two TVs, the posters. Everything is identical; only in this new image, instead of Mrs. Blakely sitting at her desk, there is another woman. The woman standing across from me now. She is talking with us; we are all laughing at something.

More of these memories start to form, details coming with them. I can see the scene, hear what is going on, and distantly remember being there, first-hand, years ago. Layer upon layer they stack up, one scene on top of another until I have nearly two weeks' worth and can remember each clearly. Yet I still perfectly

309

remember Mrs. Blakely's class. *How is it possible to live two lives at once?* I begin to feel anxious. Which memory is real? Which one is the truth and which is just a lie made up to fill the gap of time? *How is it possible?*

"How did you get the class to remember you consistently? Nikki said after normal humans come into contact with us, they forget us."

"That's true. It wasn't easy," she – Artemis is still looking at me but it doesn't seem like she is *really* looking at me. "Actually, it didn't really work. I tried for two weeks. I went the first day and you all remembered me well enough, but then I left and came back the second day and had to convince the administrators to stop panicking because they did have a sixth grade literature teacher – me. All the students and teachers had to re-meet me like the first day hadn't even existed. I still have no idea what the Gift created for each of those beginning days, what you guys thought had happened.

"It worked like that for about a week and a half. Luckily you all still remembered the information I taught so we didn't have to constantly re-learn that. It seemed that after being subjected to the same Gifted person, day after day, the exact same routine, eventually, you all really began to *know* me. By the second week of school, we were functioning like a normal classroom, and I thought it would work." Her eyes twinkle joyously, reminiscing in her achievement, but she begins to frown. "But then the weekend came again and that daily routine with me was gone. And with it went the memories."

"So that's why we all received replacement memories of that year?" My eyebrows furrow with curiosity.

Artemis nods, "The memories only stayed because you had a daily routine of seeing me; once that week ended, you all no longer saw me and were not reminded of me. You didn't see me anymore. You didn't talk to me, and you couldn't have. Once we got back that Monday, and I saw everything was once again forgotten, I left."

"Why? I mean, why did you go through the trouble of trying to get through to us even though you knew we wouldn't remember?"

"Well," she acquires an amused look on her face, "I'm sure Nikki and Trey told you they've been watching you since you were born. That year they thought the Scorned might try to reach you at school and they needed someone to watch over you. Teaching was the most plausible option seeing as I could be close to you and the Scorned would always be aware of my presence there. It shortly became clear that the Scorned wouldn't strike the school and so they said I could leave..."

"What made you want to do it? Why you?"

"All the other convenient Gifted adults were needed to teach the Gifted students, and all the ones not teaching couldn't be contacted as easily...When I was a little girl – before I knew about the Gifted, when the supernatural were a myth and fairytales were simply that: *tales* – I had always thought I'd be a teacher. So if I helped Trey and Nikki out, for a time…I could be."

"Why don't you teach the Gifted?"

"I guess I could've…" At first she trails off but she continues uneasily, "maybe after I first left the Gifted schooling, but at that time I wanted to do nothing but travel. Go see Europe and the West Coast and Australia. When I returned, I heard how my parents had died while I had been gone. After that I didn't really want to be around people so I withdrew to living alone in a rural area, some place abandoned. Now Nikki's there and she *should* be there; you guys need her."

"So you have a Gifted mind…?"

"It's the only way I could be talking to you right now," she smiles.

"Wait, so…we're in my head right now?" I ask, looking around as if expecting to see my brain but all there is is open space.

"Where did you think we were? Canada?" she asks giggling.

Not exactly…

"So what are you doing here anyways?"

"I just wanted to talk to you; see what was going on in here. Looks like you're doing well, healing pretty well…You plan on coming back anytime soon? Not that I'm trying to rush you! If you're not ready, you're not ready, but you seem to be worrying some very nice people," she smiles at me hopefully.

"Coming back?"

"To the world, to the Gifted, to reality…They need you…They *miss* you," her smile darkens slightly.

"How long have I been gone?"

"A couple days…four maybe."

"What?" I have been in and out of the two dimensions for four days! To them, I have been asleep, possibly in a coma. To the Gifted, for those four days, I have seemed unresponsive, unchanging, stoic…*Four days…*

"Yes," Artemis casts her gaze lower, "they were getting a little worried…That's why I thought I'd pop in here for a moment to see if you planned on ever coming back." She looks at me.

I realize exactly what she is implying – what she is really doing here.

"You mean I have a choice?"

She sighs, "Yes – it's only fair you know. You can choose to stay here," and she gestures around her. "There will be no more pain, you'll move on and find whatever life comes next. Or, you can come back. You'll heal, and I can't promise the pain will end there but you'll be alive in its ups and downs; you'll live," Artemis watches me hopefully, waiting for an answer maybe.

You think the choice is easy: life. But there is so much pain in it, and the option for no more pain or loss or grief is overwhelmingly optimistic. The burning torment would go away; the grief from the loss of my parents would fade. The stress of evil, creepy guy would disappear. I would be left with peace in God's kingdom (well, I hope I'd move on to God's kingdom…). I want to tell her so badly, "Of course I'll come back," but suddenly those words are becoming increasingly harder to say.

"Do I have to decide now?" I ask, conflicted.

"No," she sighs as if she was hoping I'd give her a positive answer but wasn't expecting it. "Take your time. Just know you won't have forever; your body can only remain in the in-between for so long."

"I won't take long. I just…need to think," I answer anxiously.

"I understand."

I nod absently. My mind is whirling, making a decision then questioning it.

"Do you -" I start to ask but as I look up, I realize she is gone. It leaves me more uneasy. What was once a replenishing, peaceful haven is now uncomfortable and intimidating. I am unsure of everything and that helps me in no way to make a decision. I don't know what miserable agony awaits me if I return, or if there will be joy and liveliness. I don't know whether the pattern of nightly crying will continue for years or the brokenness will start to mend. I don't know what would happen should I move on. I don't know which outcome I'd like better, which one I would regret less.

The atmosphere around me begins to disappear; the world begins to fade. I am left in dark emptiness. Just me. Alone. I open my eyes wider as if trying to see a light – *a sign*. I breathe a little deeper as if I could take strength from a fresh breeze. But it is only me.

As a little girl, I was afraid of the dark. The older I became, the less I started to fear it to the point that I sometimes preferred it. Now the dark is frightening and I am scared again. The uncertainty, the neutrality. Nothing to persuade me. Nothing to help me. Nothing. I fall to the ground – or what would be the ground – like a child, and I hug my knees. Why does life have to be so complicated? Why is it filled with such hard choices and weakening trials?

Suddenly it all changes. The blackness is here but one tiny orb of light appears in front of me, less than a foot away from me. It is the color of the sun; bright, yellow, shining a light in the darkness. It floats around like a butterfly in the wind, drifting here then there. It swirls around me then rises and moves a little farther away from me – like it wants me to follow…or I just have the cheesy desire to follow it.

As I rise to my feet, another light joins me. This one is a light baby blue, and it dances around my head playfully before going to meet the other light. They begin to move forward and I follow, dazed. We move to nowhere in particular – straight, I guess. Two more orbs fly in from nowhere on each side of me.

On my left is a beautiful sea green orb that smells of salt water, its light seeming to roll in waves inside it. It moves gracefully, seeming to float in space. On my other side is a warm brown orb that doesn't produce much light but is comforting in other ways. The two begin to circle me and one will race forward to catch up with the others but then drifts back. The other will then dart forward before slowly gliding back into rhythm with the one that had remained behind. They are dancing.

Like this, the five of us move forward, a random direction in the dark. Gently and gradually, their lights grow brighter, bigger, until they are vast moons of mixing shades. Blending, shifting, merging; one ends where another begins in a rainbow of yellow, blue, green, and brown. Yet their light never shines on anything; it simply lights the darkness. The light grows to a climax. The four orbs collide into one, ultraviolet, white light that cascades out deep into the darkness, illuminating the dark, shining through it; until this world is consumed by it. From black to white, dark to light. Everywhere.

        *   *   *   *   *   *   *

Chapter 23

I am sitting in a chair next to Kira's prone body. Nikki and Trey stand in the corner whispering what are probably formalities. Lily sits in the chair opposite me, gripping Kira's hand. Zac walks back through the door after leaving to take a nap just ten minutes ago...Guess he couldn't sleep...

He walks over and begins to whisper in the corner with the other two. I really don't understand why they think they have to whisper; the only other ones in the room are Lily and I. Really? Why is there a need for secrecy?

We've been doing this for three and a half days and nothing has changed. Not when we tried using Lily's – and about six other people's – healing Gift, not when we were able to get our hands on a human ventilator and heart monitor and hooked Kira up to it. Nothing changes, for better or worse. I know there is more to it; something is happening deep within Kira's mind.

I want Kira to wake up; we all want her to open her eyes. We only got her less than one week ago and somehow we have managed to lose her. Well, we have managed to put her in a situation in which we may very well lose her. With Trey's ever darkening brow and the deepening circles under Nikki's tired, sad eyes, I'd say that that outcome is becoming more and more regrettably real.

Lily will be heartbroken, *I think, almost comically,* almost. *It isn't the girl's fault; she has such a big heart that seems to have room to hold everyone.* Poor girl...*She cried days ago and she is out of tears by now. Only the smeared ghost tracks of her tears remain.* Would they rush back if Kira – if we - …

And so the hours – days – pass as we wait, as our own minds ramble on, trying to cope with the situation, trying to reassure ourselves that there is still hope, trying to just pass the time. Simply trying to get through this state of limbo.

Maybe this is why Kasten never saw her…because she would only be here for a short time – a glimpse…*My thoughts begin to descend into less hopeful ones, ones that have accepted a darker future that hasn't even occurred yet but my thoughts are attempting to provide answers anyways. That is, until earlier today when my mind simply wouldn't take it any longer, and I lost it as I turned from my position next to Trey to rapidly – and painfully – slam my fist into the window sill.*

"What's wrong with her?" I yell. "We've healed all and any physical injuries. We've fixed her bones, her organs, her strength. We fixed her! So why hasn't she recovered? Why won't she wake up?" I shouted to no one really; a face, then a different one, then the wall, and a table.

From the same seat she sits in now, Lily just shrugged and sighed heavily, a cloud descending over her as she admitted what she couldn't even tell herself, "We did all we could. We fixed her physically. We don't have any control, however, over her mind. We all know what a critical time it is when you're first Gifted. You've practically lost everything. How can we expect Kira to see past all the pain and hurt she feels right now emotionally? How can we ask

318

her to come back, and tell her one day she'll be okay when we can't even promise ourselves that half the time?"

I had never seen Lily so hopeless before, her eyes so empty, her voice so dull and unlively. Lily is our heart and soul. If she lost hope, we'd all be done for. I couldn't lose that yet; I wasn't ready to.

"Kira knows we're here for her. She knows she can trust us and we'll get her through this," I spoke, as if trying to convince myself – and doing a pretty good job of it.

"Give me a break Jamie! She barely knows us. She's spent two days with us; two days! As people she's known two days, we can't expect to just replace people she's known every day of her life," Lily said, her temper rising for the first time ever.

"I can't believe you're just giving up on her!" I shouted while stepping closer to her.

"It's been three days, Jamie!" Lily jumped from her seat. "You said it yourself; we've fixed her!" she yelled, stepping closer. "We fixed her days ago and she hasn't woken up yet!"

"And you -!"

I was interrupted by an irate looking Zac, blocking me.

"Hey man! Back off. None of us want her to die, but we can't afford to ignore the fact that she may not come back. I don't like it anymore then you do. I'm the one who had to carry her in here for Christ's sake. I'm the one who had to watch as her mark faded to the point that it was hardly illuminated at all. So don't tell

me that she's just fine. *Her collapsing into me, limp, isn't* fine. *The fact that her mark still hasn't brightened means she's* not *fine!"*

The tension in the two inches between us was thick and practically tangible, and the air bristled with hot strain.

"Alright, all of you, calm down," Nikki said patiently, stepping between Zac and I and expanding the distance between us by the length of her arms. "We're all just worried about Kira so there's no need for there to be fighting."

Lily looked up at me from behind Zac apologetically and Zac's face relaxed and he backed away. We all reverted to our positions as if nothing had occurred, but everyone seemed to avoid everyone else and so it has been quiet the rest of the day.

The steady rhythmic "beep...beep...beep...beep..." of Kira's heart monitor creates an eerie silence. Lily is currently drawing imaginary characters on Kira's hand while Zac has sunk into a chair in the far corner of the infirmary. He sighs and sets his head in his hands. Trey puts a comforting arm around Nikki and pulls her closer to him. I sit here, slumped against the back of my chair quietly. We are all here for Kira, but strangely no one is looking at her. Trey and Nikki are occupied in each other, Lily is blankly staring at Kira's hand while tracing invisible images, Zac probably has his eyes closed, and I am watching everyone else.

This doesn't prevent any of us from noticing when the atmosphere changes and along with it – for the first time – Kira. Her mark crescendos brightly – a good sign – except her monitor goes flat.

Beeeeeeeee....*It is unending, loud, and annoying but I block it out after its initial warning.*

Surprisingly, Zac is the first to move, practically knocking over his chair as he flies from it. He rushes over to Lily's side, "Kira!"

Simultaneously, Nikki and Trey rush around Zac, coming to stand beside me. I experience a built-up apprehension that has me standing abruptly and a death grip on Kira's hand. Zac and Lily have a joint hold on her other hand. Kira's mark continues to glow as the monitor continues to generate that flat, solid, "Beeeee...."

"What's going on?" Lily cries, standing and leaning into her twin.

No one answers her – unless you count Nikki's and Trey's pale, ghostly faces an answer.

"I don't understand," I say exasperatedly, "the mark is glowing like she's coming back but the monitor says - ...and she's not waking up!" I look at Nikki and Trey helplessly.

"Isn't there something we can do?" Zac asks Trey and Nikki desperately. "In all those chick doctor shows, at this point in a patient's treatment, don't they do that shock thing to start the patient's heart again? I can do that! It could work. Maybe that's all she needs..." he rambles frantically.

I have known Zac about two years, and in that time, there has only been one person he has ever acted this upset over and she is standing right next to him, his own DNA.

321

"Zac!" Nikki finally interrupts him, mid-ramble. She looks scared and on the verge of crying. "There's nothing we can do. We've fixed all we can. If she doesn't want to wake up...there's nothing we can do to make her." Tears run from her eyes.

Zac's mouth shuts defeated and his posture slackens. Guys never do like just "waiting around."

"Come on Kira," Lily whispers encouragingly. "Open your eyes," water seems to be building in her eyes. She turns her head into Zac's shoulder and he sets his free arm tightly around her as she silently cries into him.

Everyone stands around anxiously, on edge and rigid. The girls both have tears coming steady and Trey is nonchalantly scratching his eye as if he is hiding his own. I can only imagine the worry and panic that has to be painted on my face. In Lily's place, I mumble, almost inaudibly, "Open your eyes, Kira. We're all here. Just open your eyes."

And still no response.

Chapter 24

The blinding light fades, replacing it is a rather irritating "beeeeee…eep…beep… beep…beep…" I begin to lose that free-spiritedness from the pool. I feel tired and groggy. As the intense light clears, a completely opposite scene appears. Faces. Blurry ones I don't recognize. Ones that seem to be crying. Oh my God! Have I died and am looking down from above? No, that ache in my head isn't an effect of the Afterlife; it is unfortunately real. I blink a couple of times, chasing away the sleep that glued my eyes closed. The faces become bolder; the images I see become readable and understandable. I am awake.

Jamie. Nikki. Trey. Lily. Zac. They are all here; surprise, disbelief, and tears. The air around them seems fragile.

Almost inaudibly, Lily murmurs, "Kira?" so quietly – so frightened as if she will kill me by only whispering. Her voice is so small, like a child's.

When I try to speak, my voice only croaks; I try again, and it does the same.

"Do you want some water?" Jamie asks just as unsteadily. When I hear his voice, it is almost unfamiliar or at least not his.

I nod as he walks over to the table on the far side of the room and pours me a glass of water from the pitcher. I peek at my surroundings. This is probably one of the infirmary rooms on the first floor of the mansion. It has neutral wall paper and tile flooring. I am on one of those fancy hospital beds that recline to the position you like the best, and this time I am hooked up to some sort of monitors – nothing too scary though. There is a window on my right – behind Zac and Lily – that seems to look out over the field. It is hard to tell for sure from where I'm at, but I believe I can barely see the rocky cliffs.

Jamie brings the water back and it is indescribable how fluid and amazing it feels on my dry throat. After I down the entire glass, I try speaking again, "Funny…didn't we just do this not too long ago? I swear, I have not lost consciousness as many times in my entire life as I have around you people in two days," I smile jokingly, trying to diffuse the tension.

"Well excuse us if it's our fault you decided to run off to the Scorned like a mad woman and then proceed to nearly get yourself killed," Jamie mutters sarcastically, smiling if only slightly.

I swallow guiltily, looking down, "Are you all mad at me? I wouldn't blame you."

"We know they had your parents – don't worry, they're safe," Lily speaks slowly. "It's just – we thought, maybe you switched sides. We didn't know what was going on inside that head of yours or where exactly you were going when you drove off."

"Nice methods by the way. It took us a whole twenty minutes to beat those defenses down," Jamie looks sort of impressed.

"Yeah, and that's when we called Nikki and talked to her to see what was really going on," Lily stops and gazes at Nikki, signaling for her to continue.

"Most things had calmed down here by then. Trey had just had a vision of your parents as hostages, and then he saw you there at the Scorned mansion."

"So how did all of you get to the mansion so fast? You guys didn't even have a car," I say looking at Jamie, Zac, and Lily.

For the first time, Zac speaks, sounding comical, "Ha – well – you see, after you stole our car…we kind of – might of – stole the gas station employee's car."

I laugh, shaking my head.

"We met them at the Scorned's mansion," Nikki adds, smirking, "with a car that actually belongs to us."

"Well what else were we supposed to do?" Zac mumbles rhetorically.

"Kira…" Nikki starts, but she drops off.

"What?" I ask nervously.

She hesitates but continues, "What happened in that basement? How did you end up so depleted? Your Gift was almost completely exerted. The room was completely destroyed, and your family got out, but who were you fighting?"

"You guys didn't find him? He didn't attack you?" I ask, my eyes widening.

"Him who?" Jamie asks, looking perplexed.

The five of them look around at each other confused, almost as if they believe I have gone crazy.

"What man? There was only you in the basement Kira," Trey states hesitantly.

"Did you search the downstairs? All the doors?" I ask bewildered. Something doesn't feel right.

"Yes," Nikki answers inquisitively, "Zac stayed with you and the rest of us split up to check the entire basement. You were the only one there. We knocked out a couple of Scorned on our way in, but there were hardly any people there since most had come here to fight. Besides the fact that you were on the edge of death, we couldn't find anything that was a threat."

"Impossible! The only way for him to have escaped was the way you guys came down. He would have had to resort to hiding somewhere when you arrived, but then you would have caught him-" I stop when I realize I had started to ramble.

"Kira, who is this guy you keep talking about? It wasn't Bret. He was still unconscious, detained by Nick and his sister," Lily stares intently at me.

"It wasn't Bret; I'd never seen this man before."

"Did you catch a name?" Trey asks curiously.

"No," I answer, mentally hitting myself on the head for being so stupid. "He is darker, though, than the other Scorned, more demented. He can do things you guys never mentioned were possible, things no one else but him can do. He was arrogant and rude and narcissistic."

I watch them, waiting to hear: "Oh! Him! Yeah-" or "That's who you're talking about! I know what you mean-" They only look confused, blank, or concerned.

"Was he older or your age?" Nikki asks.

"Older, but he wasn't that old."

"And he seemed like he was in charge?" Nikki asks, her eyebrows furrowing, perplexed.

"Yeah, in fact, he acted like he was the leader of the entire free-world," I mutter sarcastically, rolling my eyes. It was meant to be a joke, but now I realize they have no idea how true my comment is – or any clue as to who the man I am talking about is. "You guys really don't know who I could be talking about?" I ask nervously.

"Not at all," Nikki shakes her head, "but Trey and I will do some research; see if we can find something out," she looks at him (I'm thinking that statement was more for his benefit than mine). She turns back to me and smiles, "All you need to do is get some sleep so hopefully by tomorrow you'll be completely recovered."

"Was nothing injured too badly then if it'll only take a day to finish healing?" I ask, relieved that nothing is permanently wrong with me – or so it seems.

"Well technically, you've been healing for the past four days -" Nikki starts.

Jamie interrupts her humorously, "No, you were pretty screwed up, but thanks to the entire Gifted healing class, they patched you up pretty well." He even winks at Lily after smiling at me.

"Thanks Lily," I smile gratefully at her.

She returns the smile and then says jokingly, smiling ruefully at her twin, "It's not like I really had a choice anyways. Zac here was a complete mess when we found you; he practically begged me to do something."

"Ok, alright, whatever; you can shut up now," he shoves Lily's shoulder playfully, and I swear I see him blushing.

"Aw, would you look at that? Zachy's just a wittle embarrassed," Lily says teasingly, as if she is talking to a baby.

"I am not," he says confidently – rather than defensively, rolling his eyes as he shoves his hands in his pockets. I think the entire exchange is hilarious and am warily trying to abate the laughing so the pain won't return. Within minutes, the tense atmosphere has evaporated, replaced by laughter and happiness and "sunshine"…What? Too cliché? But seriously, the mood has lightened dramatically. No one seems weighed down or upset any longer; there are no clouded expressions. For one instant, if just this once, I can see where this could eventually be "normal." I can see similar conversations to this with Lily tapping Zac's nose because she knows it'll annoy him and Zac tickling her sides knowing that it will irritate her; all the while everyone laughs. The words are incoherent; they don't matter. It doesn't matter what is said in these situations, but the feelings expressed. These moments

328

don't last forever though; otherwise, they wouldn't be special and this wouldn't be life. And *this* moment has run its course.

Nikki takes deep breaths to calm her laughter and says, "Well alright then." Smiling, she continues, "Now that all is well. I think I'm going to go get something to eat and take a nap…" She turns to Trey and raises an eyebrow.

He stares at her for a minute as if saying, "What the heck do you want" before recognition flashes across his face and he smiles. "I do believe that is my queue. I'll come with," he says, offering his arm.

"See you later, maybe?" I ask, trying to cover my hope.

"I'll bring you up dinner in two and a half hours," she smiles.

Jamie, Zac, Lily, and I echo in a chorus of good byes. Trey and Nikki sweetly and shortly yell as they head out the door, "Bye children!"

And so there were four…We all smile awkwardly. Something seems different; it isn't too bad but there is a noticeable discomfort.

"So…do you need anything?" Jamie asks, drawn out.

"I'm ok," I answer, rather absentmindedly, "I can wait to eat until dinner."

Oddly, Jamie glances at Zac then and they stare intently at one another a few seconds. It isn't a heated glare but it isn't a happy one either. It only lasts a minute and Jamie nods minutely as if an unseen conversation has taken place. Almost immediately after which, Jamie turns to Lily, faintly smiles, and winks at her. I look at all three of them like they are crazy, knowing something weird is happening or about to happen. My eyes flash between them until Jamie looks back at me, raising an eyebrow while breaking into a grin as if saying, "Are you going to ask? Do you really want to know?" I roll my eyes and shrug.

"Well," Jamie interjects way too enthusiastically, "I have to go…check on Liv."

"I'll go with you," Lily says.

"Wait! What happened to Liv?" I ask worriedly.

"She'll be okay. She got pretty banged up in the fight though," Lily replies, not too concerned.

"Oh. Ok," I say dejectedly, "I guess I'll talk to you guys later."

"Of course."

"Definitely."

And then, I believe, there were two.

"So do you have to leave now too?" I ask regretfully, not really wanting to be completely alone.

"No," Zac says nonchalantly, making his way to sit in the chair next to me.

I chew my lip anxiously, trying to work up the courage to ask what I want to. In the end, courage loses and I admit something I have been holding inside that needs to fly out.

"There was a little boy," I say, eyes already beginning to water. "I mean, they had a boy with them – my parents, at the

Scorned mansion and back at Wal-Mart. I didn't notice him at first in the mansion. He had been hiding behind my dad, but I saw him when I was helping them escape."

"You didn't have a brother before, did you?" he asks, but it sounds more like a statement.

I shake my head. I smile faintly, "He is really cute too. He is only about five; he has beautiful, curly blonde hair and crystal blue eyes – like the color of sapphires. He is such a beautiful little boy," I remark absentmindedly.

"I can't believe the Gift created a human being in the Covery," Zac marvels disbelievingly.

"Covery?"

"The cover-memory. The life the Gift creates when we're Gifted. Most of the time, it just recreates memories…That's incredible!"

I smile faintly, "I have a little brother…How-how is it possible? How could that entire six year process be created in an instant?" The complexity of the whole thing mystifies me. My mind races the same track over and over again, coming to the same finish, the same wall, the same problem. It can't be possible. My head feels as if it is going to explode from reeling too much, for trying too hard to compute an answer that just isn't there.

He shrugs, "I don't know. I can't even begin to try and figure out how the Gift works…"

Zac seems to dismiss the subject, but I can't let it go. I have a brother. An adorable, little brother! One that will never know me, will never know how much I already love him… Depressing, isn't it? In case you haven't figured out, apparently I subconsciously show everything I feel when I don't consciously control it.

"Hey," Zac says sympathetically, as if he knows what I am thinking. Surprising the both of us, he reaches up to gently touch my face. "That little boy – I'm positive – will be so loved, and he is so lucky to have such an amazing, loving sister like you – even if he doesn't know it."

I do believe tears are forming in my eyes as my lips fight between smiling and frowning. "Are we? I mean, are we really family? Can we be? To them, I don't exist, and to me – according to the life I had and the memories I have – *he* doesn't-shouldn't – exist. I just…I'm so confused!" I admit, crying.

"Kira," he breathes softly, "I don't have nearly as many answers as you would like me to have – or any for that matter," my mouth twitches with the beginnings of a smile, "I don't know how Coveries work. I don't know what any of us are in relationship to our families. But Kira, you have to stop thinking about it," he states, dismayed. "You can't keep trying to guess or to figure it out. You'll go crazy. All you can do is go by what your new little brother is to you. All that matters when you don't have all these answers, the only thing you have to go by, is how you feel about it. Otherwise, no one can tell you they're not your family anymore just because they don't know you. No one can say you can't love that boy any less because he's from a completely different time period-a completely different memory – than you, just because –

technically – he probably shouldn't exist. All you can do is love that little boy like I'm sure you already do and know that he would love you just like your other sister."

Zac looks so honest in this moment, so frazzled – almost upset – and vulnerable. Unhinged.

"How do you do that?" I ask wonderingly, smiling while tears are still rolling down my face. "How do you seem to know all the right things to say?"

He looks down and smiles, "I don't know. It just seems to be a rule for me: don't think about it, don't try to comprehend or understand it. I swore to myself I wouldn't, when I lost Lily for that short amount of time a couple years ago. Like you, I kept trying to figure it out. Were we still twins – even if we had the same DNA but she didn't know me? Things like that. My mind couldn't take that for very long. In fact, a week after I was Gifted, I ended up in the infirmary after having a complete nervous breakdown. That's when I decided that Lily would always be my twin. I would always love her, and it didn't matter what any Gifted know-it-alls said – not that there are any."

It does make me feel better, but I can't shake the feeling of discontent. I want that little boy to know me; I want him to know how much I love him and have him love me.

"Stop thinking," Zac says urgently, gently and comfortingly tracing circles with his thumb on my cheek.

I smile pathetically, "You have no idea how difficult that is for me. I do math for fun. My mind is can't shut off and in two minutes skirts between hundreds of different topics that shouldn't be related yet my mind connects them somehow."

"Wow," he remarks sarcastically, "you're…a major dork," he smiles teasingly.

"You have no idea," I laugh, almost bitterly.

"Why don't I distract you then…" he murmurs leaning towards me.

I believe this is the point I forget how to breathe, let alone form coherent words. Is this really happening? If I am still unconscious and this is a dream…Zac is seriously about two seconds away from kissing me. So of course – at this moment – something sarcastic would come out of my mouth.

"Well that was fast," I mutter.

He retreats a little before saying defensively, "Well you did kiss me first…"

He does have a point…Geez, now I feel bad…

"Look…I-" I say tentatively, "I feel bad about that because I did that when I thought I was going to die and there you were staring at me like I might break. There you were, that same guy that caught me two days beforehand-"

"So what? Are you trying to say I was taking advantage of you or that you would have kissed any guy who had happened to be there?" he asks, his temper rising.

"No. Can I finish please?" I fix him with a deadly glare. "I wouldn't have kissed anyone. I kissed you, because…well, girls are weird, and…I mean…I like you…well, as much as I can."

He looks happy, but then frowns, "What do you mean 'as much as you can?'"

"I've only known you six days – two if you subtract all the time I've been unconscious. So yeah, I like you, but I don't know hardly anything about you," I explain innocently.

"You know my name. You know I have a twin. You know I'm Gifted. You know every major piece of information about me. What more do you need to know?" he asks haughtily.

Again, I just stare at him as if saying "Really? Can you even hear yourself right now?"

"I want to know the little things, the less important things. I want to know more about you than just the first impression," I smile at him apologetically. "Is it really such a hard concept to accept that I don't just want to make out?"

"No, except where I'm getting a little lost here is at the part where you kissed me. Then you didn't fight me kissing you a second time, or the time we kissed in the car. And it wouldn't be 'just making out.' I do actually have feelings, you know."

"Okay Zac, I'm going to put this as simple as I can. I do like you; I kissed you because I like you and it was one of those 'what if' moments people create when they think about what's the one last thing they'd do before they die, and I'm a cheesy romantic, soap opera, dramatic freak. I wouldn't have just kissed anyone. I do like you; I just don't want to move that fast. We get caught up in our supernatural existence and we forget that sometimes things can be slow-paced and cautious. We forget to try to live normally," I state, growing more patient by the end.

"But you already kissed me," Zac reiterates yet again.

"I'm not saying it'll never happen again. I'm just saying, let's talk first," I say as evenly as I can.

"Talk first…?" he seems to deflate in an instant but approaches the concept like some foreign language. I find it funny.

"Yeah," I say giggling, "Like we did the last time I woke up from being unconscious. You know, just people…having a conversation…discussing whatever comes up," I put casually and laugh when he glares at me.

"I know what 'talking' is," Zac grumbles, rolling his eyes. "It's never been something planned before; it's been casual, normal talking. I've never had to try and make conversation."

"All I'm asking is for a regular conversation, like one between two people who just met," I smile and shrug.

"Two people who just met, huh? Hm, two people who just met…" he draws out, pretending to think quizzically. "…Hi, I'm Zac. What's your name?" He reaches his hand out, ready to shake mine, and smiles a dazzlingly, pearly-white smile.

"We can cut the intro part-"

"Nope. I'm sorry. I just met you and in order to continue talking to you, I need to know your name," Zac says stubbornly but smirks and winks at me.

"Alright. I'm Kira," I smile shyly, shaking his hand.

"So Kira…where are you from?"

Chapter 25

Well, Zac and I had a nice conversation about each other for about an hour before the making out started.

At dinner, everyone congregates in my room to eat – which is thoughtful but totally not necessary. Five people don't have to eat in this small room with me. It is decided that I am going to need more recovery time than what had been expected because of the four days of missed meals. I am undernourished and still exhausted – more mentally than physically.

They tell me how the rebuilding is going. Apparently everything is still foundationally strong, and they cleared away the rubble and broken glass in the days I was unconscious. They assure me that the Gifted mansion has seen much worse in the past. That's why everything in the mansion looks new – half of it is.

When we are all almost done, a girl walks in asking a question about a funeral. Nikki excuses herself to talk privately to the girl. When she returns, she looks sullen and I have a grim curiosity to ask her a question.

"For those that…died," I stutter over the word a little, but I force it out, "what do you do with – I mean, how do you -…" I glance around nervously, trying to think of a way to phrase the question without being blunt or offensive.

Nikki – thank goodness – seems to catch on, "Do you mean, how do we remember them after their death? What do we do with them?"

"That's what I was trying to say," I say relieved.

"Normally, we have a little ceremony – I guess you could call it a funeral, and we say our goodbyes, then we give them back to their Gift. A lot of times we end up cremating them and then releasing the ashes to their Gift; but unless they're a fire Gift, we burn them by a natural fire as opposed to a Gifted-created fire. We don't allow anyone to watch the cremation though; we bring in a practiced mortician. We let those that want to watch the scattering of the ashes."

"Where do you scatter the ashes?"

"If they were an earth Gift, we bury them. A water Gift's ashes are thrown to the lake. The ashes of an air Gift are given to the wind – we normally wait for a very windy day. A weather Gift's are thrown into a raging thunderstorm. A fire Gift's ashes are put in the bottom of the coals in the fireplace and we burn a Gifted fire in there every year on the day they died-"

Maybe I don't want to know all this…

Nikki stops and looks at me, worriedly, "Kira are you feeling okay?"

"Um, yeah," I say unconvincingly, suddenly nauseous and feeling pale. "Can we talk about something else?"

Nikki looks at me apologetically. Nonetheless the conversation moves on.

We decide I should be fine to go to Sterling's funeral on Friday, which is two days from now.

I am very nearly recovered by then.

The Friday morning we all gather for Sterling's funeral is overcast. The sky is like murky cloud soup and the wind blows in gusts, tearing at our dark clothes. It seems like most of the Gifted house has come out to grieve. Sterling's funeral is the last of the people who died; there wasn't many but any life lost is too much. We are gathered on the far rim of the woods, far enough away from where the earth class walks so we won't be reminded of it every day. It sounds like everyone knew him but he only made a few close friends here. I don't know how; I'd only known him for a day – two – and he seemed to be a really great guy. He was kind; he had been helpful and a friend when I was new and practically alone. I might not have known him well but I knew he didn't deserve to die and he definitely didn't deserve it so young.

Needless to say, I cry. Jamie stays with me as Zac already apologized in advance that he needed to stay by Lily. We'd meet up afterwards. You see, the Gifted class and the closest friends of the...*deceased* gather towards the front as they know the person best. Of course Jamie is allowed to come up front with me because everyone gets a support buddy if they want one.

The whole occasion is still so strange; there are no devastated parents and family. There are no priests or ministers officiating the service. There isn't even a gravestone; nothing to mark where the ashes are buried.

Nikki, Trey, and Reese are huddled across the burial site from us. I have a feeling each and every one of the Gifted are individually special to Nikki and Trey – are their family. Reese

339

looks the most distraught, heaving as she sobs. She has already said the group's goodbyes, the "We'll miss you," the "We'll always remember you," and then the "We know you're in a better place." Now it is almost time for the scattering of the ashes.

To give her strength, Nikki and Trey hold on to each of her arms as if grasping for dear life. I can't handle seeing people so upset; it makes me sick and I feel awful myself. I know Reese isn't going to be able to bring up the dirt to bury the ashes unless she has help.

In a leap of courage, I step out of my burrow in Jamie's side and walk over to her, also taking hold of her hand. She squeezes it tightly, even though I'm not even sure she knows who it is through all the tears.

"Together," I whisper, holding her hand tighter, "on three."
My voice wavers but it doesn't crack.

"One," I start firmly, feeling stronger. I see the Gifted earth class join hands together and step up to encircle the area designated for the burial.

"Two," I am losing volume and that strength that pushed me to step forward is fading. Luckily, Reese doesn't just have me now; she has the support of her entire class. Soon, the others – those who don't have an earth Gift – clasp hands and step forward in support of their fellow Gifted. I don't know if they can physically do anything but the morale helps.

"Three." It comes out quietly and scared but almost relieved.

Together we dig up the ground about four feet deep and three feet wide. Erik Thomas comes forward from the front line and Nikki and Trey hand him the tin box that holds his twin brother's ashes. His eyes are blood-shot red; he is struggling, but he is coping – well, grieving at least. Shakily, he walks to the hole and pops off the lid. He stares down at the contents and I can see the tears start to roll down from his eyes. With a sudden burst of strength, Reese steps out of our hold and moves over to stand with Erik, placing a hand on his shoulder. Maybe trying to share some strength, maybe trying to give guidance; in times like these, reason and logic aren't really present. There's only grief, waves of it, and questions: why him, why now, why couldn't he be saved, why isn't life fair? You can ask yourself those questions time after time and grind your mind to try and figure them out. But it's just an endless circle of twists and more questions and if you let it, it will destroy you.

In one swift motion, Erik tips the can over. Out fall and swirl and glide ashes, gray and white and black, big and small; they float down like snowflakes, drifting like pixie dust in the wind.

Realization hits us as a mass. He is gone. Sterling Thomas is gone from this world at the age of seventeen and a half. Those ashes are all that's left of him. There isn't even a gravestone to remember him. The Scorned have taken him from us and now no one will know he has been here. The rest of the world has long forgotten him. Those who still know him should have something

341

that marks their memory of him. He deserves *something* that marks his existence here.

Crazy. Stupid. Dangerous. A nearly impossible idea creeps into my mind.

Inconspicuously, I walk to Nikki and whisper simply, "Don't let anyone leave. I'll be right back." Then, keeping a considerable distance from the group, I walk around to Zac.

"Sorry Lily but do you think you could go up with Jamie? I need Zac for a minute."

"'Course," she murmurs, almost as if she knows what I am about to attempt.

I force a smile of appreciation. Zac turns to me, concern edged onto his face.

"Kira, what's wrong? Are you ok?"

"Yeah Zac, I'm fine – well fine enough. I need your help." I take his hand and I catch the faintest of smiles cross his face. "Try and keep up," I can't help but smirk.

I begin to run. To the beach. Dragging Zac behind me, but in a moment he is striding next to me. We only drop hands once we reach the top of the cliffs and I descend the stairs like water over rapids.

"Kira? Alright what's going on?"

Meanwhile I am building a mound of sand in a concentrated area and digging out its perimeter.

"I don't have time to explain everything. Just use your lightning Gift to strike the sand in this area; think tree."

"What-"

"Come on Zac, you know what a tree is. I don't have to time to tell you a tree – like with branches and leaves -"

He rolls his eyes, "Then quit interrupting me and you won't have to explain unnecessary things," he snaps. "I was trying to ask what are you attempting to do?"

I huff, annoyed I have to stop and share with someone what I am thinking, "I'm trying to make a glass tree. When you use high heat you can melt and mold sand into glass. Lightning creates abstract shapes so I'm going to use my fire Gift on top of your Gift to shape the creation as I choose. Got it?"

"Isn't this highly dangerous?"

"Since when have you taken risk into consideration?" I scoff.

"Well, I just didn't have plans to burn alive today so I'm not wearing my fireproof suit."

"I don't have plans to catch on fire either so quit being sarcastic and focus."

"Okay okay!" he pipes grouchily. "You want me to strike the pile of sand and try and form a tree shape myself as much as possible?"

"Yes and while you're doing that I'll be doing the same with my fire Gift."

"I know you said we're not going to catch on fire but there's still going to be a high amount of heat in this area very close to us. At the least it could give us a severe sunburn."

343

"I figured, so I'll also be holding up a water dome around us. You'll have to stand close to me so I don't have to make the dome too big."

"Isn't that going to take a lot of energy?" he asks nervously.

I sigh because explaining my thought process is taking a lot of energy.

"That's why I need your help. I could probably create the tree by myself but I wouldn't have enough strength to create the bubble."

Zac finally agrees with me that this might work. He steps forward, coming up next to me, and focuses on the hill of sand I created. He closes his eyes and I hear him take a deep breath.

"I'm ready."

"Well it's about time," I smirk.

He peeks an eye open to glare at me and then shuts it without voicing a remark.

I smile before concentrating myself on the sand and I close my eyes, picturing the glass tree I saw in my mind when the idea initially popped up. I picture the size I want it to be, the branches, and how they will twist and curve up to the sky.

"Alright, let's do this. I'm putting up the water dome now," I open an eye to see the water from the lake lapping around us to complete a circle and then rising over us. "I'll let you count to three."

I hear him breathe out again and begin counting, "One...Two...Three."

On three my eyes snap open and I throw the highest temperature and magnitude of fire I can at the sand pile as Zac brings down a brilliantly defined bolt of lightning from the sky.

In the gloom of the overcast day, anyone still back at the house would say there was suddenly a bright light, a piercing streak of white, originating from by the cliffs. Zac is streaming a continuous torrent of electricity. It falls down from the thick, murky clouds. It is magnificent and potentially blinding for us if the thin layer of water wasn't separating us from it. However, it means I can't see what we are creating and so I have to trust the mind of my Gift to sculpt my vision. The air is sweltering – and that is the heat that comes through the cool water; the sand hill must be an inferno. Sweat is collecting on my forehead and in the nape of my neck. My limbs are starting to tremble from the force of the heat colliding with the dome of water.

"Zac," I mutter through clenched teeth.

"Yeah?" he asks sounding as strained.

"On three let it all go, okay?"

"Just as long as you do the same."

"One...Two...Three."

On three, I cut off the tunnel of energy flow and drop to my knees, breathing heavily. I glance over to see Zac has done the same; his head hangs but his eyes are looking over at me. His face and muscled arms are red but not cheery-red which is a good thing. He smiles wearily at me, that being all he can probably muster. His eyes wander forward and I see them widen in the least (Zac probably isn't used to being shocked or surprised). I follow his eyes to see what has caught him off guard. I feel mine widen like his.

Looming before us is a glass tree. The trunk is about a foot in circumference and the branches a good six inches; the whole sight has to be about ten feet tall. The tree is nearly transparent, but more of a milky white – as if it is frosted over. It is beautiful. It is perfect.

"Wow," I hear Zac mutter with what sounds like incredulity. "It actually worked."

I smile. I'll admit, for a minute there, I second-guessed my thinking. But I was right.

We start to gain back our strength and we both move to stand. I can't take my eyes off the glass tree. In the corner of my peripheral I see Zac shift closer to me and put his hands in his pockets. He is shaking his head with a smile on his face.

"What?" I ask smiling, amused.

"We did it."

"We did, didn't we?" I turn to face him. There is only about a foot in between us.

"I have to admit, that's one of the coolest things I've ever used my Gift for."

The space between us is shortening.

"I don't know...I've done some pretty cool things with mine already," I say with mock uncertainty.

"Yes well, that's because you have four Gifts and so you don't always need other people to do things."

"I believe that's just called independence," I smirk.

"So I guess that means you can independently carry that glass tree sitting over there all the way to the memorial site," he quirks his eyebrows sarcastically.

"Actually, I planned on floating it there with my Gift," I say honestly.

"Oh," he looks disappointed.

"Unless you wanted to carry it there of course…"

"Nice try. You foiled my plans; that's all."

"Your plans?"

"Yes. Get you to beg for my help in carrying it and then make you kiss me in order to strike a deal."

"Oh, really? Well then yes, I did ruin your plans. And they were such great plans too," I roll my eyes, smiling to myself.

"I'll just have to go with Plan B then," he is smiling crookedly.

"Do tell. What has the great Zac Railey come up with now?"

"I'll have to kiss you myself."

That's exactly what he does.

This is nice: the playful bantering that normally leads to a kiss. Friendly, funny conversations with Lily and Jamie. I feel as if I belong here, or I could at least. In this group of people, who are like me but still individuals. Everyone cares about one another and

347

forms a makeshift family – like Jamie said. I guess that sort of connection would be a natural creation among a group of people who have each lost everything else and the only people they have in the world are literally each other. I like that; some kind of bond that connects everyone, bringing them together in moments of duress or amazement, standing side by side whether they know each other well or not. Whether they *want* to know each other or not.

I pull away.

"Come on, we have some people waiting on us," I wink.

"Alright," He steps away but takes my hand in his, smiling. Oh lord, he is giving me butterflies, causing the tree to nearly drop to the ground after I have lifted it into the air with my Gift. I'm really going to have to learn to control that.

Zac leads me up the stairs and the tree follows behind us. I wonder what we look like to others. Two people walking through a field hand in hand with a glass tree following them, floating along around them. As we come closer to the congregation, attention starts to turn towards us. Nikki must have heard me and she has kept them all here, waiting. They look amazed and perplexed, stunned. I hear people mutter under their breath in awe, "Unbelievable," or, "Impossible."

We near the front of the group, coming to the first row with the earth class. The hole the ashes were dropped into has been filled in. Erik and Reese don't look quite so distressed anymore.

Everyone watches Zac and me as we stop, the burial site directly in between us and Reese and Erik.

"I was wondering," I start compassionately, "if you would want a gravestone for your brother?"

Erik's eyes dart over to the still hovering tree, and for the first time today, the ghost of a smile plays across his lips. He nods.

"Oh my god," Reese mumbles, covering her mouth wonderingly as I begin to align and now lower the glass tree onto Sterling's grave.

It looks beautiful here, amongst the green of the forest. I bring Erik and Reese around to the front of the tree so they can see what I made sure to inscribe into the glass as we were creating it:

Here lies: Sterling Hayden Thomas

Born: April 26, 1994

Loving brother and wonderful friend

He will always be remembered by the Gifted

I hear Erik inhale deeply. He turns to me then.

"Thank you."

That is all he says but it holds so much appreciation and gratitude that my heart nearly melts.

I shake my head, "It's what he deserves. It's only what's right."

"I haven't really gotten to know you yet, but thank you for caring enough to do this, to be the one to finally give us a way to be remembered."

I smile humbly at his words, what he says having been exactly what I wanted to accomplish through this glass making.

"Yes," Reese chimes in, sniffling, "you'll have to teach us how to create these so we can make it a tradition."

"Of course."

The crowd is no longer formed in organized rows but has dispersed. Some have come forward to get a closer look at the tree; some have begun to head back to the mansion. I give both Erik and Reese a hug, nod towards Nikki and Trey and walk over to Zac, Lily, and Jamie. The three of them are talking over something, smiling and looking rather untroubled. As I approach, Zac takes my hand again.

"Are you okay now?" Zac whispers into my ear, disconcerted.

I turn towards him and smile, replying honestly, "Yeah."

He smiles and kisses my temple chastely.

"You ready to go?" Lily asks, smiling, looking ready herself.

"Let's go get some lunch," I say.

Jamie and Zac echo one another with, "Yes!" and "Thank God! I'm starving."

I laugh as the four of us start walking back to the mansion.

Epilogue

It's later now, after dinner. Zac wants to take a walk and I ask Lily and Jamie if they want to join us.

Right as the sun meets the lake on the horizon and begins its decent below the surface of the water, Jamie, Lily, and Zac gently sit me on the bench that over-looks the alcove of the lake. After Jamie and Zac insisted they carry me (because apparently "I am so exhausted from the day's events" – and they wouldn't let Lily do it), they nearly dropped me twice – from their own stupidity. Not to mention, Zac slipped on some water that hadn't been mopped up out in the hallway; his feet came out from under him and he fell back on his back. I would have gone down with him had Jamie not had such a steady grip of me on his side. That doesn't mean we both couldn't have joined Zac on the floor; truthfully, the only thing that kept Jamie up, who kept me up, was Lily who had a hold on the collar of Jamie's shirt. The whole process was actually funny and it only got better the farther along we got as we laughed more and concentrated less and less.

Finally – probably a half an hour after we actually left the room – we reach the bench. Zac sits down next to me and holds my hand in his. Lily walks across to the railing and leans back against it; Jamie hesitates a moment, looking down at the calm water, but eventually makes his way to stand by Lily. Right now, we are quiet; the lake below us gently rolls along the cliffs and glides up the beach with smooth ease. Because of the setting sun, the sky is orange right where the sun is falling and then it turns to a soft pink,

351

a thin shade of purple, and a navy blue encompasses everything else. This is real peace, sitting here watching the sunset silently.

I sigh, "It's so beautiful out here."

Jamie and Lily agree with me by a simple nod and, "Yeah." Zac would be the one to lean in close to my ear and whisper, "You're beautiful."

I blush and slightly turn my head to stare at him out of the corner of my eye, and smile-smirk. I turn back again, thinking this is not the time or place for it since his sister is about five feet away from us. To respond to his comment, I rest my head on his shoulder, finding it more comfortable than expected. I could fall asleep right now, in this peaceful pool. In this moment, the world seems to fade, replacing it is a pink sky, the best temperature during the day, and people, I am beginning to realize, I wouldn't be able to survive without in this new life. I almost wish I could stay in this world forever; it is serene and calm. There are no expectations or problems or duties. But this moment isn't life; it's just one instant of it. One instant we work towards. It is the instant we strive towards as we're crawling through the mud. When we reach here, it's to recover and refuel for the next long, rocky road. It's to remind us that life has happy moments, and to keep us positive. I don't know how long this whole-hearted feeling will last, but it has strengthened me enough to keep reminding myself this is why I came back.

"Hey Zac…" Lily says casually.

"Yes Lily," he says, as if he knows what she is going to ask and is already annoyed.

"Do you think we could watch a movie together tonight, just the two of us?" Lily asks, nonchalantly.

"Why? Do you miss your big brother?" he teases.

She looks at him as if saying "I'm serious" then begins to pout and says grudgingly, "Yes."

"Alright," he says, caving in.

She smiles and skips over to him, snatching his hand that isn't clasping mine, and begins to heave him up.

"Hey! Wait, you mean now?" Zac asks disgruntled as he is forcefully pulled to his feet.

"It's already almost 8:30. If we start it in the next ten minutes, I may actually be sleeping by eleven 'o clock."

"So you have to pull me away from my-....well, my almost-away from Kira *this* second so you can go to bed early?" Zac asks rather frazzled and disbelievingly.

"Eleven 'o clock is not early-"

"For you it is-"

"None of us have gotten much sleep the past four days so, yes, I'm tired. We've all been a mess during these four days, and because we almost lost Kira and we lost a couple other people, I realized I need you but you haven't been able to be there. And I'm not blaming you for anything – or you Kira -"she turns to me sympathetically and then back to Zac, "I just want to spend some time with you before the regular week starts and you're busy – and obsessed," she mutters tersely, rolling her eyes, "with Kira."

Zac stands looking at her guiltily; meanwhile, I am the one to jump up and hug her.

"Aw! Lily! I promise not to hog too much of his attention and time away from you. You just tell me when you need him – or don't; just take him and one of you can text me."

"This won't happen a lot; in fact, it only happens about once every two months. Trust me. I can only take so much of him. And besides," she begins to smile, "the more time I spend with him, the more I have to hear him ogle over you," She winks at me.

I giggle and turn around to look at Zac who is standing with his mouth hanging open.

"Well why are you just standing there?" I ask smiling. "Say goodbye to 'your...well, your almost – to me,' so you and your sister can go spend some quality time together."

"Hey man, I'd do what she says," Jamie, who has been patiently and silently observing this take place from his spot against the railing, stands up straight and takes a step towards us, smirking. "Your sister and your whatever-she-almost-is are not a pair you want angry with you. Together they have great power."

Lily turns around to look at Jamie, feigning a bright smile, "I knew there was a reason I've always liked you!"

"Traitor," Zac mumbles, grudgingly.

While Jamie and Lily are busy talking, I stroll closer to Zac and wrap my arms around his neck, bringing the sum total distance separating us to about a foot.

"Go hang out with your sister," I say encouragingly. "I'd give anything to spend time with mine right now," I look down, trying to keep telling myself what Zac said earlier about "not thinking." "If Lily feels anything like I do, then she does need you."

"I was going to go anyways," Zac says, huffing, but his frown grows into a smile and he pulls me even closer, "but thank you for showing me how much you care about my sister. It means a lot."

"I know how much she means to you. Not to mention, she's such an amazing person anyways that it doesn't really have anything to do with you," I explain, leaning in closer, mimicking him until we meet in a kiss.

It doesn't last as long as either of us would like it to, because in the next second, Lily has somehow squeezed her way between Zac and I and is pushing him away.

"Ew! Well, I think that's enough of that. Time to go!" she says nauseously.

"Bye to you too, Lily," I smirk, but act as if she hasn't just been a grossed-out sibling, like a little girl who thought boys still had cooties. Although, I can see where it would be perfectly reasonable to assume your brother always has cooties. I laugh to myself.

"Bye Kira," she begins pushing Zac with one hand – which I'm sure isn't really necessary anymore – and waves back with the other. "See you tomorrow! You too, Jamie!"

"See 'ya Lily!" Jamie shouts so she can hear him, going to sit on the bench.

I walk over to sit next to him. I say more to myself than him, smiling, shaking my head, "She is so adorable."

"Yeah she is," he says faintly, and I look up at him to see him smiling absentmindedly. I know that smile!

"You like her don't you!" I say excitedly.

He rapidly loses his wondering look to stare down at me as if I have lost my mind – or I am high or something. He pauses for a moment before saying, "Me? You think I like Lily? Okay, maybe it's time you go back to the infirmary. I think you're just a little mentally confused."

I will not be refuted though.

"You do! That's why you're trying so hard to deny it -"

"No, I really don't -"

"-want the entire world to know?" I finish for him, jokingly. "Yeah, I understand. I won't tell anyone -"

Jamie looks as if he is becoming annoyed as I keep interrupting him and finishing his sentences – and not the way he would have ended them.

"There's nothing -"

"-To hide? Oh good! I'll go see Lily later and we'll talk. Maybe she likes you too!" I exclaim, sounding like an excited five year old girl.

"You wouldn't dare," he says, glaring at me.

During this process, let me point out, that I have been doing all this as a joke but have kept a completely straight face while doing so. Jamie is now three shades paler than he normally is, and has a combination of fear and desperation on his face. I can't hold it in anymore and I burst into laughter. Loud. Whole-hearted. Annoying. Laughter. I am laughing so hard my face turns red and tears start to pool.

Jamie slowly relaxes, and smiles warily, "It's not funny!"

I just nod and clutch at my stomach.

"Come on, cut it out," he says, playfully bumping into my shoulder.

It takes a full minute but I eventually calm down, taking heavy breaths and little fits of giggles sneaking in here and there.

"Okay, okay," I sigh, finally settling down, "but seriously, do you like her?" I ask him calmly and casually, like a normal human being.

His face twists hesitantly, "I don't know…maybe. She and I didn't hang out a ton until you got here; a lot of times it was just Zac and me that hung out…She seems pretty cool though."

I don't respond but smile at him knowingly.

"And what about you?" he smiles, poking me in the side. I raise my eyebrows quizzically. "You and Zac, huh?"

357

"Yeah," I say casually, nodding.

"He can be great sometimes, and others a real jerk, but most of the time he's fine."

"I'm pretty sure I can handle him."

"I'll tell him if he hurts you though, I'll kick his ass," he winks at me.

"Lily might kick yours then," I say, smirking.

"Nah, she'll probably help me," he snorts.

"I wouldn't put it past her," I mutter, brushing the hair away from the place near my eyes where it has fallen.

Silence takes the reins and it is awkward in a sense that it feels as if we should be talking and we're not. I sift through topics I could bring up or ask him. I think of one, but it is grimmer and will darken the mood depending on the answer. Of course I actually want to know the answer and after a while of more silence, I decide to ask it.

"Do you believe me – about the guy in the basement? Do you think I'm making him up?" I ask, and my eyebrows crease with worry.

"Of course I believe you," he says with conviction. "I don't know how it's possible, but that doesn't mean it's not the truth. I'm sure Nikki and Trey will figure it out, and if he seems to be the powerful, controlling guy you say he is, then we'll probably hear of him again," He looks at me reassuring. I leave the conversation at that; we'll cross the bridge of "what if they don't find anything and he doesn't show up" if we come to it.

I glance up at him and find something worrying his features.

"What's wrong Jamie?" I ask concerned.

He looks at me for a second but now turns away. That's not like him.

"Jamie -"

"I keep trying to figure it out but I can't seem to understand. Why did you leave without us? Why was it so necessary for you to go without us?" he asks, and a flash of anger appears in the corner of his face I can see.

I have been expecting this; in fact, I have spent all day anxiously awaiting the moment one of them would work up the courage and frustration to ask me.

"I had to," I say urgently. He looks back at me, defiance clear on his face. Before he can say anything, I continue, "Bret and Tessa were right. The Scorned were there for me – and some serious revenge – but they wouldn't have an excuse without me. I was tired of you all getting hurt and dying; it's not fair. If you three had come along, someone might have died in that basement -"

"Or maybe with the four of us, we could have taken the guy down," Jamie replies, his voice rising.

"Or someone would have done something stupid and heroic and gotten themselves killed and then everyone would have been upset and not thinking clearly. Down there was the absolutely wrong place to be distracted – I almost killed myself because I wasn't completely focusing -"

"Kira, someone did do something stupid and heroic and almost did die. You! So what? You can decide what can and can't be done, but you don't know how to follow your own guidelines? People *were* worried and upset. You hurt us. You should have seen Zac! I swear, I have never seen him so rattled. I don't know how you managed to, but that guy is somehow already crazy about you. You didn't even think about what it would do to us! You didn't think about how much we need you. More importantly, you didn't think about how much we have already accepted you! For a lot of us, this is our family. We have lost our old ones and now we almost lost another member again because you were selfish.

"I get that you wouldn't be able to live with the guilt, but a lot of us can't live with much more pain! I can't! Every person I've loved in the past has been killed so I don't get attached to people anymore. And then I met you and – you've just been different – and I thought-I thought I was going to have to go through it all again. Kira-I-it is indescribable how much it hurt when my parents and my sister died. I don't want to go through that again."

"I know it was selfish," I splutter, heavy tears fall down the curves of my cheeks, "but it was selfish staying! I couldn't hide around as people died. You don't get what that feels like! They weren't just getting hurt; they were dying! Sterling, a guy I just met the day before, that had been nice to me, died right in front of me! He was *nice* to me and I'm the reason he's dead! The evil, crazy guy said if I did bring you, he'd just kill you all. What if he really had the power to do that?" New waves of guilt rack my conscience, unlocking the gate that held the pain inside. As I continue to cry, I watch Jamie's face relax, sink even. He sighs heavily and comfortingly wraps his arm around me.

"I know," he says crestfallen, "but they didn't die because of you. They died because we were under attack and they were defending themselves, the mansion, and the people around them which includes you. The Scorned and the Gifted have gotten into fights before. This happens, but no one should blame themselves because of it. Yes, maybe you were the reason the Scorned were here but you're not the reason that anyone is dead. The people who attacked us are the reason. The people died for you, not because of you – wow, that sounded incredibly cheesy and like a line from *Harry Potter*," he grimaces, awkwardly.

I'm not exactly sure what happens but I snap. In the most annoying, unattractive way, a very loud fit of laughter explodes out of me and won't stop. Apparently, I find something highly hilarious because I keep laughing. Tears are still falling down my face. Now there are tears of laughter – stupidity even, mixed in. My sides start to hurt considerably and my hands clench at them.

At first, Jamie humors me and laughs along with me, probably getting a kick out of my complete insanity in this moment. However, now, like for any other normal person, it starts to get old and he attempts to move on – except I am still sitting here laughing hysterically.

"O-K-well I think it's time I get you back to the infirmary…"

"No, no, I'm calming down. I'm fine," I say, as the laughter splutters to a stop, and then explodes again.

"It's official. The Gifted healers' power must work like morphing because you are absolutely loopy," he looks at me, grinning, his eyebrows raised humorously. The whole episode only makes me want to laugh harder. He throws his hands up to the sky with mock frustration. "I don't get it," he says chuckling, confused. Slowly, with a "Ha!" and then a "Haha!" his laughter builds up until it matches mine and we are sitting here, two idiots laughing hysterically about nothing in particular.

This is how Nikki finds us five minutes later.

"Well that's a happy sound to hear," she comments, amused.

This of all things finally causes us to settle down, aside from the heavy breathing and sore stomach muscles; not to mention, I have to wipe the tears from my eyes so I can see clearly.

She arches an eyebrow sarcastically, "Better?"

In response, I give a short, subtle giggle and nod vigorously – still dabbing at my eyes.

"Good," she smiles warmly, "you deserve to be. In fact, we all do. We've all had a set of exciting and trying few days." She casts her gaze lower and to the side, dismayed. The atmosphere almost immediately darkens and my head drops with a sudden overwhelming exhaustion and slight dizziness – but the latter is probably more from the laughing and lack of oxygen.

"Just so you know, classes are canceled for a couple of days. We probably won't start them again until next week – but you didn't hear it from me," Nikki smiles slyly and winks at me. "I think the students are planning something special one day this week that they're trying to keep from us teachers," she smiles ingeniously. "Of course, I know nothing of this either. But I bet Jamie could probably tell you something," she looks at Jamie, who is still sitting next to me and smirks. I look over at him and find that he is blankly staring at the ground, as if concentrating on something unknown to Nikki and me.

"Jamie...You who?...Earth to Jamie...Jamie?" I say slowly.

With a jolt, his gaze snaps back to us...and reality, "Oh, uh, what? Sorry."

I turn back towards Nikki, expecting her to ask him. Instead I find her staring at me, giving me a funny look.

"Um...Oh, uh, Nik-" subtly, Nikki steps on my foot – gently, but it still catches my attention. Short and evasively she shakes her head. I start again after realizing what she is attempting to convey, "-I heard from some people that there's something going on. I don't know what they were saying exactly, but something about planning an event. I was wondering if you knew anything."

He gazes at me warily and now turns to Nikki and narrows his eyes suspiciously. He is clearly lying when he replies, turning his nose into the air, "I have no idea what you're talking about.

However," he is standing now, looking back at us snootily, "Matt just Minded me, saying I'm needed for something very important."

"Like what?" I ask, giggling. I mean, really? What could be so important this late that Nikki wouldn't know about too? "Don't tell me. It's top secret, too."

"No, it is a very critical game of Call of Duty in which case they are a man down, and apparently I am the first on the recruiting list," he shrugs.

I gasp, overdramatically, "So you guys are just like normal guys obsessed with mindless video games and get excited over them like little girls and their dolls? And here I thought I was in some alternate dimension all this time. Darn."

"First of all," he states, "they are not mindless. They require skill, hand-eye coordination, and strategy. Secondly, what do you mean normal guys? What made you think we weren't normal to begin with?"

"Oh I don't know…the fact that your birthmarks glow…that you can kill people with lightning, blast people with fire, control people's minds…I guess I just assumed," I count off, rolling my eyes.

"So you were wrong?" He states more than asks, smirking.

"Well I guess so. Are you going to freak out over the fact that a girl is admitting she was wrong?" I ask, cocking an eyebrow.

"No, I'm more mature than that," he replies proudly, puffing up his chest. "Besides, why would I?" He begins walking away but turns to walk backwards so we can finish this random, miniature conversation.

"Because that is what a normal guy would do," I smirk.

Un-phased, he smiles, "Whatever you say darling…"

"That is so cliché," I say, rolling my eyes before winking at him.

He laughs and replies sweetly, "See you tomorrow, Kira."

"Bye Jamie," I smile.

"Hey! What am I? Chopped liver?" Nikki shouts at him, seemingly offended but turns half her face towards me and gives a crooked smile.

"You know, if you had given me a chance, I was getting there," Jamie says defensively, obviously lying.

"Ah-huh, sure," she says sarcastically and disbelievingly as if she is telling a four year old she believes he can fly.

"Bye Nikki!" he turns around and waves back at us.

"Good bye Jamie," Nikki giggles, probably because he said he was leaving what feels like ten minutes ago and he's only now walking away. She strolls over and sits down beside me where Jamie – and earlier, Zac – sat. "So how 'ya doing girlie?" she asks.

"Actually…I'm doing pretty well," I say honestly, and find myself smiling. Who would have thought, with as much pain I was in just five days ago, that today I can find myself happy – really happy. I still feel the reality of the loss of my family and I still feel that darkness, but I also feel the light. Sometimes all you need is a little light to struggle and stumble through the dark.

"Good," she says as if she had already known we'd be sitting here now. As if she knew that I would find a new, different family here, one I am beginning to need. Then again, I do recall her saying something about that a couple of days ago.

"Hey! Your seventeenth birthday is in a few weeks, isn't it?" Nikki asks excitedly.

"Um, yeah," I smile brightly, "August eighth…Did Zac tell you it was coming up?"

"No actually," she smiles shyly, "when a Gifted baby is born, everyone else is alerted by a lighting of their mark. Most of the time we don't remember the exact day one is born, but because it was such a monumental event I can remember everything about that moment. Trey and I had been taking a nap, so of course that would be the time he would get a premonition and wake me up, mumbling 'something big is coming.' About five minutes later, we got the Warning."

"That's cool that these marks," I speak while feeling the skin where my mark lies, "know when new Gifted are being born."

"Yeah it's incredible how much power they possess. We figure the point of this part of their power is so we know that there's another person out there that's going to need us one day, and so maybe we can find them before they're wondering around lost, alone, and forgotten in this big world. When we get the Warning, we normally put a team of Gifted psychics on it. Most of the time we find them quickly."

"You found me…" I murmur with a half-smile.

"Yep," she says proudly, "took us quicker than we thought it would too. We got the Warning at 7:45 and an hour later we had located you."

"Wait…What?" I ask suddenly and abruptly bemused.

"Sorry. What are you confused about?" she asks.

"I was born at eight o'clock and I thought you said the Warning comes when you're born…I don't understand…" I say hesitantly.

"Neither do I," Nikki replies, paling almost.

"Maybe you remember the time wrong…?" I suggest helpfully.

She shakes her head though, "No, I remember it perfectly. Everyone does because it was such a big moment."

"My Mom and Dad have always told me eight o'clock…They even have it on tape…"

Nikki stares at me, bewildered; her face is set in deep thought.

What does this even mean?

I state in almost a bewildered sense, "I wasn't born at 7:45."

So who was? Who am I?

Just like that, the world is a frightening, confusing, unsteady place once again.

A pain grows behind my eyes, located somewhere in the center of my brain. It is a mild form of the searing headache that attacked my mind in my room. I cringe. I know what this means now. I know what – more like *who* – causes it.

"This is only the beginning Kira. Just remember, you know nothing. Absolutely nothing. You have no idea the skeletons, the devils, and the secrets that are waiting for you."

Made in the USA
Charleston, SC
06 March 2014